AN

Abundant
Woman

ELIZABETH NEFF WALKER

San Francisco

Belgrave House
190 Belgrave Avenue
San Francisco, CA 94117

Cover design by Andrea DuFlon

Cover painting by Judith Swirsky

Manufactured in the United States of America

1 3 5 7 9 10 8 6 4 2

Library of Congress Cataloging-in-Publication Data

97-94542

ISBN 0-9660643-7-2

Visit Belgrave House on the World Wide Web at:
http://www.belgravehouse.com

With love and gratitude to Paul, Laura and Matt, as always.
And special thanks to Miranda Coffey and Kay Turner.

PROLOGUE

Nigel drove me to Heathrow in his Rover because the amount of luggage I was taking wouldn't easily fit in my MG. But he was late picking me up, which added to my already overburdened nerves.

Leaving for six months, with only a week's notice, seemed to me a tricky sort of thing to do to one's husband. But Nigel had waved aside my concerns, saying, "I know this is something you'd give your eye teeth for, Mandy. You should thank your lucky stars Doug Lattimore had a heart attack. I'll be perfectly fine on my own."

Maybe that was what worried me most. He *would* be all right on his own. In fact, I often thought he preferred being alone, and my going away for six months might just decide him to live without me permanently. I didn't dare voice that concern, because he would have dismissed it as he dismissed all attempts at a serious discussion of our marriage. "We've managed just fine for twenty-two years," he was given to saying. "Why rock the boat now?"

If Nigel didn't consider my going to America for a six month exchange "rocking the boat," it seemed to me a breathtaking example of at least swaying the canoe.

"Have your tickets?" Nigel asked as he pulled onto the M4.

I patted my purse. "Yes, and American currency for when I get there."

"Did Doug give you last minute instructions?"

"Naturally." My boss, Doug Lattimore, had insisted that I come by the hospital, where he was still recuperating, for his words of wisdom on how to behave in Wisconsin. He was not at all happy to see me take his place on the exchange.

Nigel grimaced. "He's an idiot."

That wasn't precisely true. Doug was actually the head of OB/GYN at our hospital and intelligent enough. The problem was that the American exchange ostensibly hinged on a set of pregnancy and childbirth studies with which I was far more knowledgeable than he. This because I'd had to do his contribution to the research for him several years previously. Unfortunately, we held opposite views on the usefulness and implementation of the ultimate findings.

"He said he'd faxed Dr. Hager in Madison with all the necessary information about me," I said. "That's exactly how he put it—necessary. He didn't mention giving her a glowing account of my abilities."

"He wouldn't."

"Perhaps not." Doug doesn't acknowledge my abilities, though he depends on them. "There was just the hint of a threat that I'd better see things his way in America. He told me he didn't want me harassing Dr. Hager about ECPC data."

Nigel glanced over at me. "That's what the exchange is about, isn't it?"

"It's supposed to be." I sighed heavily. "For the next six months I just know he'll be trying to undermine my reputation at the hospital." When I was there, I had no difficulty standing up for myself. In fact, if anything, I was too blunt and straightforward in my approach to people and problems. More than once my tongue had gotten me in trouble.

"No one is going to listen to his grumbling," Nigel said absently.

That wasn't quite the point, but I let it go. After all, I'd recognized the possibility of Doug's treachery when I pressured him into letting me take his place. The whole American project had from its inception seemed more appropriate for me than for him. Not only the subject matter, but I liked Americans, felt a kinship with them, which Doug certainly didn't seem to. Doug had been prepared to abandon the exchange altogether after his heart attack. Fortunately, the American OB/GYN coming to England on the exchange hadn't been so sanguine about canceling his own plans.

Nigel frowned at the heavy traffic ahead. "We're running a little close, I'm afraid."

"Yes, I know. Just drop me off with my luggage. You don't have to come in."

"That might be best," Nigel agreed.

Disappointed, but resigned, I changed the subject. "Cass didn't think she'd be able to visit me in Wisconsin. She has definite plans for her holidays."

Our daughter, Cass, was away at university, studying physics. I think Nigel had wanted her to become a biochemist like him, and I know I'd wanted her to become a medical doctor. Cass had a mind of her own, however, and insisted that she knew precisely what she was doing. Probably she did, but she was ignoring an artistic streak a mile wide to pursue a scientific career.

Nigel grimaced. "The holiday camp. I really can't picture Cass catering to a bunch of tourists for the entire summer. She'd have done something different if the trip to Italy was still on."

We'd had a summer holiday planned—two weeks in the Florence area—for the three of us. It was impossible to tell if its cancellation was an irritant to Nigel. Cass had merely shrugged it off. "It would have interrupted the summer, anyhow," she'd said, indifferent. The chances of our vacationing together as a family seemed to have dwindled dramatically the older she became.

"I really regret having to call off the trip," I said. "But I thought Cass might grab the opportunity for a trip to the States."

Nigel gave a snort of disbelief. "To visit her mother? I think not. Now if she were offered a chance to tour around the U.S. on her own . . ."

He was right, of course. Cass preferred to associate with people her own age, both men and women. She preferred to study. She preferred to travel. She preferred to hike and ski and do yoga. Her parents made a rather weak showing in any competition for her attention.

Traffic remained heavy the entire trip to Heathrow, and I watched the minutes tick away on my watch with increasing alarm. Nigel, as always, remained calm. On either side of the highway the May morning sparkled with the newness of spring. Inside the car my tension mounted, but I held my tongue. There was absolutely no sense in blaming Nigel for getting us off to a late start. Better to part from him with a smile and what appeared to be a light heart.

As he negotiated the turnoff to the airport, he said casually, "Cass seems to think this is a separation of sorts for you and me."

Immediately alert, I could feel my pulse speed up. "What do you mean? She knows I'm simply taking Doug's place."

"She doesn't think you'd go away for six months unless you were considering leaving permanently." His eyes remained locked on the traffic.

"That's ridiculous," I said. Snapped, probably. "This is a career opportunity. When did she say that to you?"

"When she called last night before you got home."

"Well, it's nothing of the sort," I insisted.

Nigel glanced briefly across at me and returned his attention to the demanding pile of cars all attempting to be at the same place at the same time. "I suppose it *is* a kind of separation, Mandy. You may not say so, but it's something you've thought about, I know."

My scalp prickled. My stomach sank. My palms grew suddenly moist. Why was he bringing this up *now* when there were about two minutes before we pulled up to the British Air doors? What did it mean? "I'm just taking advantage of a serendipitous opportunity, Nigel," I protested.

As if he hadn't heard me, he said, "Consider it a separation, Mandy. Do what you have to. I'll understand."

What the hell was he talking about?

The Rover stopped with a jerk and Nigel hopped out of the car. Waving a porter over, he pulled the three large suitcases from the boot and set them on the curb. I watched numbly as the porter loaded them on his dolly.

Nigel moved to stand beside me. He was tall and thin; I was short and round. Dressed for work in a dark conservative suit, he nonetheless remained conspicuous amongst the hurrying business travelers around us. He was not someone who had mingled all his life with indistinguishable, bland, public-school types.

Nigel's features betrayed his origins. Despite his academic brilliance, he could trace his family through generations of seafaring men who had lived near the London docks. Nigel's face was imprinted with the rugged handsomeness of a nineteenth century sea captain.

Compared with his restrained presentation, my own clothing showed a taste for flamboyance. To travel I had chosen to grace my zaftig figure with a purple suit and fuchsia blouse, complemented by a vivid and flowing silk scarf. Nigel tucked the scarf under my suit jacket collar, saying, "We're late, Mandy. You must be a nervous wreck. You'd better run."

"But, Nigel . . . "

"Have a good trip, and enjoy your time in America."

Frustrated, alarmed, I couldn't find a thing to say except, "All right, Nigel. I'll miss you."

He nodded and gave me a little push in the direction of the waiting porter. I wasn't going to let him off that easily. I stood on tiptoe to kiss him, a hearty, enthusiastic kiss which he returned with a familiar peck. But there was no time to continue our discussion, to sort things out. My plane would take off without me.

As I tucked my purse in tight to my body and started to trot off, Nigel smiled and waved. Before turning a corner to the check-in counter, I looked back. But Nigel was already gone.

CHAPTER ONE

When the cab dropped me off at Mayfield House, I have to admit that I was pleasantly surprised. In the last of the May evening light the red shingled building looked almost enchanted, with the sun gleaming off the west windows and new foliage bursting on a phalanx of bushes. There were charming gables and odd turrets, giving the place an almost humorous appeal. From the driveway I could just see spring flowers blooming wildly in the untamed garden, where gravel paths wound past leafy shrubs and trees. With luck, I thought, my room would overlook the elms and irises, reminding me of my childhood home.

The door of the house opened before the cab driver had finished unloading my suitcases. A young woman with lovely auburn hair stepped hurriedly down from the stoop and hastened toward me. An enormous man with unruly hair and bristling eyebrows followed at a much more leisurely pace. From my insignificant height he looked at least seven feet tall, but I realized later that was merely the impression he gave, and liked to give, I think.

"Dr. Potter?" the young woman asked, holding out her hand. "I'm Angel Crawford. This is my husband, Cliff Lenzini. I'm *so* sorry we didn't know in time that you'd be arriving tonight. Dr. Lattimore had arranged to be in tomorrow."

"Not to worry," I assured her as I shook hands with each of them. "I only called from Chicago so you'd know I was coming on through. Doug had planned to visit a friend there, but I wanted to get in and get settled."

"Of course." She picked up one of the suitcases and waited while her husband gathered the other two. "It must be incredibly late London-time. We'll show you to your room."

I would never myself have chosen a rooming house for my lodging. Give me a kitchen to cook in and the privacy of my own place any day. But Doug had entirely different needs than I did, and for the time being I was willing to accept the prearranged situation. Later I could find an excuse to move to a small apartment of my own.

The front door swung into a spacious hallway with polished hardwood floors and gleaming white surfaces. Oak tables scattered against the walls held vases filled with a variety of spring flowers. A delicate scent wafted across to us and Angel smiled. "Sherri loves freesias," she said, setting down my suitcase. "She manages the place and cooks the meals here."

"Welcome to Mayfield House," Dr. Lenzini said, waving a hand at the spacious hallway. A meaningful glance from his wife inspired him to continue. "Angel wanted me to assure you we don't expect you to stay here unless it suits your needs."

There, his look seemed to say to his wife, I did it, like I promised. But he turned back to me and added, "I think you'll like it. We're a mixed batch. The two students from Australia who share the top floor don't always get on very well, but I'm sure they won't bother you. On your floor there's a pediatric neurosurgeon going through a divorce, a retired education expert who taught in a one-room country school, and a sculptor my sister discovered."

"Let's show Dr. Potter her room, Cliff. She's probably exhausted."

"Please," I said, "call me Amanda." Just before falling asleep the previous night, I had decided that Mandy would sound entirely too casual to Americans. They love the formality of the British accent, and they expect a degree of reserve from us which seemed to make Amanda more appropriate.

"And I'm Angel," my hostess said. As she climbed the stairs she explained that her husband had the suite on the east side of the house. "I don't actually live here," she explained, "but Cliff is here fairly often."

Hmmm, I thought. What's that all about? I'm nothing if not curious. My daughter sometimes refers to this as being nosy.

"And Sherri, the woman I mentioned, has a set of rooms at the back," Angel added.

Her husband, easily hauling the two large suitcases up the broad staircase, said, "The living room, dining room and TV room are for everyone, and the kitchen, too, when Sherri isn't fixing meals. There's a booklet in your room that explains our routines."

Gratefully I followed the two of them up the stairs while Cliff pointed out features I might not have noticed—like the wall sconces and the intricate turning of the handrail. Americans tend to forget in the face of Old World visitors that our stately homes often date from a period before America was *discovered*, but I find their enthusiasm charming. That probably sounds patronizing, and I don't mean it that way. We British are entirely too diffident, acting as though we regarded the whole of our lengthy history with a most unbecoming ennui.

Angel was the one who pushed open the door off the upstairs hall and I was instantly struck by the feel of walking into a leafy arcade. The trees outside seemed to frame the window both close at hand and far into the garden. The room's furnishings were simple, good-quality pieces of rugged craftsmanship, not the elegant antiques and frou-frou fabrics I'd found in restored Victorians on other trips to the States.

This first room was a sitting room, with a windowseat facing the garden, a comfortable-looking sofa in a boldly striped material, and numerous bookshelves with a few paperbacks scattered on them. There were two chairs, one a rocker, and a low table, what the Americans call a coffee table. There was a colorful rug (from one of the Native American tribes indigenous to Wisconsin, I later discovered) on the dark hardwood floor. A small television sat on the table opposite the sofa.

"We get cable downstairs," Cliff explained. "The ones in the rooms only get local stations. And there's a radio in the bedroom because people from abroad don't bring that kind of thing."

The bedroom was smaller but just as tasteful. The bed was a good size, larger than the cramped double bed Nigel and I shared in London. He would have appreciated the spaciousness and the down comforter that Cliff pointed out. Though Nigel had urged me to buy a queen-size bed, I'd never gotten around to doing it.

"The bathrooms have all been remodeled," Angel said, leading me through a door off the room. "But yours is especially small because it was a closet. I hope you won't mind."

Actually, it was dismayingly small for a woman of my generous proportions, but so was my MG, I reminded myself. So I smiled graciously and merely said, "Not to worry." I am nothing if not polite.

Cliff did look concerned, however. With a glance at Angel and a tsk of annoyance he said, "I hadn't thought of that. It wouldn't be big enough for me, either."

The moment's awkwardness was broken by a voice calling from the hallway. "There's Sherri," Cliff said with relief, moving back into the sitting room. "She's the one who handles all the problems around here."

A very young woman with a mop of brown curls bounced into the sitting room at Cliff's summons. You could tell before she said a word that she was one of those people with energy to spare. On the tray she carried was a small basket, covered with a napkin, from which fragrant steam rose, and a pot of tea with tiny pewter containers of milk and sugar. "It's probably a strange hour for tea, but I thought it would make you feel at home," she said, placing the tray on the nearest table and extending her hand. "I'm Sherri Hartman."

"Amanda Potter," I said, caught up in her enthusiasm. One could accomplish a great deal in life if she had that kind of unremitting vigor. I'd always had my share, but then I came from a family of manic-depressives. They call it bipolar disorder now, but manic-depressive is so much more descriptive. "How thoughtful of you. I shall enjoy it immensely."

Before I could say more than a quick good-night, they had all decamped and left me alone to my tea. I kicked off my shoes, removed my silk scarf and purple suit jacket, and sank into the enveloping sofa. As the sounds outside my door dwindled, I poured a mug of tea (Americans believe the bigger the cup, the more satisfying the beverage) and smiled at its being one of my favorites, Earl Grey. In the basket were two enormous blueberry muffins and a curl of butter.

Right off I knew Sherri and I were going to get along well. Here was a woman who'd provided delicious sustenance without having the first clue of my roly-poly figure. Nor had she shown the slightest sign of dismay when she did observe it. Not that Angel or Cliff had, except for Cliff's concern with the size of the bathroom. But Sherri would be providing meals, and I had a hearty appetite, for food as well as for life. I ate every bite before stripping off my remaining clothes and heading for the closet-sized bathroom.

Birds were already singing outside my window by five in the morning. I'd been awake since four, just lying there drinking in the fact that I really had arrived in Madison, when barely over a week ago I'd planned to spend the entire summer in London, with the exception of the brief holiday to Florence with Nigel and Cass.

Most of the flight from London I'd thought about Nigel's parting words, pecking at them from one direction and then another, as though I could unearth their hidden meaning. To very little effect. Nigel, master stonewaller, had once again managed to totally bewilder me. Wasn't he the one who professed to see no reason to change the status of our marriage?

Well, I wasn't going to spend a beautiful morning worrying about Nigel's intentions. Here I was in Wisconsin, and not just for a holiday. This was a six-month fellowship. Having done an obstetric/gynecology residency in the South while Nigel did a biochemistry fellowship at Duke many years before, I had maintained my American medical license ever since. And my tenacity was finally going to pay off.

My boss wasn't qualified in America, and could have done nothing more than observe and pontificate—which were his favorite activities in any case. But I would be free to absorb the whole experience, to do procedures, to learn new methods, to see how well a typical American university OB/GYN department had adopted the ECPC guidelines we'd all agreed to.

There would be time to think about my marriage later, now that I was thousands of miles away from Nigel. I'd been putting off doing that for far too long.

But I was not going to start now. I scooted out of bed and walked over to the window. My view encompassed the green bower of rear garden, shrubs and trees, but on the fringes I could see neighboring houses. None of them was as unique as Mayfield House but they looked large and well-kept.

It was a cluster of purple flowers in the garden that caught my eye, however. From this distance I couldn't tell what they were, but I suspected they were lilacs, and couldn't believe I'd find them in Wisconsin in early May. Which led me to throw on a pair of slacks and a boldly-patterned jumper, and, pocketing the key I found beside the tray, I quietly let myself out of my "unit," as Cliff Lenzini had called it.

The house was silent at that hour. On a Saturday morning people probably didn't stir until well past their usual hour, if London was any example. Not that London isn't always throbbing with activity, but it's a different kind on the weekends. If I'd been up most of the night for a complicated delivery, before going home I loved to sit with a cup of tea in Hampstead Village to watch the area come alive. And remember how different it had been when we'd first moved there almost fifteen years ago.

The Mayfield House hallways had carpeting that deadened the sound of my footsteps, but I could faintly hear from above me the raised voices of a man and a woman. Ah, the Australians, I remembered, glancing at my watch. Now what were they doing arguing at five-fifteen in the morning?

Downstairs I wandered through the attractive public rooms, thinking that it might be pleasant to sit in the parlor and chat with the other guests over a cup of tea or a glass of sherry. The table in the dining room was set for breakfast, which apparently was served in warming dishes on the sideboard. There was a variety of fruit in a vividly colored bowl, so I helped myself to an apple and pocketed a pear before wandering through to the telly room.

This contained a group of comfortable old chairs with plump pillows scattered around, and a large bowl of popcorn leftovers which made the cozy room smell like a cinema. An abandoned video tape of *Casablanca* remained on an oak table near the door. There was a list on the table, too, which apparently allowed tenants to choose what programs they wished to watch, or which hours they hoped to use the VCR. Very efficient, I thought; possibly Sherri's idea.

The building itself, though fascinating, was not what beckoned to me. I found a door at the back of the entrance hall that led toward the kitchen. This was a delightful, sunny space with copper pots hanging from an iron ring above the stove. Off this room, as I'd suspected, I found a door into the rear garden. Just opening it brought in the fresh, damp smell of a spring morning, and the sound of drowsy birds twittering. There were two semi-circular gravel paths leading off, which probably joined each other deeper in the shrub-crowded garden. I took the one to the right.

Along the path were the green tufts of perennials that would bloom later, and just beyond them yellow daffodils, purple iris and red tulips in marching clusters. I wound my way back toward the red brick wall covered with green vines that would become wisteria, or possibly jasmine. Shrubs were everywhere, blocking the view here, offering a peek of color there. I couldn't identify all of them, but thought perhaps the one I was passing was a flowering quince, not quite in bloom yet. The purple I had seen was indeed early lilac, which would come to full flower in another month.

Toward the rear of the yard, where a trail of shrubs formed almost a hedgerow, I slipped through a grassy opening to see what was beyond it. I was startled, and a little alarmed, to find a clearing with a green wood-slatted bench, occupied by a very real human being.

CHAPTER TWO

Naturally I had been told before I left England that there were homeless people all over the United States. "And they aren't always harmless, like here," Doug had insisted from his hospital bed. "These are the mentally ill that their government doesn't want to know about or pay to treat."

Well, Doug loves to knock the United States whenever he can, and he was annoyed that I had been offered the opportunity to take his place, so I expected nothing less of him. Still, I stopped instantly where I was, planning to back through the hedges before I was noticed.

That wasn't possible because the man sitting on the bench was already staring at me. He appeared just as surprised as I was, and glanced at his watch as though to confirm it was still extraordinarily early for someone else to be abroad. It was hard to determine his age, as he had one of those timeless faces that indicated he might be prematurely aged by the weight of his problems, or again look younger than he in fact was because of the openness of his countenance. His expression gave no hint of shuttering up, though a wary light darkened the depths of his sad blue eyes. He was probably close to my age, forty-three or four.

He was barefoot, with a University sweatshirt over a pair of maroon and navy striped pajama bottoms. Obviously he hadn't come very far. He was clean, his dark hair damp from a shower. One of the residents of Mayfield House? But what was he doing out here in the middle of the night?

"I beg your pardon," I said, stepping back toward the shrubs. "I had no idea there was anyone here."

"Don't let me frighten you away," he protested, rising to a not intimidating height. "I live here."

"Do you? In the garden?" I asked, amused. "I arrived last night. Amanda Potter."

"Jack Hunter," he responded, though he didn't move to shake my hand. Which was for the best, because there was something unnerving about him—the lack of a smile, or the fleeting impression that he could tell what I was thinking. "You would be the English OB/GYN, then."

"Yes."

He nodded. "You haven't adapted to local time yet. And you're probably hungry. Would you like me to show you where to find a snack?"

I produced the apple from behind my back, where for some reason I appeared to be hiding it, as though he might snatch it from me. "I picked this up, and a pear. Would you like one?"

Very much to my surprise, he accepted, choosing the pear and motioning me to a seat on the bench, which was still damp with morning dew. Ah, well, I could change my slacks when I returned to the house. "Why are you up so early?" I asked.

He seated himself as far as possible from me on the bench. "I wake up early every day."

I regarded his sad face and said diffidently, "I suppose you know that can be a sign of depression."

For the first time his lips twisted into something resembling a smile. "Do OB/GYNs practice psychiatry in England?"

"I beg your pardon!" I said, a little stiffly. "I had no intention of diagnosing you. It was merely an observation. You'd be surprised how many of my patients are depressed. I've trained myself to look for the signs, and refer them for proper treatment."

"And you think you see the signs in me, after an acquaintance of three minutes?"

That tongue of mine, it did get me in trouble. I sighed. "I was only trying to be helpful, Mr. Hunter. Forget I said anything."

He considered the pear in his hand for a moment and then took a bite from it. Suddenly I realized that I was famished. Though I knew the apple would have been washed by the efficient Sherri, I automatically rubbed it against my sleeve like we'd done as kids in Yorkshire after we'd swiped them from a tree. Mr. Hunter appeared amused at this piece of gaucherie, and I gave him my haughty English aristocrat look. He laughed outright.

"You probably grew up in the East End of London," he taunted without rancor.

"Hardly," I said dryly. "I'd have been lucky to come across an apple there."

"Where then?"

"Yorkshire, until I went off to university. But I'm very good at depressing pretension because I'm a doctor. American doctors know all about depressing pretension. Sometimes I think my British accent was the only thing that got me through the residency at Duke."

"You're licensed in the States?" he asked, surprised.

"Mmm-hmmm." I took another bite of my apple. The sun had risen enough now that a bright ray shone directly through the canopy of greenery and into my eyes. The new spring leaves swayed slightly in the breeze, allowing glimpses of a sky almost too blue to be real. I had just momentarily transported myself to that Florence vacation spot when Mr. Hunter said, "I am depressed."

Blinking to bring myself back to the present, I frowned and asked, "Well, have you done anything about it?"

"Oh, it's not a clinical depression."

"How do you know?"

"Because I've never been depressed before. There have just been some things getting me down."

"Now who's playing psychiatrist?" I quizzed him. "You may not be the best judge of your own clinical diagnosis. Has anyone else suggested that you see a psychiatrist?"

His brows rose. "I beg your pardon?"

"If your friends and colleagues have mentioned that it's a problem, you can be sure they've seen something you're trying to ignore."

"Oh, for God's sake," he said irritably, bouncing one knee up and down in place. "Everyone wants to help me. I don't need any help."

"Maybe not from your friends, but possibly from a professional."

He sat there glowering at me for a full minute. Then, astonishingly, he shrugged and said, "I suppose you're right. I'll see someone this coming week."

"Good," I said. "Tell me who keeps up the garden. Surely Sherri is too busy to do this, too."

He looked disoriented—or disappointed?—at the abrupt change of topic, but responded, "Some fellow comes around in a truck. I don't know who he is, or how often he comes, but he manages to keep it looking wild without looking messy. You're probably a garden fancier, being English."

"I am," I admitted. "We have a house in Hampstead with a small garden. That's where I work off my frustrations, and even indulge in a little creativity from time to time. I'm half afraid of the condition it will be in when I get back."

He considered me for a moment before asking, "How long will you be here?"

"Six months. The head of my division was supposed to come, but he had a heart attack and bypass surgery. He'd planned to stay at Mayfield House, so I filled in that spot, too. At least temporarily."

"You don't like it?"

"It's charming, but not perhaps what I'd have chosen for myself. Rather close quarters with a lot of strangers."

"Which is a good way to get to know some people quickly. They're an interesting group."

"So I've heard."

He actually grinned. "How did Cliff describe me?"

"He didn't give names to anyone. Let's see, there were the Australians who don't get along (I heard them as I came down), a sculptor his sister had discovered, a one-room school teacher. Are you the sculptor?"

"None of the above. Actually I'm a pediatric neurosurgeon."

"Ah, yes. He did mention you—going through a divorce."

A frown lowered his dark brows. "The divorce was final some time ago. Well, half a year, but I suppose it was Cliff's way of saying I've become a sullen, reclusive bore. Not that he knew me before all this happened. He and Angel only came to Wisconsin last summer, though Angel grew up here. I remember her from when she was in medical school. I was surprised she didn't choose to do her residency here."

"A charming woman." I wasn't sure what to say about Cliff Lenzini, my impressions being mixed, so I said nothing. I rose, pocketing my apple core. "Is your real name John?"

With a gentleman's natural courtesy he rose also, his sturdy, athletic body more apparent at its full height. Surprised by my question, he said, "Yes."

"John Hunter. Amazing."

He knew what I meant, and nodded. "I think the only reason I became a doctor was because I read a biography of him when I was in high school. And the only reason I read the biography was because he had the same name I had."

"Wonderful! He was part of my inspiration for becoming a doctor, too. The brilliance of that uneducated mind took my breath away. I memorized some of the truths he taught: 'Never perform an operation on another person which, under similar circumstances, you would not have performed upon yourself.' We don't do half as well today. And I loved that he'd come from such a simple family, like mine."

"And mine," he admitted. "So few people know his name. I think you're the first person who's ever made the association, and I'm delighted."

A surprising amount of warmth seemed to pass between us, as though we'd identified each other as kin, or something. But he was standing there in his pajama bottoms, so I said, "I've imposed on you quite long enough, Dr. Hunter. I'll just make my way around the rest of the garden."

"No one else will be up for hours. On Saturday breakfast isn't even set out until eight. Are you sure you don't want me to help you find something to eat?"

"Thanks, I'll manage." As I turned away, I said, "I hope you won't think I've interfered, but I'm glad you're going to see someone."

I could feel him stiffen slightly, but he murmured, "Not at all. A pleasure to have met you, Dr. Potter."

"Amanda," I responded, automatically, and strolled off as though with the intent of identifying down to the last spring bulb the variety of plants in the Mayfield House garden.

In truth I was a little distressed by the meeting. I had only been away from Nigel for a day and already some tenuous feelings of liberation were stirring in me. Not that I'd never felt attracted to some man in London, but one didn't usually run into them in their pajamas, in rather acute depression, in one's garden. Probably it was the doctor in me, I thought with a sigh. And didn't believe it for a minute.

Because of the time difference, I realized I could call Nigel. My hours of en route debate had provided me with no answers, except that I had no wish to refer to our "separation." Let him bring it up if he chose. My guess was that since he'd only raised the issue when there was no time to deal with it, he wasn't ready for a full-fledged discussion. He'd never been ready for a full-fledged discussion of our marriage.

Nigel had phrased his talk of a "separation" almost as though I'd requested one, almost as though it was for my convenience. And though an actual separation had not occurred to me, I had certainly realized from the moment I decided to leave for six months that I would be reevaluating my marriage while I was away. Did Nigel's bringing it up mean that he would be doing the same?

One of the first things Nigel had said when I told him about the sudden opportunity to go to Wisconsin was, "Now I'll feel better that I dragged you to North Carolina all those years ago. You'll get some benefit from having done that hellacious residency."

Nigel himself had benefited immediately on our return to England from getting his biochemistry doctorate at Duke. Biochemistry is his life, in many ways. He eats, sleeps and breathes his work, and he's brilliant at it. His family, Cass and I, run a good second, mostly because he's trained himself—or we've trained him—to remember birthdays and appointments and all the trivia of life that escape so many dedicated people. With both Cass and me away, he must have had a shining vision of six whole months in which he could totally immerse himself in his research.

"How was the trip?" he asked when I finally reached him at his lab.

"Not bad. And the rooming house is a charmer, though I'm not sure I'll stay here. I'd like a place with a kitchen of my own."

"It might be helpful to have someone else providing meals on a schedule," he pointed out. This was one of Nigel's subtle ways of referring to my weight management, or lack thereof. Nigel assumes that one day I'll decide to lose weight—as if it were a choice one could make, like picking a set of curtains. I had long since given up trying to make him understand.

"Well, I haven't made up my mind yet. I suspect the woman who cooks here is quite talented."

"Save your energy for your work," he recommended. "Cooking for one is a bore, and this is the experience of a lifetime, Mandy. You have an opportunity to make first-hand comparisons in treatment and outcome between the two countries. By the time you come back, you'll have an article for The Lancet. Doug will be green with envy."

An inspiring thought. "There's a delicious garden here, with spring flowers in riots of color. You'll be sure to look after my garden, won't you, or have someone come around?"

"I promised I would, and I'll take care of it. Sybil left a casserole, thinking I'd starve with you away. But she mentioned in her note that her gardener might be able to squeeze us in."

"That would be perfect. And you will remember to eat, won't you?" Unlike me, Nigel is thin as a rail with no apparent hunger signals to guide him toward a meal at the proper time. "I left lots of frozen things in the fridge."

"Please don't worry about me, Mandy," he said, a little abruptly. "I'm perfectly capable of finding enough food to sustain myself."

"Of course you are. Sorry." It was always hard to determine where Nigel's boundaries were. He could be astonishingly prickly if you overstepped them, but they seemed to shift with his mood. We'd been married for twenty-two years, and I still couldn't judge them with great accuracy.

"I'm just going to get settled in and walk around town and the university today and tomorrow," I plowed on. "Monday I'm supposed to report to the department head. I didn't get much reading done on the plane, so I'll need to catch up with that before I start, too."

"They won't expect you to have read the whole manual before you start, especially since you only agreed to come a week ago."

While this was probably true, I didn't want to be at a disadvantage or make them regret allowing me to substitute, but I decided not to mention this point. Nigel knew very well that he would have memorized the manual by now in the same situation (he's an incredibly fast reader, with a photographic memory), and he thought he was offering me a dollop of reassurance.

"Yes, I'm sure they'll make every allowance," I agreed. "Let me give you my number here in case you need to reach me."

Though we chatted briefly after that, I had this feeling of increasing distance between us, as if Nigel were impossibly far away. It wasn't the phone connection, and it wasn't necessarily impatience or distraction that I detected. Hearing his voice simply didn't make the emotional connection I had hoped it would. He was thousands of miles away, and it was as though each of those miles had erected a barrier to real union between us. Shrugging off the uncomfortable feeling, I said, "I miss you, Nigel." Did I mean that? Did I miss him? "I love you."

"Love you, too, Mandy. 'Bye."

It was a mildly satisfying conclusion to a mildly unsatisfactory conversation. The distance that I recognized sitting on my sofa in Madison, Wisconsin, wasn't all that different from the distance that occurred between us every day, was it? I was just more aware of it here in America.

Nigel and I hadn't behaved like a married couple for a long time. Meaning we didn't have sex. Which didn't seem to bother him, but it had always bothered me and the urgency of my concern was increasing. In England it was easy enough to keep up a facade of being a comfortably married academic couple, too busy to spend much time together but not so grown apart that a divorce was necessary.

But I ached for our lack of closeness, both physical and emotional. I didn't want a housemate; I wanted a husband. Living with the father of my child wasn't enough, even if it had provided Cass with such a solid family setting. Worse, I suspected that Nigel's withdrawal from me had been caused by my weight, though I had been round all my life, round when he married me.

For myself, my extra pounds were not a source of pain. I could look in the mirror and accept my generous body. I could dress it in splendid clothes, in vivid colors and flowing fabrics that became me. I could wear bold jewelry and outrageous scarves. I could understand that this was me, that I was meant to be this full-sized woman.

But no amount of self-acceptance could totally counter the constant knowledge that so many people viewed being fat as ugly and weak-willed. Nigel's disapproval was the most unendurable of all because I needed him to love and approve of me. And he could no longer do it. That was far too great a burden for a marriage to sustain.

I set the phone back on its stand and rose from the sofa, my heart heavy. At least there was breakfast to look forward to.

CHAPTER THREE

Some American breakfasts are better than others. On the whole, I'll take English breakfasts, kippers and all, over cold cereal and Pop Tarts. But I have to admit to a real partiality to pancakes, those thick, light ones with both butter and real maple syrup on them. As luck would have it, Sherri apparently made pancakes either Saturday or Sunday morning, and today was the day.

When I came down the stairs I could smell the griddle warming up. I was a little afraid I'd be the first one there but I needn't have worried. Angel and Cliff were already discussing whether they'd leave town for the rest of the weekend, and the Australians were bickering about who had left a coffee cup in their shared bathroom. Dr. Hunter was fully dressed in gray cords and a green turtleneck pullover, and acknowledged that we'd met when Angel introduced us. This seemed to puzzle her, but she moved right on to the remaining guest at the table.

This was a woman in her eighties, I guessed, wearing a dress right out of the forties, which looked perfectly appropriate on her. Sophia Granger had wisps of gray hair which she tried, unsuccessfully, to capture with white bobby pins. The effect was truly bizarre, as though her head had been stapled between fluffs of gray cotton. "How do you do, ma'am?" I said with a smile.

"Not at all well this morning," she claimed, in the loud voice a deaf person sometimes uses. "It's my gallbladder, you know. They'd take it out if I weren't so old and my heart in such rickety shape. Can't promise me I'd survive the surgery."

"That's distressing," I said in a raised voice. Dr. Hunter pulled out the chair next to his for me. "Fortunately, you seem to have a number of medical people surrounding you here."

"Oh, they're of no use! Don't know a thing about old folks." With a nod toward Angel, she conceded, "Well, perhaps Dr. Crawford does, but she's not here very often. Just surgeons and such."

"I guess that pretty well takes care of you two," Angel said with a grin at Cliff and Dr. Hunter. "When you get right down to it, a family practitioner is a lot more useful to a lot more patients than you two cutters are."

"But for the ones who need us," Cliff insisted, "we're absolutely essential. Isn't there a statistic that when doctors go on strike the morbidity rate goes way down?"

"I'm sure that statistic includes surgeons."

"Surgeons never go on strike," Cliff, the high-powered general surgeon, claimed.

The woman of the Australian couple, Crissy Newman, interrupted their exchange to ask, "What kind of berries is Sherri offering in the pancakes today?"

"It was on the menu, Crissy," her male compatriot, Mark Bird, taunted her. "Didn't you see it? Blackberries. Frozen from last year, no doubt. They'll be wanting to get rid of them before the summer crop."

"You can have them without," Angel explained to me. "Sherri's pancakes are great plain, too."

"The blackberries sound delicious," I said.

"That's because you don't have dentures that will stain," Ms. Granger protested, baring her yellowed set at me. "You're from England, aren't you?"

"Yes. I only arrived last evening."

"I don't understand why all these foreigners come here. What's the matter with their own countries?" She frowned at me and pointed a finger at the Australians. "They're foreigners, too."

"I can't think of any reason why foreigners *shouldn't* come here," Dr. Hunter said. "After all, we've been visiting other countries for as long as I can remember."

"They don't come to visit," Ms. Granger said. "They come to sponge off the government."

Dr. Hunter laughed with real amusement. "I think you have it a little backward, Sophia. The government in England is considerably more liberal with their benefits to their citizens than we are."

"Nonsense. I've read about it in the papers. They come and get on our welfare roles and drain money from our health care system."

Cliff had had enough of this kind of talk, apparently, because he snapped, "Not at the breakfast table, Sophia. If you want to start an argument, you'll have to wait until we're finished."

"She always starts arguments," Mark Bird muttered. "And she's always saying something rude about foreigners, as though we'd personally robbed her of her pension."

"No," Cliff said, "we're not going to discuss personalities, either."

The young couple were casually polite to me, as Australians are. Naturally I'd known about a zillion Australians in my lifetime, living half of it in London. They were some of the most adventurous souls I'd ever encountered, with a real penchant for traveling on their wits. These two didn't seem to quite fit that mold, but it was hard from such a spare acquaintance to pinpoint why I thought so.

Angel inquired of Dr. Hunter whether he would be spending the weekend with his children and he nodded. "I'm taking them to the Oconomowoc house. After May they get pretty busy with their summer activities, so this might be the last chance for a while to spend a whole weekend with them."

"How old are your children?" I asked.

"Luke is seventeen and Sandra is fifteen. They're both sports crazy."

"What a surprise," Angel remarked with pretend innocence. "I rarely see you when you aren't on a bike, or driving off with skis on your car."

Because a plate of blackberry pancakes was set in front of me at that moment, I lost track of the conversation momentarily. The apple several hours ago had not been enough to take the edge off my appetite. I noticed, too, that a plate with American sausages and bacon was being passed down the table, and though I preferred English to American sausages, these were more than acceptable to me at the moment.

Something we don't have very often at Netherhall Gardens is real maple syrup. Nigel isn't very fond of things like pancakes and waffles and French toast that call for maple syrup, so I usually eat them out, at places where they wouldn't know real syrup from the artificially-flavored variety. It was delightful to let a dab of butter melt into the pancake and then pour the real thing over it. As I'd expected, the taste was heavenly.

I helped myself to a slice of bacon and a sausage when the warm plate arrived. And there was a variety of chilled chunks of fruit in a big blue bowl which Dr. Hunter, with a suspicious gleam in his eyes, passed to me as well. Since I had every reason to be hungry, I gave him my superior English sniff and he laughed.

Angel regarded us curiously, but said nothing except, "Cliff and I won't be around Mayfield House much this weekend, Amanda, but Sherri may be, if you need any information."

"I plan to explore downtown and the University, familiarize myself with the layout of the hospital. I believe it's possible to walk to the University from here."

"Well, it is," Dr. Hunter said, "but riding a bike is more convenient. An old bike of Sandra's is in the garage, if you'd like to use it."

"Thank you. That's very kind." I was not going to tell him that I'd never ridden a bike in my life, because people simply refused to believe that. My mother credits my having become a doctor to the fact that I'd spent two weeks in hospital when I was very young, having been run down by a cyclist. When asked to what she attributes my choice of specialty, since it wasn't orthopedics, she usually says with a bland smile, "Her contrariness, of course." Not that I am the least bit contrary, but she *will* have her joke.

"I'll show you where it is right after breakfast," Dr. Hunter volunteered.

"Please don't inconvenience yourself on my account. You must be in something of a hurry to pick up your children. I'm sure I can find the bike if I decide to use it."

He regarded me somewhat curiously, but nodded. "It's the purple one hanging on the back wall. If you like, I'll lift it down for you before I leave."

Obviously I deserved this, for commenting on his depression. He was being as persistent a do-gooder as I had been. "I'm sure I can manage."

"I doubt it. You're far too short."

Perhaps he would have liked to add—"and stout"—but he didn't. The Australian, Mark, said, "I'll be around, studying. Just give me a hoot if you want help."

"You're going to stay in on a day like this?"demanded Crissy, indignant. "It's perfect weather, for God's sake. And you know you promised to go with me to the Farmers' Market."

Angel and Cliff exchanged a look that said, "Let's get the hell out of here now!" Which they did. And shortly I rose, too, replete with the delicious breakfast and ready to tackle my new environment.

Madison is a charming town with a luxuriant Farmers' Market on Saturday morning from spring through summer. Sherri drove me there, and while she shopped, I wandered around the capitol area, joining her for a ride back to Mayfield House. Then I was eager to get a look at where I'd be working, and if it hadn't gotten quite warm that day, I would probably have been perfectly comfortable walking to and from the University hospital. I frequently walk to work in London.

As it was, I found myself perspiring when I arrived, and even after a cool drink I was wishing that I didn't have the walk back to contemplate. The hospital consists of a number of tall towers connected at the corners, and each tower contains several floors. Without their grid system patients and visitors could have wandered through it for years without finding their way back out.

This modern edifice made me feel almost nostalgic for my dank, lumbering London hospitals where only the insiders had any idea where they were going. Though I wandered all over the attractive hospital building, including the obstetrics and gynecology areas, I didn't introduce myself to anyone. The heat and the time change had me slightly disoriented and before long I decided to start the walk back to Mayfield House.

People of all ages whizzed by me on bikes, looking as comfortable as if they'd been born on them. I had to admit to the tiniest smidgen of jealousy. Perhaps I should have tried learning to ride a bike as a grown-up, but I couldn't even imagine negotiating the traffic in London. A few young people were on rollerblades, and I felt sure I could master those, but as no one my age was on them, I assumed it would be undignified to travel to the University that way.

Walking was obviously my best bet. Another day I would wear something cooler; I already had on my most comfortable walking shoes. For May it was a great deal hotter than I'd expected, more like the middle of summer. Sherri explained, when I arrived back at the house, that they didn't always have heat like that in May, but I'd have to expect the occasional day. She also suggested that she pour me a glass of iced tea. I was dubious, but agreed.

"I always keep a pitcher of tea in the refrigerator on hot days," she said, beckoning me to follow her into the kitchen. "But it's not a mix; I brew it from tea leaves, or tea bags if I'm in a hurry. For iced tea I use something a bit spicier than for hot tea."

"Do you take a full load at school as well as running this place?" I asked, impressed with her attention to detail.

"Not quite, but usually I make up for that with a course or two in the summer." She had brought out a tall glass from the freezer, and now filled it with ice. From a wonderful old-fashioned pitcher of cobalt blue, she poured an amber tea into the glass. "Here, this should help. Can I get you something to eat with it, Dr. Potter?"

"No, thanks," I said, though I would have adored one of the puddings I'd seen in the refrigerator when she opened the door.

They were doubtless for dinner, which on Saturdays and Sundays, according to the brochure in my room, took place at six, six-thirty week days. "I'll save my appetite for dinner."

"That's almost two hours." She waved toward a cookie jar on the spotless tile counter. "There are always cookies in there, for between meals. And I keep a container of veggies in water in the fridge. Please help yourself any time."

"In that case . . ." I helped myself to a biscuit from the stoneware jar. It looked like what Americans called a ginger snap but was soft in the center, and rich with molasses. "Delicious. Perhaps I'll take two."

Sherri smiled appreciatively. "Please do. Most of the boarders ignore them, and they're best fresh."

Such a pleasant young woman, I thought, as I ascended to my room carrying the iced tea and the extra cookie. For a variety of reasons, not just the availability of food, I had come to think I might stay at Mayfield House instead of looking for an apartment of my own. I would have more than enough to do, adjusting to a new country and university.

That evening I sat in the television room for a while with the Australian couple. One of them had rented an Australian videotape, and the other criticized it in a continual low-voiced commentary. Like most of the Australian movies I'd seen, this one was a bit bizarre, but interesting.

When the movie ended and the Australians were having a full-voiced discussion of its merits and demerits, I quickly escaped to my room. Resisting the temptation to call Nigel again, I picked up the manual I'd been sent and began to study it in earnest. Beside every item with which I had decidedly conflicting views, I placed a large red X. Beside those I didn't understand, I placed a black question mark. When the manual looked like a strange game of tic-tac-toe, I put it aside.

Though the miniature bathroom posed some problems for a short, round woman, I pride myself on my flexibility and I was learning to adapt to its limitations. Yoga was one of the more useful passions of Cass's life that I had adopted some years ago. Under no circumstances would I have embraced her vegetarian diet.

Thinking about Cass sometimes tripped my guilt switch. Not that she wasn't a wonderful person, and doing extremely well academically, but I often felt I hadn't quite done enough for her. Because of my medical career, I hadn't always been there when she needed me—as mother, advisor, or friend.

I regarded myself in the small, round mirror, trying to search out in those green eyes and that rosy face whether Cass was the reason I'd stayed with Nigel. If I hadn't been able to give her as much time as I wished, at least I'd given her a stable home. And unlike so many families that might have dissolved, ours had not been a contentious one. Nigel and I got along perfectly well.

Cass had responded to the paucity of parental supervision throughout her life by becoming independent, which was all to the good. What was perhaps not so terrific was her tendency to withdraw into herself. As outgoing as I am, and as self-controlled as her father is, Cass appears alongside us as neither wholly self-confident nor particularly sociable. In her own circle she was simply acknowledged as shy and brainy.

As I lay waiting in the large bed for sleep to come, I remembered the last time I'd lived in the U.S. That had probably been the most difficult period for Cass, when we were all in North Carolina, where she had started kindergarten. She hadn't understood the American children, and they found her accent and mannerisms amusing. Instead of capitalizing on this—as I had done—she became bashful and reserved.

Though Nigel and I had tried valiantly to temper these characteristics, our love and encouragement weren't completely successful. For one thing, I was too naturally energetic and her father too absorbed in his work to always recognize the symptoms.

Really, Nigel and I were well-meaning people, but frequently so challenged by our demanding careers that we were able to give attention only to someone or something that exploded with urgency in our faces. Cass's gentle self-effacement sometimes failed to alert us to her needs.

Having only one child had not been my idea, but, looking back, I think it had been a good one. At least what time and attention I had to give, had been given to her, I thought as I finally fell asleep.

The dreams I had that night were a melange of scenes from my youth to my present age, with characters who weren't quite what they should have been. My father, a lorry driver, was meticulously stacking crates of newly hatched chicks at the city dump while my mother, disguised as a nun, dragged my pushchair over a track of computer disks. And then it was Cassandra in the pushchair, except that she was sixteen, and I was explaining to her that sex had to be a mutual decision, a responsible decision. "But it should just be fun," she insisted, pouting, her enormous brown eyes glaring at me.

The scene changed again and I was riding a bicycle down an English country lane at dusk. A baby was crying somewhere ahead of me, but try as I would, I couldn't find it. Rain started to fall gently, and then in earnest. I heard Nigel's voice cry, "I've found the baby, Mandy," but I could locate neither of them. A feeling of despair overwhelmed me and I awoke in my bed in Mayfield House with tears sliding down my cheeks into my ears.

How bizarre! I thought, rubbing ferociously at my eyes and swinging my legs over the side of the bed. I hadn't cried in years, and I certainly didn't have any reason to do so now. Nigel and Cass were both safe in England, doing what they wanted to be doing, and I was in America, excited about comparing the current practice of obstetrics and gynecology in the two systems.

It must have something to do with jet lag, I decided as I glanced at the clock and found it was almost time for breakfast.

CHAPTER FOUR

Sunday was an even better day for touring Madison. Everyone seemed relaxed and welcoming, from the bus drivers to the shopkeepers to the pedestrians. The weather being slightly cooler, I wandered around downtown with map in hand. But as I explored the campus the temperature rose, so that once again I arrived back at Mayfield House overheated. After a refreshing glass of iced tea and cookies, to which I helped myself, I wandered out to the old carriage house that served as a garage.

The interior was cool compared with the yard. It took my eyes a few minutes to adjust to the gloom. There were spots for three cars there, but they were empty. Hanging on the walls were a variety of tools and sporting equipment. Dr. Hunter's daughter's purple bicycle wasn't hard to spot, but it was indeed far too high for me to reach on my own, and I had seen no one around the house to ask for assistance.

Not that I was sure I wanted to attempt the bicycle, but I could see that riding one would be extremely handy. I had no intention of buying or renting a car for the entire six months. My idea had been to rent one when I wanted to leave town for a weekend or a week. Probably I could hitch a ride to the University with someone, but that seemed a dicey proposition. The purple bike was a ten speed, I knew, from having witnessed Nigel and Cass on theirs many times.

A ladder resting against the workbench at the southern end of the garage looked sturdy enough to give a try, and I moved it to where I could maneuver the purple bike off its unnecessarily large hooks. Why does everyone have to make things so difficult for us short people? In the process of shifting the bike off its hooks, I managed to knock it against the bike beside it. Fortunately that one didn't come crashing down on me, but apparently I'd loosened a pack of some sort, which fell to the ground.

Thinking that I'd take care of it in a minute, I slowly lowered the purple bike onto the concrete floor, which turned out to be a little lower than I'd expected. This kicked up a bit of dust which made me sneeze and almost topple from the ladder. Eventually I climbed down and picked up the pack, from which several maps of biking trails were extruding. In my attempt to dust off this pack, I dislodged a sheet of paper, making the words on one side partially visible.

Now, contrary to Cass's opinion, I don't think I'm more nosy than the rest of the world, but I do admit to an untamed curiosity on occasion. It was probably a list of supplies, or directions to some mountain lake. What harm in just peeking at it and then returning it to its snug resting place amongst the folded maps? When I saw that it was something personal, something that looked very much like a poem, I knew I should have tucked it away, but one of the lines caught my attention, and I could not resist reading the whole.

"The angiogram looks very hopeful," I told him.
"I'll go to Crete," he said, "and see the Minotaur."

That maze, so like his arteriovenous malformation,
Where human beings were consumed.
"When you're well again," I said.

But he was a boy, twelve, scarcely begun.
"Or to Alaska, to see the aurora borealis."
That wild display of flashing colors and images,
Like the performance in his head.
"When you're well again," I said.

Sometimes pain overwhelmed him,
Fear raged through his hairless chest.
"I can give you something," I said.
"Let me travel to a special world."
"When you're well again," I said.

That last night I was so sure.
He sat with book in hand, entranced,
His head bowed to the wonder.
No hands could save him, not mine.
I will forever see him there, imagining.

A hot flush rose in my cheeks. This was a *very* personal poem
and I'd had no right to read it. Hastily I refolded and tucked the
sheet back in the pack with the bike trail maps. Then I climbed
the ladder again and tried to figure out where the pack might
have been hanging. There was no obvious spot, so I tucked it
under the seat and hoped Dr. Hunter wouldn't notice that it was
not perhaps where it belonged. Damn my curiosity.

The heat had begun to ease by the time I wheeled the purple
bicycle from the garage. But outside there was merely a gravel
drive and then the street, a sloping road where cars trundled past.

Certainly it was not the place for a neophyte bike rider. There was a sidewalk, but it seemed impossibly narrow to me, like the three-inch balance beam gymnasts do all those incredible things on. Walking the bike up and down the drive did nothing to bolster my courage. Despite the fact that everyone in the world balanced the things, the chances of my managing to do so on my first effort seemed very small.

As I was considering returning the purple machine to its place in the garage, Dr. Hunter drove into the driveway. It had not occurred to me that he would arrive home so early. After all, he had wanted to spend time with his children. Surely he should have taken them out to dinner. He drove the car to where I was standing and stopped there, his face only three feet from mine.

"How nice of you to take the bike for a walk," he said.

"You should have treated your children to dinner," I said crossly. "Kids love to eat out."

He had turned off the engine by now and was climbing out of the car. "Mine get fed better at home. Their mother is a gourmet cook."

"It doesn't matter," I insisted. "It's the excitement of being in a restaurant."

"My kids are far too sophisticated to think of restaurants as a treat. The opera is a treat." He cocked his head at me, amusement twisting his lips. "Why aren't you riding it?"

"I don't know how."

He pinched the bridge of his nose, eyes squeezed shut, as though attempting to absorb this was as trying as coping with a teenager's moods. "Very few people don't know how to ride a bike at all."

"Well, I'm one of them. I was run down by a cyclist when I was very young and have never had the least desire to learn."

"Until now."

"I'm not sure I do now, either. Unfortunately, I don't have a car, and I've found the walk to the hospital irritatingly hot these last two days. But I understand this isn't typical weather for this time of year."

"It's typical weather for the summer, when you'll also be here."

Suddenly I remembered the poem and felt a flush rise in my cheeks. Turning away from him, I started to wheel the bike back toward the garage. "Maybe you'd help me get it back up on the wall."

"I'd prefer to teach you to ride it. Hop in. I'll take you to a deserted parking lot and get you started."

"Thank you, no. It was a stupid idea."

He was already lifting the bike out of my grasp and onto a bike carrier at the back of his car. "Where's your helmet?"

"I don't need a helmet. I'm not going to try riding the bike."

"We always wear helmets when we ride. Didn't you see them on the wall?"

"Dr. Hunter . . ."

"Jack. Were you going to try to ride without one, when you don't even know how?" He sounded astonished. Maybe it was the neurosurgeon speaking. He'd probably seen plenty of broken heads from bicycle accidents. But it put up my hackles.

"I don't suppose I ever really intended to get on it. And I didn't notice the helmets." Maybe that was where the pack had been stuck, in a helmet. I had been concentrating on the bikes so firmly that I hadn't paid any attention to the helmets.

"Well, get in the car and I'll bring you one."

"You're not listening to me. I don't plan to learn to ride after all."

A trace of irony gleamed in his eyes. "Too late. Once the idea of learning a new skill has you in its grip, there's no denying it."

"Nonsense. I only thought it would be convenient."

"It *would* be convenient. And it's not all that difficult, even for an adult." He considered me dispassionately for a moment. "You need a good sense of balance, though."

"I have a perfectly adequate sense of balance," I assured him, "my weight not withstanding."

"Right, then. Let's get on with it."

Well, I thought, I would accept his challenge. If I managed to make a fool of myself, who cared? I climbed in the car, which was black and rather elegant-looking, but not a model with which I was familiar.

In a short while he was back, a slight frown wrinkling his brow. He opened the door and placed a helmet on my lap, then climbed in as he said, "I usually keep a pack of maps in one of the helmets. Did you see it?"

It hadn't occurred to me that he might not notice the pack under his bike seat. Trying desperately to control the flush that attempted to steal across my face I said, "Something like that fell on the floor when I took the purple bike down. Since I didn't know where it had come from I put it under the seat of the bike beside it."

He nodded, satisfied. "Good. I just didn't see it, coming in from the bright sunlight. Do you think you should change to older pants?"

My slacks were crisply new, to be sure, but I didn't have anything really rugged upstairs either. There hadn't been room to pack my hiking clothes. Another problem had occurred to me. "We might miss dinner if we go now."

"Sunday is always something of a buffet. There will be plenty left if we're a little late." He grinned at me. "And if there isn't, I'll treat you to dinner at a real restaurant."

"Very funny. I'll probably be too bruised to have an appetite left, anyhow."

As we drove toward the University, he offered a running tour-guide commentary on what we passed. It was obvious that he'd shown a lot of people around Madison. When I queried him about it, he said, "Mostly people applying for residency, either from medical school or further into a neurosurgery residency who want to specialize in pediatric neurosurgery."

"Why don't you have a junior staff member do it?"

"Sometimes I do, but I like to get a feel for what the applicants expect. If they're too far into wonderful-land, I offer them some hard truths, along with the potential rewards. I'm on the committee that selects who gets offered a position."

"Do you find they correlate—your impressions when they come to visit, and after they've been in your program a while?"

"Fairly well." He glanced over at me and shrugged. "There are always some surprises, and occasionally in the right direction. We had a man through here a few years ago who struck me as an arrogant jerk when he visited. I would have turned him down, but the others were impressed with his credentials, and he came. For a couple years he was a real pain in the neck, but something happened, and he changed—practically overnight."

"What happened?"

His eyes narrowed thoughtfully. "Nothing obvious. No patient died because of any incompetence. He still maintained a little distance from the families. But the kids themselves . . . I think some little girl or boy got to him. I think he finally realized that we couldn't do everything we promised, that these kids weren't going to be brand new again, that most of them would always be affected by physical problems."

He pinched the bridge of his nose again and pointed out the hospital administration wing. "That's probably where you'll present your credentials tomorrow. The department chair is Lavinia Hager. Have you met her?"

Alerted by a different quality to his voice, I turned back to observe him, shaking my head. "No. Doug knew her from meetings. The two of them dreamed up the fellowship idea last year." I remembered overhearing one of their conversations, but I wasn't going to mention that to *him*. "Since my counterpart insisted, Dr. Hager allowed the exchange to go forward after Doug's heart attack. Doug thinks she's a terrific physician."

"She's developed a department high on technology. I'm not sure how that will sit with an English OB who's used to midwives and less intervention."

"I'm here to learn. And I imagine I'll have a few ideas of my own to share. I'm not easily intimidated."

He flashed a smile at me. "I thought I'd just intimidated you into learning to ride a bike."

"So you did," I agreed easily. "But that's not my field of expertise."

Which was certainly an understatement. When we came to an empty parking lot, Jack abandoned the car and set the bike on the ground. He was dressed in jeans and a short-sleeved plaid cotton shirt, with a pair of sports shoes that had seen much service. No doubt he'd done something energetic with his athletic children that day. Now he held the bike and motioned me to climb onto it.

"Show me first," I urged, reluctant to put my life in jeopardy so soon.

Obligingly he straddled the bike, which was definitely too small for him, and a girl's bike at that. He rode the purple contraption in tight circles around me, explaining about the gears, the brakes, and how to use your feet to keep from falling if the bike tipped too far in one direction. "It's pretty much a matter of balance, as I said before. With kids we use training wheels, but adults don't have that luxury." He climbed off the bike and held it invitingly for me.

With a deep sigh I stepped up to it and nervously clasped one of the grips. When he let go, I found I had to hold both grips to keep the bike from falling. So how did one climb onto it, balance oneself, and start to pedal all at the same time? The prospect looked impossible, and yet almost everyone in the world somehow managed, didn't they? Of course, all of them had started when they were kids, not forty-four years old. Jack handed me the helmet.

The helmet made me feel only slightly more secure, and I assumed it made me look ridiculous, since Jack was attempting to keep a straight face. The bike was probably a little tall for me, even if it was his daughter's. Lots of fifteen year olds are taller than five-two. I attempted to hop up on the seat, only to hopelessly lose my balance and thrust my legs out to save myself. Jack took an iron grip on the seat. "Do it now," he said.

People of my size are always a little afraid that their weight will defeat others, but I did what he said and found the bike held solidly in place. "Now start pedaling," he said. Wobbling and jerking, I moved the bike forward. Jack stayed with me. "Now faster, and feel your balance."

My attempt was initially successful, but ultimately failed when I lost my footing on the pedals. Instantly I dropped my feet to the ground to secure myself. "Use your brakes," Jack said. He was right there beside me, had been the whole way. "Try again."

After a while that was all Jack said: "Try again." Long after I was ready to quit trying, he insisted that I was making progress and that I should "try again." He always let me start with him holding the bike steady, but after I learned to use the brakes and drop my feet properly at a stop, he no longer ran alongside the bike. When I was good and exhausted, he said, "Ride around the edge of the parking lot without stopping. If you can do it once, I'll let you quit."

Naturally I wanted to tell him that I could quit any time I wanted to, but it's hard to do that when someone is showing infinite patience with you. It took me about a dozen tries to go all the way around the parking lot, with him stabilizing me each time I started, but when I'd done it I felt a real sense of accomplishment. He clapped and held up a V for victory sign, just as though I were one of his kids who'd made him proud. It gave me a very strange feeling.

"Next time you'll practice getting on by yourself," he said as we lifted the purple metal frame onto the bike rack. "This one's a little tall for you, but ultimately that won't make any difference. You'll learn to adapt to any size bike within reason. Before the week's out you should be able to ride to the hospital."

"Thank you. You've been very kind."

"Actually, I like teaching skills," Jack replied as he climbed into the driver's seat and rolled down his window. "I suppose that's why I stayed in an academic center. Originally I'd planned to set up a private practice in Milwaukee or Chicago."

"You certainly have the patience for it. I'm afraid my store of patience is much smaller."

He turned to look at me for a long moment. "But you have perseverance, obviously. Probably a much more valuable quality than patience."

Was it? I doubted that very much. Nigel was patient, and I was persevering. Even the combination didn't seem to have moved us to the right place. "I'm starved," I said. "Let's get back and see what Sherri's created for her buffet."

CHAPTER FIVE

On Monday I was admitted to Dr. Lavinia Hager's office by an administrative assistant who appeared unusually flustered by my arrival. Since I was on time and dressed with my usual care, this struck me as odd. Dr. Hager herself, an attractive woman in her late fifties, regarded me with a certain coolness. Though she shook my hand, there was little warmth in her greeting.

The chair she waved me to was a totally inappropriate item with more the appearance of a narrow wheelchair than a comfortable seat. This might have been the height of modern design, but it was difficult to wedge myself into its skimpy confines. I grimaced; so did Dr. Hager.

Because we had spoken on the phone several times, when Dr. Hager had been more cordial, I was puzzled by her attitude. She immediately asked for a detailed description of my training and practice, something which I would have thought quite unnecessary under the circumstances.

It occurred to me that Doug's recent fax to her from his hospital bed might have been less than flattering. Perhaps he had mentioned how alert I was to allowing even high risk labors to continue at their own pace, without undue monitoring or rush to intervene. Like Doug, Dr. Hager was reputed to be a high-tech practitioner. Give them a new toy and they would find a way to use it.

Dr. Hager's attitude disturbed me. Her contention that I would have much to learn, that the American practice of obstetrics was far in advance of England's, was nicely calculated to rouse my defensiveness. Nigel has taught me well in this regard, however. All Dr. Hager was able to elicit from me was a passive nod and smile—and the occasional recitation of the figures which indicated England was far and away a less dangerous place for a child to be born.

"That's only because you give every pregnant woman prenatal care," she remarked, rather carelessly.

"But that's necessary for a good outcome," I reminded her. "It only makes good medical and financial sense."

The National Health has its faults, heaven knows, but it does provide health care to everyone. Americans are apparently convinced that *government* administration of health care is inefficient and wasteful. But their private insurance companies add a very expensive layer between doctors and patients, which seems totally unnecessary to me.

Dr. Hager took me on a brief tour through her department, introducing me to the OB attending doctors, but with a half-hearted instruction to them to see that I be given any assistance I needed in my research. When she deposited me at the office I'd been assigned (quite a nice one, obviously meant for Doug's comfort), she flashed the briefest of smiles.

"I'll take under consideration your desire to do clinical work, Dr. Potter," she said.

"It's in my contract," I reminded her.

"You have to be included under the department's insurance. That's a matter I have to approve." And without further explanation, she turned on her stylish high heels and left me.

My purpose in coming to Madison had been not only to engage in the agreed-upon comparisons of Effective Care in Pregnancy and Childbirth (ECPC), but to actively participate in obstetrical care. Since I had a valid medical license to practice in the U.S., this was not a matter for debate, so far as I was concerned. But I couldn't practice if I wasn't covered under the department's insurance.

If Doug had planned to be only an observer, there was no reason why I had to be, so I set about establishing a foundation for myself in the department. I managed to woo two of her attendings to my side of this debate. Both Dr. Sarah Jamison and Dr. Willard Kyle seemed to appreciate my frustration with the idea of being prevented from participation in clinical work.

Sarah, who was a new member of the staff, probably had a great deal to lose by championing my cause, but that didn't seem to deter her. On the Wednesday after I started, Sarah took me along to the weekly morbidity and mortality conference. (Dr. Hager hadn't mentioned it to me.) The conference met in a small, attractive auditorium with facilities which would have made Doug Lattimore's eyes pop out.

Referring to the case under discussion, Sarah said, "Dr. Potter mentioned that she's had experience with this kind of cultural problem in handling high risk deliveries in England. Apparently some ethnic groups view at least an attempt at labor as highly desirable, even when the likelihood of a caesarean is high. There have been men in these groups who have spurned their wives for not attempting to deliver vaginally."

Dr. Kyle called on me to give an example, and I succinctly described a not-uncommon situation in London of a Bengali couple I'd dealt with the preceding week. Dr. Hager thanked me for my participation and turned the discussion to other matters. After the meeting, both Sarah and Willard helped me corner her.

"I would very much like to have Dr. Potter work with me, as we'd planned," Sarah urged. "I've arranged for her to have access to our ECPC data, but I feel I have a great deal to learn from her about clinical practice as well. Not only is the cultural set-up different there, but the English experience of what's successful high-tech-wise may be different. Even more than that, Dr. Hager, I want to learn about their system of midwifery care."

Dr. Hager waved aside Sarah's arguments. "Dr. Lattimore felt the ECPC research would occupy him quite sufficiently for the duration of the fellowship. Dr. Potter would be diluting her efforts by maintaining a clinical practice as well."

Willard Kyle, who was an older attending, merely raised his brows at this. "If Dr. Potter feels she can manage both areas, I think we have an obligation to let her try. She's obviously familiar with our American system, Lavinia. After all, she trained at Duke."

"Many years ago." Dr. Hager smiled kindly to show that this wasn't meant as an insult. She was, after all, perhaps fifteen years older than I, though a striking-looking woman with silver hair and intelligent eyes. "A lot has changed in our practice of obstetrics since those days."

"I assure you I'm abreast of the literature," I said, trying to keep a sardonic edge from my voice. "Doug Lattimore must have given you some idea of my competence. We've worked together for many years."

She was unrelenting. "Dr. Lattimore has no way in which to judge your performance by our standards."

"Dr. Hager, I'm qualified to do clinical work in the United States. We agreed that I would on the phone last week."

"Perhaps that was rash on my part," Dr. Hager said, but there was no trace of apology in her melodious voice.

"Not at all," I assured her. "I wouldn't have come if the only inducement had been the ECPC work. Statistics are all well and good; I've produced most of the studies from my hospital. But the real pleasure and learning experience is seeing first-hand what is being done, especially in a first-class university environment."

Flattery obviously was going to get me nowhere. Dr. Hager responded flatly, "Our patients expect cutting edge knowledge and experience here, Dr. Potter. We're not familiar with either your knowledge or your experience. You can appreciate the dilemma that produces."

Dr. Kyle snorted. "It's no worse a dilemma than any resident produces, Lavinia. And Dr. Potter's licensing automatically makes her eligible for our hospital insurance." He offered me a good-natured smile and said, "I think we should welcome her into the fold."

When Dr. Hager didn't accept his suggestion, Sarah grew impatient. "Lavinia, you promised me access to Dr. Potter's English experience. I've made all my arrangements for the next few months based on that. Why don't you stand in on a couple of procedures to see for yourself how she does?"

Though I could see it was a necessary ploy, I found this suggestion somewhat demeaning. After all, I'd practiced obstetrics in a university setting for so many years it seemed absurd anyone would question my credentials. When Dr. Hager said she didn't have the time to do that, Sarah said, "Well, I do and Dr. Kyle does, so we'll handle the matter."

Dr. Hager did not flat out veto this arrangement, and our meeting disbanded. I couldn't help believing Doug had somehow sabotaged me, which made me madder than hell. As if I hadn't put up with enough from him over the years, now he was crippling the one opportunity I had for a stint away from his irritating authority.

While awaiting opportunities to prove my capabilities, I spent a fair amount of time questioning my new colleagues and exploring the hospital floors and patient charts. One of the fellowship stipulations had been that the records for the past few years would be made available so that I could study how patients were indeed being handled, and what I could make of the outcomes.

My understanding was that American insurance companies currently were trying to shorten patient stays (to save money, of course) and that their method for determining when to do this consisted of going through patient charts to ascertain if morbidity or mortality issues entered the picture during the patient's hospital stay. If they didn't, obviously—in the corporate mind— there was no sense wasting money keeping the poor sods in hospital, despite their potentially vulnerable physical and psychological states.

A few years ago determining length of stay would have been considered in vast, monitored studies of the issues. Today it was being plotted out of wishful thinking by people intent on that bottom line. They were doing outpatient mastectomies in the United States, for God's sake! Greed is a nasty motivator.

In any case, the whole matter of effective care in obstetrics was a passion with me. From everything I'd seen at the University, Dr. Hager had a similar concern. Though she was far more geared to high-tech practice than I was, her department was run for the benefit of the patient rather than the practitioner. And Lavinia knew her department would ultimately benefit from my research, which was why no doubt why she'd allowed someone to take Doug's place when he was unable to come. So her animosity toward me was both confusing and distressing.

Though I spent hours working on the ECPC data, it was the sort of thing which required regular breaks in order to give it my best concentration. With no clinical practice to distract me, I used the bike riding as a diversion, but I was not very successful for a while. Actually mounting the purple monster and getting started without Jack's supporting hand on the seat proved harder than I'd expected.

But I persevered. I had no intention of asking the neurosurgeon's assistance again and made sure that I worked with the bike when he would not be around. Sherri frequently came to cheer me on. I learned to prop the bike steady against the garage and she'd give me a shove off. With this start I managed to stay astride for quite some time, often making it up and down the block. When I didn't, I pretty much had to walk the bike back to start again.

After watching for a few days, Sherri made a suggestion. "Let's try you on a pogo stick. It requires a similar kind of balance and getting started."

Pogo sticks must not have been around when I was a child, because it was something I'd seen only in movies. To me it looked just as complicated as the bike. "Not at all," she protested and showed me how to hop on and keep hopping.

Imagine me hopping around on a pogo stick. Nigel would have been stunned, if for no other reason than that it looked totally undignified, even when Sherri did it—and she did it well. Still, it turned out to be a good idea because once I got the idea of the balance of the pogo stick, I was able to transfer the knowledge to the bike, concentrating on the pedals instead of keeping my seat.

Just before dinner Thursday, after an hour of working on it alone while Sherri got dinner, I managed to mount without the assistance of the garage siding. I rode off steadily around the block, merrily forgetting that Americans drove on the other side of the street than English folks.

Cliff was not expecting someone to try to enter the driveway at the same time he was, and we nearly collided. When he recognized that it was me, he merely shook his head in mock despair and said, "You're going to have to remember where you are, Amanda."

"How true! And all week long being at the University has felt just like being at home," I remarked rather tartly.

"Dr. Hager giving you a hard time?" he asked, his ferocious eyebrows raised.

"She's making things difficult."

"She's usually rather accommodating, from what I've heard. She's had the position for at least half a dozen years, so she's got a solid hold on it. Angel said she was widowed two or three years ago. Maybe that's changed her. Is this going to make a problem for you?" he asked, climbing out of the car he'd pulled off to the side.

"I hope not. I seem to have two champions on her staff. They'll help me bypass her where they can, but it's a bit of a nuisance."

Cliff frowned and pursed his lips. "Let me know if I can help. Though I'm not beloved of everyone here either, coming from the outside. There were several people who apparently expected to get my job." He shrugged and added, "And they probably should have. Sometimes you lose perspective when you're at a place like Fielding. You think no other medical center in the country has the same kind of talent, and you're wrong. At least partially," he couldn't help adding with a twinkle in his eyes.

"God, and think where that puts people at universities in England," I said as I rolled the bike toward the garage. "No wonder Dr. Hager doesn't trust me."

He frowned as he followed me. "Doesn't trust you? But you couldn't have done anything wrong yet."

"No, and she's not about to let me. Maybe my boss wrote a less than flattering synopsis of my career. Not to worry." I leaned the bike against the wall and dusted off my hands. "Doug and I are old antagonists and I've learned a lot about working with some-one who doesn't appreciate your strengths and overestimates your weaknesses."

We started to walk toward the house, Cliff easily outpacing me with his long legs and energetic stride. When he came out of a brief abstraction he slowed his pace to mine and asked, "Are you still thinking of trying to find another place? Or haven't you had time to consider that yet?"

Surprisingly, it had completely slipped my mind. "I'll stay," I decided instantly. "Mayfield House is working out perfectly."

"Great. Angel hopes to get you out to our house one of these days, too, for a meal." He paused on the back steps and turned to me with a worried look. "Sometimes I think it's too much for her, you know, the medicine and the child and me not being available to help much. I'm useless at arranging childcare."

How many fathers had I heard say that over the years? But I held my tongue, saying only, "Could you give her a break, Cliff? Could you stay with your son and let her take off alone some-times?"

"I don't think she wants time alone."

I frowned. "Really? She'd be the only mother I know who didn't. Maybe just a few hours now and then. You'd get to know your son better that way."

His expression turned almost comically dismayed. "I'm not good alone with Roger. I hate changing his diaper and I don't really know how to bathe him."

"Those skills are easily acquired," I said, trying to sound patient. "If you spend time with him, you'll learn. Mothers have to learn, too, Cliff. They don't come with built-in knowledge."

"But it's not the same," he objected, holding the door for me to enter in front of him. "It will be better when he's older and I can actually do something with him."

Remembering my own days when Cass was a baby, experiencing both the overwhelming love and the trapped frustration, I couldn't help but ask, "Yes, but can you wait that long to do something for your wife?"

Before he could figure out how to answer, I hastened up the stairs. I've met a thousand fathers like Cliff—well-meaning, loving even—who allowed their wives to shoulder an unfair share of the household work and childcare. If these husbands and fathers felt they were being asked to do too much, how about their wives? Life was even less of a picnic for them.

My concern for my patients, and in this case for Angel, often led me to voice my strong feelings on the subject. I wasn't blessed, or cursed, with the usual English reserve, and it was a tenet with me that it was better to speak up than regret not taking the opportunity to right a wrong. If Cliff was miffed with me, so be it. At least my words might give him pause, I thought as I brushed my hair in preparation for returning downstairs to dinner.

There were only five of us at the table. Jack wasn't there, and the sculptor, Rob Sharpe, seemed to be away for the week, so I had yet to meet him. Sophia Granger was as contentious as ever, and if Cliff had intended to continue our discussion, he stood little chance. Ms. Granger complained about the food, the facilities and the other guests.

For the sake of peace at the dining table, which we English value rather highly, finding it conducive to digestion, I set myself the task of finding something that would make a difference in Sophia Granger's life. When I questioned her about her daily activities, they turned out to be few. She wrote letters to old friends ("But half of them come back because they've died," she complained) or read books of an uplifting nature which could not have failed to irritate her.

"With your experience, I should think one of the literacy projects would need you," I said. "Haven't they been beating down your door?"

"What literacy projects? No one has mentioned literacy projects to me."

"Surely you must have them here in the U.S. They're a very active function of libraries in *my* country. Wiping out adult illiteracy is a pressing goal for us, because it's something of a scandal. We have an impressive education system, especially during those years when children learn to read."

"I'm sure ours is every bit as good!"

"Mmmm," I said doubtfully. "Perhaps the problem isn't as great here, but I'm sure I've read that it exists. I'd be very surprised if a town like Madison didn't need experienced teachers to help with adult illiteracy. Many of our retired schoolteachers volunteer their time to worthy projects like that."

Never much for subtlety, I would have told her exactly what I thought she should do, except that Sophia Granger would probably have become stubborn as a mule if I pushed any further. And since I'd finished my meal, I could see no reason to linger. "See you tomorrow," I said, by way of excusing myself.

Cliff's amused gaze fell on me when I rose to leave.

CHAPTER SIX

There's nothing as exhausting as minding other people's business, so I sat down in my windowseat and refreshed myself by watching the changing light in the garden. Which reminded me of my own garden, and I was sorely tempted to call Nigel to check whether he'd made the arrangements we'd spoken of. Which would have annoyed him, of course. Fortunately it was the wrong time of day to call England, anyhow, and I told myself I would call Saturday, when it had been a week.

But thinking about home made me a little restless, and I decided to take a walk around the immediate vicinity of Mayfield House. As I was approaching the front door, Cliff called to me from the communal living room, where I found him talking with Jack Hunter. Cliff motioned me to sit down opposite him, on one of the wing-backed chairs.

"I won't be around this weekend," he said, "because of a family get-together, but I think Angel would like me to arrange something more for you to do than sit in your room. And here Jack was telling me that he's going to Oconomowoc this weekend without the kids. That area would give you a real taste of Wisconsin, and Jack has tons of room in his house."

Obviously Cliff was a worthy opponent. All I'd said was that he might give his wife a little free time, and look how he was repaying me. If he meant to embarrass me, he certainly accomplished his goal. Jack looked as though he'd swallowed a walnut whole.

"Nonsense," I declared firmly. "There's plenty to do in Madison for someone who's just arrived. And there's no reason on earth poor Dr. Hunter should have a companion dropped on him."

"Well, I . . . it's not that I wouldn't enjoy having you along, if . . . " The man was so taken aback he couldn't think of a single reason not to have me. "You're welcome to come, Dr. Potter, but I wasn't planning anything special. Canoeing, hiking, maybe fixing one of the windows."

His gaze at Cliff was a plea for help, at which Cliff merely cocked his head and grinned.

"Don't give it a thought," I said, frowning at my host. "Cliff is merely getting even with me for suggesting that he isn't perfect."

"I *am* perfect," Cliff protested, a devilish gleam in his eyes. "Not everyone can see it. Some people, for instance, believe I'm not holding up my end of my familial obligations. But look what I've just done: I've found you a delightful plan for the week-end. Just what my overburdened wife would have wished."

"Your overburdened wife would have far preferred your arranging a few hours off for her to spoofing poor Dr. Hunter into thinking he had to take me off with him somewhere."

"Poor Dr. Hunter," said poor Dr. Hunter, "is far from understanding this entire conversation. I presume it has nothing whatsoever to do with me."

"Right," I said.

"Wrong," Cliff said. "If I were to go home and tell Angel I'd arranged for Amanda to spend the weekend at Hunter's place in Oconomowoc, she'd be impressed."

"Not if she knew how you'd done it, and that poor . . . that Jack had been thoroughly embarrassed by your methods."

"I was not thoroughly embarrassed," Jack insisted. "I was simply taken unawares. Of course I'd be happy to take Amanda with me, if she should want to go."

"That's very kind of you," I said, "but I have other plans."

"Oh, sure," Cliff drawled. "She's going to ride that bike on the wrong side of the street, and call England, and read the Department of Obstetrics, Gynecology and Reproductive Services' dull and forbidding manual for the next few days."

"You're riding the bike?" Jack asked. "You can get on it by yourself now?"

Cliff looked entirely puzzled by this. "Of course she can get on it by herself, but she hasn't figured out that our traffic is opposite England's yet. I damn near ran over her."

"That's an exaggeration," I assured Jack, who was looking alarmed. "I carelessly didn't notice Cliff when I was pulling into the driveway this afternoon. I've lived in America before and driven extensively on the continent. I'll get used to it."

But Jack knew that riding a bike was all new to me, and his eyes narrowed. "You'd do better to practice out of town where there isn't so much traffic," he said. "There's a bike at the lake that you could use. And you'd have plenty of time to read the dull manual, and call home. It's not like I don't have a phone there."

"Thank you, but I'd prefer to stay right here."

"Oh, don't be so stuffy," Cliff teased. "Jack's not going to bite you. Oconomowoc is a delightful area, and Jack's place is an old family retreat that everyone I know would give their right arms to own."

"He's exaggerating again," Jack said. "But the area is perfect for escaping from city life and disagreeable departmental stresses."

I glared at Cliff. "So you've been bruiting about my problems at the University, have you? And I thought *I* had a big mouth. Give Angel my regards," I said as I propelled myself out of the wing-back, no mean feat in a chair that one sank into like a boulder on a pillow. "I'm going for a walk."

"Now, wait," he protested, but I didn't. I can be as stubborn as the next person, especially when I suspect that I'm as much at fault as he is.

I had reached the sidewalk and decided to turn left when I heard the door thud shut and hurried footsteps behind me. Assuming it was Cliff, I refused to slow my page. But it was Jack who came bearing down on me.

"We haven't finished our discussion," he said, falling into step beside me.

"Certainly we have. There's no reason on earth why you should take me to this retreat of yours. Cliff was just paying me back. Sometimes I can't resist telling people what to do; it's a horrible failing of mine."

"Like telling me to see a psychiatrist?" he suggested, only partially teasing. "I did, you know. Yesterday. She had no hesitation in diagnosing me as clinically depressed. Gave me a prescription for Prozac straight off. Don't they usually do tests or talk to you for hours? She said it would be a few weeks before the drug was really effective."

"It has to build up in your system for maximum benefit." It surprised me a little that he was being so open, but I liked it. "Prozac has been a blessing for a lot of people." With very little effort I could have come up with the names of about two dozen—family, friends, colleagues, patients. For a lot of them the medication had made a permanent change in their lives, almost always for the better.

Jack walked beside me, his gaze abstracted, his hands clasped behind his back. Only the hair at his temples was lightly touched with gray, the rest was a wiry brown, trimmed fairly close to his head but looking thick and healthy. He had eyes of a deeper blue than most, almost violet in the evening light. His mouth turned down slightly at the corners when he wasn't talking or interacting with someone, but the cast of his face was inherently strong and trustworthy. If you'd seen him in the supermarket, you'd have known he was a responsible, and probably highly intelligent, man.

"I've taken Cliff to Oconomowoc, one weekend when Angel was out of town at a conference."

"Who took care of the baby?"

His brows drew down in concentration. "Her mother, I think."

I sighed. "That's just the kind of thing he needs to rethink. Angel should be able to count on him in those situations."

Jack snorted. "Amanda, you don't know a thing about their arrangements. Maybe Angel doesn't trust him with the kid."

"Exactly!" I smiled triumphantly. "Which makes it necessary for her to do all the arranging and shifting and compromising. She has no choice, does she? If Cliff pulls the incompetency defense, he forces her to carry the whole burden."

With a wave of his hand he dismissed the topic. "That isn't why I mentioned that I'd taken him to the retreat. I was trying to point out that I've had people stay up there with me before, and there's no reason why you shouldn't come."

"There's no reason why I should. Cliff is a man. What would your neighbors think if you brought a woman up there?"

"Who cares what they think? It's none of their business."

"Oh, sure. And the next time you take your kids, some neighbor will ask, 'Who was the woman up here with your father in the spring?' People are curious."

He regarded me with a rueful expression. "You know very well you wouldn't let that kind of gossip bother you. Why do you think it would bother me?"

Having no pithy answer to that, I countered, "Look, Jack, I'd be in the way. You have plans for the weekend, things you want to do. If I went you'd think you had to entertain me."

"No, I wouldn't. I'll do precisely what I expected to do, except in the evening, when I'd just have read a book, anyhow. It'll be nice to have someone to talk to." He shrugged a little uncomfortably. "It's actually better when I'm not alone too long. I get to brooding."

"Obviously Cliff has hit on the perfect solution for you," I said, mocking him gently for resorting to this tactic. "You just hadn't realized you needed someone to keep you company."

He grimaced. "If you don't want to come, you don't have to. I'll be leaving after dinner tomorrow, barring any medical disasters at the hospital. It's not a long drive, less than an hour. The house isn't primitive, but I've always liked to keep it simple—no formality or fancy furnishings. There are five bedrooms and a sleeping porch, and usually enough food around to not starve before I go shopping."

We had made almost the full circle of the block, and were heading toward Mayfield House again. Jack looked down at me in a speculative way. The evening light softened his slightly stern features. "It wouldn't be a big deal, Amanda. You don't have to decide now. Let me know tomorrow evening if you like."

There were scattered lights on in our building. It felt comforting to know I'd already settled into my new home. Jack unlocked and held the front door open for me. "I'd enjoy having you along, Amanda. Think about it."

"I will," I promised, though I knew the answer had to be "no," if only because of Cliff's intervention. Never in a thousand years would Jack have thought of inviting me to go along, and that had to be my guiding principle. Otherwise I'd be taking advantage of his courtesy, something I had no intention of doing.

Which was a pity, because the scheme had, the more Jack talked, sounded appealing to me. Nigel and I spent several weeks each year at a cottage near Ullswater in the Lake District. I would sit for hours by Aira Force where the waterfall slid under a stone footbridge and plunged seventy feet into a wooded glen. The seclusion, the escape from London, the physical and mental freedom, all refreshed me in a way no other experience could do.

But, good heavens, everything in Madison was new to me, and certainly different from London. I had my own space in Mayfield House where I could think my way through the dilemma I was posed in the OB/GYN department. I could read their weighty manual and digest the important differences in our systems. Obviously this was much the better way to spend the weekend, I assured myself as I entered my room and closed the door. And married women simply didn't go wandering off alone with single, attractive men . . . did they?

On Friday Sarah Jamison was my guide, introducing me to her colleagues, her residents and students, and to a number of patients with interesting findings. The department chair appeared on several occasions to quiz me the way they do American residents. This was the kind of treatment one might have expected her to give a GP in from the countryside, rather than a consultant and senior lecturer from a major teaching hospital in London.

Despite my enormous annoyance, I answered her thoughtfully with how we would handle a similar situation at home. When she challenged me on an issue, I regarded her with surprise. "But surely, Dr. Hager, the ECPC guidelines are quite clear on this. Data-based research from a variety of countries has proved that use of corticosteroids for women threatening preterm delivery should be increased."

"We realize that, and were pursuing it long before the ECPC guidelines were adopted," she said, her nostrils flaring slightly. "But each case has to be determined on its own merits. The guidelines serve best for local doctors who haven't changed their practice since they left training and don't have the advantage of being in an environment where they are constantly kept up to date."

Sarah was not going to allow me to fight this battle on my own, apparently. "Effective Care in Pregnancy and Childbirth has to be a goal at our university level, too," she protested. "If we want practitioners in the U.S. to change their methods, we have to start with the doctors we're training."

Dr. Hager's eyes narrowed at Sarah. "We're always attempting to improve on existing practice, and we'd do that with or without ECPC. Our goal is safe mothers and babies, which requires nothing less than the most exacting care for the high risk patients we handle."

"Exactly," I said, trying to smooth matters over. "Implementing the ECPC has taken time in England as well as here. All of us are trying to root out the obsolete practices and the old wives' tales that have no place in obstetrics."

One of the passing residents caught the edge of my flowing tunic with his clipboard. The tug startled me and embarrassed him, but we both managed to laugh the matter off in a matter of seconds. When my attention returned to Dr. Hager, she was regarding me with something that looked very much like disgust. Before I could react to the expression, she abruptly left us.

"Thanks for your help, Sarah." I pushed back my short, wavy hair with a frustrated gesture. As we walked together toward her office, I asked, "What's going on here? Cliff Lenzini told me Hager has a reputation for being accommodating. Hardly the way she's behaved toward me. Do you understand why she's being so oppositional?"

A flush rose in Sarah's cheeks, and she didn't meet my eyes. "It's embarrassing to explain," she finally admitted.

Enlightenment. This had nothing to do with Doug. "She has a thing about weight," I said flatly.

Sarah, blinking guiltily at me, nodded. "It's been obvious for years. We haven't had an overweight resident in our program since I've been here, and she's terribly hard on the medical students she can't avoid working with."

Every fat person has run into that kind of prejudice, either subtle or overt. It made my heart sink every time. "So she thinks fat people are lazy, inefficient, and self-indulgent, huh? How unfortunate."

Sarah, herself willowy slim, bit her lip. "It doesn't seem to matter how much research comes out showing the physical and genetic basis of obesity. She can't absorb it. So far no one has been willing to call her on it. I'm really sorry."

So was I. "Not to worry. At least it probably means my boss doesn't have everything to do with Hager's attitude, though I still wouldn't put it past him to have written something unflattering."

We continued down the hall, passing an empty conference room and several offices. My mind was turning over options, considering possibilities. But I was curious, too. "You seem particularly alert to the issue, Sarah," I remarked.

"My sister is bulimic."

"Oh, dear. Is she getting help?"

"Some."

We had arrived at her office and she waved me in. Though the room was small, the visitor chairs were large and comfortable, just the way a pregnant woman would want them. There were bright watercolors of spring flowers vying for space with her diplomas on the walls. It was a cheerful space, warm and welcoming. Sarah took her chair behind the desk and sighed.

"I wish I weren't so far away from my sister, and so damn busy." She grimaced and pushed her shoulder-length brown hair away from her face. "Medicine is such a contradictory profession, isn't it? We go into it to help other people, and as often as not end up not being able to help the ones we most want to."

I smiled in sympathy. "I like to think that help gets passed along. I give it to someone, someone else gives it to me and mine."

"A heart-warming if slightly quixotic view of things," Sarah said with a grin. "How do you philosophize about people with Dr. Hager's problem?"

"I haven't had to deal with that so much in my career. Being a doctor has been an advantage, so far as the weight is concerned. You wield enough power and influence to neutralize the prejudice against fat. Usually."

Sarah looked troubled. "Lavinia is the only one I know around here who's so hostile about it. Makes me wonder if she had a weight problem earlier in her life or something. But you wouldn't think she'd be so judgmental if she had, would you?"

"It doesn't follow, I'm afraid. American women seem to be especially terrified of carrying extra pounds."

"No wonder." Sarah raked her fingers through her hair again. "I hate sitting with my sister watching TV. Weight is the butt of at least one joke on every sitcom. And some of the models they use are so painfully thin, they look anorexic. We Americans are a strange lot."

"It's not just an American prejudice."

She laughed and reached down to open a file drawer. From the back of it she took out a bulky file folder which she slid across the desk to me. "My obesity collection," she said. "My sister Joan clips articles and ads and cartoons and sends them to me. They're quite impressive, especially in total."

She picked up newspaper accounts at random and read the titles to me: "Study Says Brain Chemical Linked to Weight Gain." "Gene Discovery Reveals Why Folks Get Fat." "Second Protein Is Found That Stifles Appetite: Substance in rats' brains makes them eat much less." "Protein Discovery May Help Obesity: Scientists say leptin receptors tell brain to suppress appetite."

I picked one up that read, "The Burdens of Being Overweight: Mistreatment and Misconceptions." The *New York Times* had put out a three part series on "Fat in America" which had a callout quite clearly declaring: "Research finds weight depends more on genes than willpower."

"Maybe I should show this one to Lavinia," I said. "Doesn't everyone in America believe what they read in the *New York Times*?"

"Not when it's about obesity," Sarah said. "Doctors don't believe their own studies, for that matter. They just keep telling people to diet, as if diets served any long-term purpose other than gaining weight."

Sighing, I slipped the article back into her file folder. "Weight prejudice isn't easily overcome. This could be a tricky six months for me."

"I hope it won't be."

I rose to take my leave. "Thanks for being so honest with me, Sarah. I'll find a way to maneuver around Dr. Hager. If you'll clue me in on department politics, maybe I can use them to my advantage."

She smiled and extended her hand. "It's a deal."

CHAPTER SEVEN

Staring out the window of my office, I forced myself to acknowledge the conflicts in my own personality about weight. Though I firmly believe being fat is not a character flaw, I'm aware of how people like Lavinia view it. They *do* see those extra pounds as a physical manifestation of moral laxity. They firmly believe that what causes excess weight is eating more than your body needs, and/or exercising less. To them, losing weight is a matter of will power, and if you're fat, you obviously don't have any.

Doctors should know better, but they're as susceptible to the "obvious" as everyone else. That diets don't work has been proven to them so consistently and over such a long time that it's embarrassing they haven't grasped the truth—that being overweight is a function of a person's genetic, physical and chemical makeup. But it's easier to blame a fat person for her own problem.

The fact of the matter is, as all those newspaper articles of Sarah's explained, the body has a highly sophisticated, complex system for regulating its fat stores. The brain mechanisms that determine appetite or efficiency in storing fuel are not the same in everyone, so everyone doesn't have the same tendency to gain or maintain weight.

When I'm confronted with someone like Lavinia, I don't find it so simple to hold onto my confidence in my own appearance. Every day of your life you can look in the mirror and say: *I'm an attractive woman. I dress becomingly. I'm well groomed.* But if the Lavinias of the world say, *No, you're not,* it's not so easy to ignore them.

I've developed a high tolerance for such attitudes, and a remarkably strong sense of self-acceptance. But it fails in my most personal life. When my nearest and dearest don't understand, when they reject that part of me, I weep inside. Nigel no longer comments on my weight, but he has a tendency to indicate that I've "had enough." He doesn't approve of my having sweet things in the house. He can't help frowning when I order something he considers fattening at a restaurant.

And Cass. Cass has become a vegetarian. That might be a personal choice or have something to do with animal rights, but I suspect, deep down, it's an attempt to keep her figure from becoming like mine. And that hurts me in profound ways. Even my child rejects so forcefully that part of me that is overweight that she'll do anything to avoid having it happen to her.

Like Sarah's bulimic sister, I thought, and realized how grateful I should be that Cass had chosen to be a vegetarian.

Though it was only three, I rose from my desk and gathered up the department manual to take with me. I'd had enough of the University for one week. As I rode the purple bike back to Mayfield House, I realized that I was considering going to Oconomowoc with Jack.

It was not unusual for me, when I wasn't on call in London, to come home at the end of a rough week and throw some clothes in a case and take off for Cambridge or Bath or anyplace else that appealed to me. Sometimes Nigel came with me, mostly he didn't. That independence was one of the more useful elements of a pseudo-marriage such as ours.

On the other hand, my getting away wasn't always a need for time alone. If my relationship with Nigel had been different, if he'd been loving and warm and giving when he was with me, of course I would have preferred to have him along. Not just to receive the benefits of such bounty, but to offer them as well. Sometimes I felt as though I had years of such giving stored up in me, just waiting for an opportunity to flow out onto someone.

My patients were the legitimate recipients of the overflow of this desire to give. And Cass, of course. But she had reached the age where she felt smothered by too much attention. And the illegitimate recipients were people like Jack and Cliff, who tripped my need to "make things right"—to offer advice and see negative situations converted into positive ones.

Because Nigel wouldn't accept my offerings. He wouldn't accept my body, or my expressions of love. He had made it clear that he wished us to remain married, and to remain friends, but he was not interested in me romantically any longer. So sometimes getting away from London meant getting away from Nigel and a situation where I felt unwanted.

Things in Madison were different, but they were proving stressful in their own way. Without a car it would be difficult for me to leave town, and I disliked the feeling of being trapped here. Renting a car was a possibility, but not one I relished. I hadn't much idea where to go, either, having been in Wisconsin less than a week. Obviously the logical thing to do, if I felt I had to get away and could silence my conscience about imposing on him, was to go with Jack. If he was still willing to take me.

But going off with Jack was hardly like going off on my own, or with one of my women friends. He was an unattached male, a rather vulnerable male at this point in his life. And though I was attracted to him, there was no reason to suppose that the feeling was mutual. Given my current frame of mind, there was every reason to suppose that he wasn't. Obviously we could carry off a friendly weekend together.

Before I quite realized what I was doing, I found myself packing my suitcase.

Jack appeared at my door with my note tucked between his fingers just as I was about to go down for dinner. He looked so tired that I immediately said, "Oh, dear. You need to just sit in your room and vegetate. Don't give me a thought."

"I can't possibly look that bad." He frowned and rubbed his face. "I'm still going to the lake, and you're welcome to come. Dinner will revive me, and if I'm too tired to drive, you can do it."

"I haven't driven in America yet this trip."

He shrugged. "It will come right back to you, like it does on the continent."

"Hardly the same as here," I grumbled, "but of course I'd be happy to help."

He crumpled the note in his hand and stuck it in his pocket. "Very accommodating of you. Let's have dinner and get on the road."

He did appear to revive somewhat over Sherri's lamb curry, which was surprisingly good, and obviously made with the real spices—garam masala, coriander, cumin, turmeric, ginger, chili. Usually Americans make it with curry powder and it tastes like a particularly nasty yellow pudding. Serving it with brown rice was a good idea, too, and the two kinds of chutney—mango and cranberry—were delightful. I made a mental note to ask her for the recipe for the cranberry chutney.

After the meal Jack hustled me right along. He wore a pair of jeans he'd changed into and shook his head ruefully at my skirt and jumper. "It's *very* casual there," he said. Refusing to let him carry my one suitcase (he had only a backpack with him), I gracefully descended the staircase with it thumping against my leg and the department manual clutched awkwardly in my other arm.

He stowed everything in the trunk of his car and unlocked the passenger side for me. But he still looked so tired that I offered to drive and he accepted, only staying awake long enough to direct me onto the freeway and telling me the exit I should look for. Friday evening traffic had already thinned a bit by the time we were out of the urban area, and the driving was relatively easy— certainly compared with getting out of London at that time of day.

The scenery was pleasant but not distracting. I had expected my thoughts to drift to my departmental problems, but I was very conscious of Jack sitting there, his head slumped against the door. In the fading light his face looked both vigorous and relaxed, as though he'd fallen asleep after running a particularly challenging race. Knowing that he was a troubled man may have had something to do with my reaction to him then. Certainly I tried hard to tell myself that what I felt was a friendly concern, a sisterly interest in seeing him through his difficulties.

But the truth of the matter was that a bolt of sexual desire struck me so hard I thought for a moment that I'd had an accident. However, the cars in front of me were in the same positions, the ones behind me moving with notable regularity. Nothing had changed at all. Except for the intensely aroused state of my own body, the tingling in my breasts, the longing between my legs. Most inappropriate, I thought, putting my standard regimen into practice.

Like a man trying to delay his orgasm during intercourse, I had developed a routine for dealing with unwanted sexual arousal. Mentally I forced myself to attend a particularly dull lecture on the human body which a senior lecturer had given when I was in medical school.

It was an anatomy lesson on sexual response, but given in such a dry, overbearing manner that there was nothing the least bit titillating about it. We'd had to memorize hormones and chemical reactions, and minute body parts that were peripherally involved. Ordinarily the mental exercise was a very effective way of tamping down any physical desire. I had used it successfully on many, many occasions.

Starting with Nigel, I had refined the procedure over a desperate, lonely period of months, and then years. My desire for him had been useless against his indifference to me sexually. At first it had been almost unbearable, the pain of his rejection. But with time my physical desire for Nigel had diminished and eventually died.

Odd spurts of desire had been elicited from my perfectly healthy body by other men over the last years, but nothing that wasn't susceptible to my firm control. And though the present excitement was not yielding well to my command, I felt sure I would eventually be able to get this unruly desire in hand.

"Where are we?" Jack asked, shaking himself and sitting up straight in his seat.

Actually, I had no idea, my thoughts having been too distracting, but he knew the highway well. His forehead wrinkled and he said, "Amanda, you've missed the exit."

"Have I? Sorry. I'll get off at the next one."

He continued to regard me curiously, but finally shrugged and relaxed back against the seat. "We've only come about five miles too far. Were you worried about something?"

"Not at all," I assured him, pulling into the right hand lane to exit. "Just thinking, I guess. Everything's a bit new to me here."

Though he seemed to accept this explanation, I could imagine him deciding that maybe he'd better not fall asleep when I was driving again. He probably thought I'd revert to my English driving habits. But he adopted a perfectly patient attitude, and it wasn't long before we were passing through the downtown area of Oconomowoc, such as it was.

Passing along Main Street and then Lake Road, he pointed out some astonishingly large and beautiful mansions (considering the size of the town) on both sides of us. Those on the east faced onto Fowler Lake and those on the west to Lac La Belle. The architectural style was predominantly Queen Anne, but there was an example of the Swiss cottage style and a French Provincial manor among the others. I began to wonder if his family "retreat" was going to be one of these gems.

He dismissed this idea pretty much as soon as it popped into my mind by saying, "I'm further on, on the west, a shed compared with these beauties."

But he was exaggerating. When we drove up the lane to his retreat, we crossed a clearing and then encountered a screen of trees that almost entirely hid a very old stone house with a wrap-around veranda that absolutely exuded charm. "Some shed," I commented.

But the sight of the property had a decidedly invigorating effect on him. "It's beautiful, isn't it? I grew up here." He climbed out of the car and sucked in a large volume of fresh air. "Sometimes I think I could live here year round, if only there were a metropolitan hospital nearer than Madison."

A breeze ruffled the leaves on the trees that stood guard around the ivy-draped building. Though I knew the water wasn't far away, I couldn't actually see it, even when I climbed out of the car. When I opened the trunk, Jack came to lift out my suitcase and manual and his backpack, which he carried over to the house. On the veranda was a set of ancient wicker furniture—chairs, a coffee table, a chaise, and several footstools. Jack dropped my manual and his backpack on the table, unlocked the door and set my case inside the house.

"Come with me to the lake before it gets totally dark," he said.

He walked rapidly down a short dirt path at the back of the house that led to the boathouse and dock. "We have a canoe and a kayak and some other equipment in there," he said, pointing at the dusty window. "The kids and I went out in a canoe last weekend, but the water's still too cold for swimming." Without ceremony he seated himself on the end of the dock, removed his sneakers and socks and dangled his feet in the water.

There was a rural stillness to the scene. The water looked black and deep. You could see the pale images of other docks dotted along the shore, but nothing moved. I was tempted to sit down beside Jack, but the hum of attraction remained in me and I stood quietly by an old wooden post. It seemed almost sacrilegious to speak, so I surveyed the vista in silence, firmly keeping my gaze from alighting on Jack, who sat as though in a trance.

Probably this spot was for him like the cabin in the Lake District was for me. When we arrived, I would walk down to the water and stare at the ruffled surface while the stresses of London and work and family dissolved within me. Sometimes I could achieve in minutes what a trip to the continent never did produce—a feeling of peace and renewal.

After about ten minutes, Jack abruptly stood up and said, "Sorry. I just need a few minutes when I get here to let it seep into me."

"It's lovely, and incredibly peaceful."

He nodded. "Come on, I'll show you your room. The kids keep their stuff in theirs, and I do in mine, but either of the guest rooms should be in good condition."

"Anything will be fine," I said, following his lengthy stride as he started up the path.

All five bedrooms were on the second floor, but one of the two guest rooms faced out toward the water and I chose it. He smiled. "I felt sure you would. Though in daylight you'll see that the other one feels something like a treehouse. I'm across the hall," he added.

"That will make me feel very safe," I teased.

He regarded me curiously, and I wondered if something of my feelings had leaked through my carefully guarded expression. Finally he said, "It's very safe here, Amanda. In areas like this, America isn't the crime-ridden place you see in our television programs."

"I'm not the least bit worried." I pushed my suitcase in front of me into the room. "You won't mind if I explore the house a bit, will you?"

"Everything is at your disposal. It's early. Maybe we could have a drink and play a board game. The kids have a remarkable collection downstairs."

"Unless you'd rather read or turn in early . . . "

"No, I'm not ready for bed yet."

After he left me, I put away my clothes in the empty bureau and stuffed the department manual on a shelf. The room was sparsely furnished, but with attractive pioneer-type pieces and simple matching curtains and a bedspread of a Native American design. The floor was a soft polished pine, marked by generations of visiting guests dropping suitcases and sporting equipment. When I didn't hear him come back out of his room, I wandered into the hall and peeked in his kids' rooms, since their doors were open.

They were slightly larger rooms than mine, and reasonably neat for teenagers. Apparently the boy was into baseball, as there were posters on two of the walls. The girl's room had a number of trophies in it, lining the shelves. Though I couldn't tell for certain, they appeared to be sporting trophies, and I could see framed pictures of a girl in a variety of different sporting poses—diving at the lake, on skis, fishing, swimming. Sometimes another teenager was in the photos, sometimes Jack.

The stairs were polished pine, too, and uttered continuous protests as I made my way downstairs. The living room was central, with the kitchen, an enclosed dining porch, a bathroom and a storage room coming off three sides. On the fourth side was a room taken over by entertainment equipment—TV, VCR, stacks of games, a rack of videotapes, a wall full of books, a sound system and a library of CDs. There were tables for playing games and some comfortable chairs for reading or listening or viewing. It was a crowded, cozy room, quite different from the living room.

When I looked back into the large main room, Jack was standing there, his gaze abstracted, his lips pursed thoughtfully. Something about his stance reminded me of the poem I'd read, as if he were thinking about all the wrenching losses he'd suffered professionally. Probably it was nothing of the sort, of course. He was as likely wondering why he'd agreed to bring me along and deciding how to best keep me from interfering with his plans.

Eventually, Jack drifted into the game room. His voice sounded both amused and friendly when he asked, "Would you like me to put some music on?"

"Please. Unless you'd rather not."

We debated the merits of classical or jazz as background for a game of backgammon, and settled on classical. He put on a CD that was resting atop the console. "See if you recognize it," he said as he slipped it in.

Oh, great, a pop quiz, I thought. But the strains of Dvorak's New World Symphony filled the long, narrow room and I nodded. "This has always been one of my favorites. Mother played it constantly for a while, maybe in one of her manic stages, when I was eight or nine. I'd come home from school and the house would be filled with it. She never played it when she was depressed."

"Your mother's manic-depressive?" he asked, startled.

"Um hum. And her sister. And my grandfather. The family is full of them."

He looked rueful. "No wonder you notice the signs of depression. What would you like to drink?"

"Nothing, thanks. You go ahead." I get a little flirtatious when I drink sometimes, and this would not have been a propitious time to do so. Though I felt that I had myself under tight control now, it was better to be on the safe side.

Jack returned with a glass of white wine and sat down to the backgammon game I'd set up. He set a bowl of pretzels on the table between us. "In case we get hungry," he said with a complicit smile.

Actually I was feeling like a nibble and I stretched out a hand to help myself. "I do like an understanding man." As soon as the words were out of my mouth, I thought how provocative they sounded and I fought to control a flush. "My husband," I added firmly, "doesn't believe in encouraging my eating, but then he's naturally thin."

Jack had a good solid body, neither thin nor heavy. Muscular, I suppose it would be called, undoubtedly from all that sporting activity. I enjoyed watching the way he moved, with a fluid, vigorous grace that made the breath catch in my throat. He was a few inches shorter than Nigel, but still a good half foot taller than I. So that he didn't misunderstand, I added, "He's a sweetheart, Nigel. Caught up in his work, of course. We both are. Have I mentioned that he's a biochemist?"

"I don't think so."

"And Cass is studying physics. This was her first year at university. I'll miss them, being away so long." Babble on, Amanda, I thought.

Jack regarded me with a singularly bland expression. "I'm sure you will."

For some time we concentrated on the backgammon game. Though I was no expert, I found myself wanting to beat him. There was an aura he gave off, of being a winner, that set up my back. I rolled a number that would allow me to send him back, but would leave me vulnerable. Without hesitation I did it.

A flicker of something sparked in his eyes, and he set himself to battle back. We were silent for long minutes, only breaking the stillness to throw the dice or grunt with annoyance at each other's luck. His compact surgeon's hands moved precisely each time it was his turn, and rested with aggressive ease when it wasn't. I could hardly take my eyes off them.

As we approached the denouement, there was a palpable tension in the air. Academic medicine is extremely competitive, as are most sports. I don't think Jack was used to losing.

When I rolled the perfect combination to end the game, Jack grumbled, "You didn't tell me you were good at this. We could have played something where I would have for-sure beaten you."

"There is no such game," I declared dramatically. "When challenged, I play my best. And I'm always lucky."

"Oh, I doubt that." He grinned at me and pushed the bowl of pretzels toward me. "Have another pretzel."

"Too late. I can always be distracted by food, but you have to do it while we're still playing."

"Aren't we going to play another game?"

Considering my state of awareness of him, I thought that would be pushing my luck. "Not a chance," I said. Tucking the bowl of pretzels against my stomach, I rose and grinned at him. "I'm going to take these along in case I get hungry later. Good night, Jack. Thanks for bringing me."

"My pleasure."

The last glimpse I snuck of him before I slipped out the door was disturbing. His face had a naked, hungry look that stung my heart. Jack Hunter was a very needy man, no doubt about it. He needed someone to comfort him, to ease the burden of his professional losses, to be a psychological support to him. And since he was a man, chances were he would settle for the "comfort" of a sexual encounter. Which was a very tempting thought to me at that moment, with my body still uncalmed. With great force of character I marched up the stairs.

CHAPTER EIGHT

Rain was beating against my window in the morning. I groaned and rolled out of bed, pushing back the curtain and staring mournfully at the gray clouds and dripping trees. This was going to put a bit of a damper on my plan to explore the area, or to ride the bike, or just sit outside and drink in the country air. Though I was tempted to climb back in bed, it was already half eight and I'd look like a slug if I stayed holed up in my room any longer. From my suitcase I chose a salmon-colored cotton shirt and brown corduroy pants, and donned the least elaborate of my silver earrings. I decided I would call Nigel first thing.

When I came out my door I could smell bacon cooking and it occurred to me that Jack was cooking breakfast for the two of us. Probably I should have offered to do that. Nigel was awkward in the kitchen, possibly because he wasn't much interested in food.

Downstairs I could hear the clatter of pans in the kitchen, and I presented myself at the door with a smile. "Morning," I said cheerfully. Jack looked like he hadn't slept well, but I had no intention of commenting on that. "The rain is disappointing, but you probably have a dozen things you do in the rain, eh?"

"I stay indoors like a sensible person," he retorted. "Pancakes okay?"

"Sure. I love pancakes."

"We usually eat on the porch, but if you think it will be too cold or wet, we can eat in the living room."

"I'll set places for us out there," I said, indicating the porch. His irritableness seemed to be directed at me, for some reason, so I went about my task with few questions. Maybe he'd been waiting for a long time to hear sounds that I was up. After all, the Prozac would take several weeks to offer the full effects of its magic, and Jack had only been taking it for a few days, if he'd actually begun. Rather than ask him, I decided to take a peek in his bathroom cabinet when he was out somewhere being a jock.

We ate in comparative silence, with me commenting on how good the pancakes were, and Jack asking me to pass him the syrup. Jack was looking everywhere but at me, which seemed a little odd, until I noticed the guilty flush in his cheeks. Then I realized as if he'd spoken it aloud that he'd dreamed of me the previous night. Which was only fair, since I'd dreamed of him and could still feel a lingering arousal.

Jack's embarrassment was endearing, if misplaced. He'd probably forgotten how potent proximity could be to a sexually deprived individual. I myself had experienced the problem many times, and had long since ceased to blush for my uncontrollable dreams. I had always assured myself that they had no more significance than a song on the radio, buzzing through one's mind one moment and gone the next, occasionally with a lingering wisp of interest.

As we rose from the table his hand accidentally brushed my arm and he jerked it away so quickly I almost had to laugh. "I'll do the washing up," I said, "since you cooked."

"Fine," he murmured. "I have a few calls to make."

That reminded me of my own call to Nigel. While I sudsed the dishes—and rinsed them, Americans being particular—I thought about what I would say to my husband. Most of the week I hadn't thought of him at all, but it had been a busy week. I would tell him about the problem in the department, of course, and he'd offer me sage advice. I'd tell him about learning to ride a bike. I'd tell him I'd gotten away for the weekend, but perhaps not that I was at Jack's. Not that there was anything wrong with my being there, but I didn't want to have to go into a long explanation.

Jack was still on the phone when I appeared in the living room, so I went into the game room and picked up a *People* magazine to peruse and keep me from training my ear to hear his conversation, which seemed to be with someone local about a repair job. His deep voice continued for some time, and when it finally ceased, he appeared at the game room door.

"Were you waiting to use the phone?" he asked.

"For my call to London, but there's no hurry."

"I'm finished. Go ahead."

Instead of disappearing off somewhere in the house, he followed me back into the living room and sat down in a cushioned chair there. Was he trying to see if I'd put the charges on his phone? I distinctly told the operator that it was to be charged to my calling card, but Jack remained in the room, intent—apparently—on the newspaper he was holding in front of his face.

The phone rang at the London house, and much to my surprise was picked up on the second ring. But it wasn't Nigel's voice that answered. "Tony? Is that you?"

"Amanda, darling! So good to hear your voice. How's America, love?"

"Just fine. Is Nigel there?"

"We just got back from a set of tennis. He's up in the shower and I'm raiding your fridge. I was about to take him off to mother's for dinner."

"Have him give me a call before you go, please. I'll give you the number." Which I proceeded to do, while Jack looked over the top of his newspaper, with brows lifted questioningly.

Tony had rung off and I lowered the receiver to the cradle. For no reason I could think of, I began to explain the situation to Jack. "Tony's a great friend of ours. He lives with his mother not too far away, in Finchley Common. Mrs. Growalter has us to dinner regularly, and she's a fabulous cook. She's rather adopted Nigel."

Jack looked thoughtful rather than bored by this unnecessary tale. "Her son still lives with her? How old is Tony?"

"Mid-thirties, I should think. No, wait, thirty-seven last birthday. I remember because of the party. He runs the other biochemistry lab. The whole group came to our house. For a bunch of lab rats, they do enjoy a party, as long as there's plenty of liquor."

"Not unlike my very own colleagues." His gaze turned to the window, which was still dripping down rivulets of rain. "We have a great assortment of puzzles for days like this. Want to start one?"

"Maybe in a while. I think I'll just wait here for Nigel to call back." How long could it take, right? But I waited for ten minutes, and then twenty, when I finally had to go upstairs to the bathroom. Naturally it was while I was completely indisposed that I heard the phone ring. I hurried when Jack called me and arrived breathless in the living room.

"Where are you?" Nigel asked.

"At a friend's retreat not far from Madison. Tony said you were going to his place for dinner. Give my best to Lydia. Has it been a good week?"

"Not too bad. The grant came through."

"Splendid! That will rid you of a whole layer of worry. Has Tony heard about his?"

"No, but I think there's little doubt he'll get it. Tonight, though, we're celebrating mine."

When I mentioned that things hadn't been going smoothly in the OB/GYN department, Nigel said, "You can be a diplomat when you try, Mandy. You'll get things sorted out in no time."

This vote of confidence seemed a little detached to me. Usually Nigel would have very specific advice, but he sounded a bit rushed, telling me Lydia would be expecting them.

"Have a lovely time, then," I said. "Congratulations on the grant. I miss you."

"Have a good weekend."

"Thanks." Looking pointedly at Jack so he wouldn't miss my message, I added, "I love you, Nigel."

"Good-bye, dear," he said, and rang off.

Jack folded his newspaper and set it aside. "Everything all right at home?"

"Fine. Nigel got the research grant he'd been counting on. That should keep his project very much alive for the next three years."

"I'm glad for him." But Jack looked neither glad nor impressed. He looked restless, and a little downhearted. "Interested in the puzzle now?"

"Sure," I said, having established that I was more or less a happily married woman who took an interest in her husband's work.

Jack poured the pieces of an incredibly difficult puzzle onto the card table we'd used the night before. The picture on the box was of trees, and lake reflecting trees. With a sigh I began turning pieces right side up. "I haven't done many jigsaw puzzles in my life."

"They're fun, and not a source of competition."

I regarded him with a skeptical eye. "Oh, I'm sure you could make anything a competition."

He nodded in acknowledgement. "But with puzzles you can't quantify it, so it doesn't count. I'm sorry about last night. When I'm edgy I get more pushy."

"Well, this seems the perfect place to 'mellow out,' as you Americans say. Or can you only relax when you're getting a lot of exercise?"

Jack shrugged. "Exercise does get rid of my aggressive impulses, but I can relax if I try."

Unable to resist, I asked, "Have you started the Prozac, Jack?"

"Two days ago. But it doesn't work for everyone."

"It will work for you," I promised, though what did I know? "You're not drug aversive, are you?"

His fingers paused on the puzzle piece he was holding and his lips twisted ruefully. "Maybe a little. I like to solve my own problems."

"In this case you're likely to solve them by taking your medication."

"Yes, ma'am."

He said it lightly, but there was an edge to his tone. For some time he worked on turning over the cardboard pieces, and then began sorting out the edge pieces. In ten minutes he had most of the flat edges connected to each other. I began to work on one area of the water that was churning with foam, making it different from the rest. Fairly soon I had a three inch square more or less lodged in its correct spot. Pleased with myself, I glanced over at him.

His gaze was already on me, moving from my eyes to my lips to my neck—no lower. Personally, I have always thought my eyes, being an interesting shade of green, my best feature. But men have told me—obviously when they shouldn't have, me being a married woman—that my lips, which are rather full and red, look very kissable. Jack was probably noticing the two streaks of gray in my hair and the "laugh" lines radiating from my mouth and eyes.

He dropped his eyes hastily to the puzzle and asked, "How old are you, Amanda?"

"Forty-four."

His brows rose. "Really? I'm forty-three. You look younger than me."

"Only because you've been depressed. That will ruin your looks if you're not careful."

"And you, on the other hand, have no worries at all."

"Quite the contrary." I slipped a puzzle piece into a section he'd been working on and sat back in my chair. "But heavy people often look younger."

"Hmmm. Why is that, do you suppose?"

"Because there's not as much possibility of deep wrinkles or an aging gauntness in our faces. And overweight people often look robust in a way thinner people don't."

His amused gaze ran over the part of me he could see. "You *do* look robust," he admitted. "You look healthy and energetic, and . . . and full of mischief."

I don't know if he'd meant to add that last quality, but I could feel myself grinning. "And you think that perhaps I'm teasing you."

He shrugged, not quite meeting my gaze. "Maybe. You seem to be radiating a . . . playful aura. I'm not sure whether you're doing that intentionally or not."

"Hmm. Playful. Yes, that might be how I feel. On the other hand, there's something more voluptuous to it than that. I think a rounded body can make a woman feel earthy, nurturing, rich with possibility. I don't suppose most men look at a large woman that way."

Jack swallowed rather painfully. His thumb rubbed the glossy side of a puzzle piece in unconscious circles. "I'm sure many men are attracted to larger women."

"Not many, I'm afraid."

"But how would you know? You've been married forever. Men aren't going to let you know they're attracted to you."

"What century are you living in, Jack?" I asked mildly. "If a man is attracted to me, he often lets me know, subtly, husband or no husband, just in case."

"That's reprehensible. And probably harassment." He dropped the puzzle piece and shifted his hands to his lap. "Just in case of what?"

"In case I'd be interested in a little dalliance. Men never like to miss a chance for lack of trying."

He paid close attention to trying to fit a missing piece into the bottom of the puzzle. "And have you been interested?"

I sighed. "No. I've been a very good girl."

"Well, of course you have," he said stoutly. "Why shouldn't you be?"

Better not to ponder that one. "Indeed. Why shouldn't I be?" I rose and said, "I'm going to make myself a cup of tea. Would you like one?"

In the kitchen I paused for a moment to lean against the stove and get a grip on myself. There was no excuse for my behaving so provocatively, but I seemed to have a playful devil urging me on. Jack would be better, I told myself, for my having brought the sexual tension out into the open. And my honest declaration that I'd never fooled around would no doubt act quite effectively on him, even if it didn't seem to be making any impression on my own body.

Going through the motions of preparing tea, a time-honored ritual where I came from, I worked to calm myself and gain control over my impulses. There is something infinitely soothing about familiar tasks, and I allowed tranquility to seep into me while the tea steeped in a chipped golden teapot I found on the shelf. By the time I brought Jack his cup of tea, I was able to say, "I really ought to study that departmental manual for a while. Maybe I can work on this later with you."

"Sure." He scarcely looked up. "Thanks for the tea. I'm probably going to go for a walk in the rain in a little while. It's too claustrophobic inside."

Wasn't it, though? "Good idea."

CHAPTER NINE

In my room I did indeed attack the manual. By focusing my entire concentration on it, I managed to skim my way through most of it in two hours. Pleased with myself, I set it aside and walked over to stand at the window. The rain continued beating down and a mist made it difficult to see very far. My stomach was telling me it was close to lunch time, and I hadn't heard Jack return. Well, I was perfectly capable of making my own lunch.

But I stayed at the window, gazing out for a long time, my mood a tangle of conflicting emotions. A longing so strong I could scarcely credit it seemed to tug at both my body and my heart. A sadness just as strong battled to overwhelm the longing, and everything else I felt.

Looking out over the misty, dripping scene, I also experienced joy in some corner of my soul, a sliver of pure sunlight. What that small, surprising pocket was all about I couldn't imagine. Alongside it was the desire to laugh, almost hysterically, at my present situation. But I am basically a practical person, so I shrugged off all these disturbing emotions and went downstairs to find food.

The refrigerator had a minimum of supplies—a carton of milk that was not outdated, orange juice, part of a dozen eggs, some bits of reasonable-looking cheeses, various relishes, spreads, and jams, a partial loaf of 9-grain bread and a plate of fruit. The freezer had a number of TV dinners, frozen juices, ice, ice cream and a variety of Sara Lee frozen desserts. Someone — possibly Jack but more likely his kids — had a sweet tooth. There were also a few packages of frozen meats and vegetables, more appropriate for an evening meal.

All things considered, I decided to make myself a toasted cheese sandwich and a cup of cocoa, and have some fruit after. Or possibly the frozen pound cake with some of the canned mandarin orange sections I'd found in the cabinet alongside the cocoa. It was pleasurable to putter around the kitchen, though it had very few of the modern conveniences I had in my own—no microwave, no Cuisinart, no fancy pots and pans. The utensils almost belonged to an earlier period, and I couldn't help but wonder if Jack's ex-wife had moved any gourmet equipment back home with her.

The cocoa was warm and the cheese sandwich toasting on its second side when I heard Jack stomping on the back porch. "I'm in here," I called, and he showed up in the doorway looking fresh-faced and relaxed. Obviously a walk did him good. "Would you like a toasted cheese sandwich and cocoa?"

He shrugged out of the slicker he was wearing and hung it on a hook on the porch. "I brought some lunch meats. Salami, sliced turkey. I was going to make you sandwiches."

"That sounds great, but the toasted cheese is hot," I coaxed. "Why don't you start on it and I'll make another one for myself?"

"Okay." Jack handed down two mugs from the hooks under a cabinet and poured steaming cocoa into them. His equilibrium was restored, and with apparent ease he touched my fingers as he passed me a plate for the sandwich. "Let's stick this in the oven for a minute to keep warm, while you make more. I'd like one and a half, please."

Since I'd been contemplating whether one would be enough, this was welcome news. I made two more sandwiches and stood chatting easily with him while they browned. As it was a little chilly for the open porch, we took our plates and cups into the living room, where I snuggled into one end of the sofa and he took his chair across the room.

"How long has it been since your parents lived here?" I asked.

"At least ten years. The area was getting too crowded for them, so they bought a property in the back of beyond, where they're happy as turtles. Even when they lived here we came up for many weekends, though Karen never felt particularly comfortable with them around." He grinned ruefully. "They're not particularly polished people, just solid, intelligent folks. They still own the place. I offered to buy it, but they said I'd inherit it when they died."

"No brothers or sisters?"

"No. An only child."

"Me, too. And as you can see, I'm spoiled rotten."

"I never had to worry about that with my folks. They believed in character building."

"They seem to have done a good job."

He frowned. "You hardly know me."

"Yes, but it takes a lot of discipline to become a pediatric neurosurgeon, and a lot of strength."

His face took on a despondent cast. "Recently I've wondered whether I can keep doing it. It's so incredibly sad to see some of these kids and know that no matter how much you do for them, most won't lead normal lives. They're so courageous, and so hopeful, and their parents expect so much. I try to explain the realities, but it's hard for them to absorb what they don't want to hear."

Remembering his poem, I said, "And sometimes you can't do as much for the kids as you'd hoped."

"That's the worst, when things look so promising and turn out to be a disaster." His left hand tightened on the arm of his chair. "Sometimes you wonder if another surgeon could have done better."

"But you know he couldn't," I said with all the firmness at my command.

His glance was curious. "You never lose confidence in yourself?"

"Not completely, or I couldn't operate. You couldn't either, Jack."

"I know. But this past year has been difficult, with the divorce and the patient losses. Sometimes I've wished I'd gone into a different line of work."

There are doctors who say that frequently, but I suspected Jack had never even considered it until recently. He didn't need platitudes right now, and the only thing I could think of to say was, "Every line of work has its disappointments and frustrations," so I said nothing.

Jack had finished his sandwiches and sat holding his cocoa mug as though to warm his hands. He stared into its depths for a minute and added, "I wanted something demanding, something worthwhile, something where I could make a difference. And then you realize, when you have kids, that every parent makes that kind of difference, or could. You don't have to be a neurosurgeon to change lives. But I screwed up at the parenting thing."

"How?" I asked, almost afraid to interject myself into his musings.

"Kids need both parents. I had that, I meant to give it to mine."

"So you were the one who wanted the divorce?"

"No." He blinked at his mug and set it aside. "Well, I've told myself it was entirely Karen's idea, but just lately I've come to understand that it wasn't, really. I'd lost my belief in her."

"Why?"

"Oh, she's a good mother, does all the right things, teaches the kids about life. But her world started to seem so superficial. She's interested in maintaining a place in local 'society.' Her dad is a doctor, a urologist, and her mother comes from blueblood stock. Karen had been raised to believe she was a chosen person."

He grimaced and met my interested gaze. "I thought that was independence, self-confidence, when I met her—strength that came from her knowing she had a place in the world. Later I felt disillusioned."

"But it was Karen who asked for the divorce?"

He nodded. "And it came as quite a surprise. I thought I'd hidden my feelings well, and they were only part of the story, in any case. She has a lot of excellent qualities. When she told me she wanted a divorce, she said, 'If you'd just once be honest with yourself, Jack, you'd know it's what you want, too.'"

He sat brooding for a long time, and I said nothing. "Actually, she was wrong about that," he said finally. "I didn't want a divorce. But I *didn't* value her the same way I had originally. I suppose she sensed that, don't you?" Fortunately it was a rhetorical question and he continued, "It was my blindness that caused the problem, and I wouldn't for the world have had her pay for it, or the kids."

"You'd have continued in the marriage as if there were no problem?"

His shoulders rose and fell. His gaze met mine briefly and swung away toward the window. "I think so. Probably if I hadn't been a doctor, faced with life and death and disability, I wouldn't have considered the social world so shallow. I would have been proud to be part of the set who made things happen culturally in Madison. They're not a bunch of dilettantes just indulging in their own pleasure. They're on the boards of worthy institutions, they volunteer for meaningful organizations. At the time I'd lost sight of that."

"But now you recognize what a rich and fulfilling experience it can be to be one of the first families of Madison."

My sarcasm was meant to bring a little reality to this discussion, and Jack acknowledged it with a lopsided grin. "Okay, so I still think society is superficial," he admitted. "But I'd have put up with that small annoyance for the sake of keeping my family together."

"Laudable, I'm sure. But you can't blame your wife for not staying with someone who basically disapproved of her."

"I don't blame Karen. I blame myself."

I leaned toward him, hands clasped earnestly around my knees. "How about not blaming anyone? How about just accepting this as one of the little tricks life plays on us?"

"Too simplistic," he retorted. "It was my faulty judgment that created the whole mess."

"Since when is one's judgment perfect when one falls in love? We see what we want to see in people we're crazy about. Jung had a whole lot to say on the subject, I believe."

Jack ran a hand through his wiry brown hair. "You know what's sick? I can remember thinking she'd make a great doctor's wife—independent, capable, knowing the routine because of her father. Where did I get off, seeing her in terms of what I needed?"

I couldn't help laughing at him. "Jack, my dear, we all see other people in terms of what we need. Do you think she didn't consider what it would be like to be a doctor's wife, and choose that because it would indeed feel comfortable to her? That's not calculating on either part. It's a reasonable consideration, among all the other things you consider when you decide to marry someone."

I could remember telling myself what a good father Nigel would make because he was so gentle and so thoughtful and so accommodating. He very much wanted to have children at the time, perhaps because friends were starting to have their families, perhaps because he'd been an only child and wanted to raise a bunch of his own.

But these were only some of his traits, the ones I'd needed to see then. All of his other traits were just as visible—his devotion to science and research, his reclusiveness, his irritation with people who distracted him, his intelligence, his respect for his parents, his enthusiasm for long, solitary walks in the country.

Jack had just asked me something, and I'd been too caught up in my thoughts to hear. "I beg your pardon?"

"Did you want any dessert? There's fruit in the fridge."

"What I really want is the pound cake with mandarin orange sections on it."

He shook his head with amusement. "You've been scouting out the kitchen. Why don't you get us each some? This seems to be your meal."

Just to be on the safe side, since he might be mocking me, I gave him my superior sniff and departed for the kitchen. He soon followed me and stood leaning against the door frame as I sliced and set the pound cake in the warm oven to defrost and opened the can of orange sections.

Because the house wasn't over-warm, I had changed into a sweatsuit while reading the manual upstairs. This outfit was a teal color which tended to make my eyes look greener. On the other hand, the sweatshirt and pants were a loose fit, suggesting that I lounged around in them, rather than taking any exercise seriously. Jack seemed to be considering my clothing with a jaundiced eye.

"Do you actually go outside in that outfit?" he asked.

"What a rude question! Of course I go outside in it."

"But you look like a cuddly teddy bear. Don't people want to take you home?"

My heart nearly arrested, I swear it. Probably some valve misfired in shock, like when you swallow something the wrong way. "No one," I said, "has ever wanted to take me home."

"I doubt that."

"Well, if they have, they've resisted the impulse. Besides, in England you're more likely to see Paddington Bear in his slicker and galoshes, than you are to see some roly-poly Winnie-the-Pooh."

"Yeah," he said thoughtfully, his gaze still on me, "I remember reading the Pooh stories to my kids. As I recall, Pooh had a sweet tooth."

"For honey," I informed him. "Paddington Bear probably eats vegetables."

His eyes glinted with laughter. "Don't you like vegetables, Mandy?"

Again my heart did one of those unruly things. "Why did you call me Mandy?"

"That's what your husband calls you, apparently. He asked for Mandy when I answered."

"Well, I haven't been using it in America."

"Would you rather I didn't, then?"

There seemed something pointed about his question, and yet it was a very simple one. Would I rather he didn't call me by that familiar name, insist that he use the more formal one? I gave a tsk of confusion and said, "I don't mind your using it, Jack, but I don't really want everyone to adopt it. At the boarding house, at the University, it seems more appropriate to be Amanda, or Dr. Potter. In England I'm Mrs. or Ms. Potter."

"Ah, yes, a surgeon. It's a quaint custom."

"We're full of quaint customs," I said, taking the pound cake out of the oven and placing two slices on each of our plates. they weren't very large slices. Jack watched as I spooned the orange sections with their syrup over them. "There's an OB/GYN office here with a poster on the door saying: *But we've always done it that way.* I like how Americans mock themselves. It's more honest than all our little tricks of habit and tradition."

He took the two plates and carried them into the living room, where he joined me on the sofa. Though he didn't sit particularly close to me, I had felt more comfortable when he was in his own chair. We each took a bite of dessert. The pound cake wasn't completely defrosted, but in my opinion it tasted better cold. I raised a questioning brow at him.

"Delicious. You never answered my question about vegetables."

My nose automatically wrinkled upwards. "Have you eaten vegetables in England? When I was a child they were always overcooked, and I can't say it's that much better now. Raw vegetables I like; cooked ones I can as often as not pass up. Actually, I always refuse cooked cabbage. I remember the smell of it too well in the hallways of overcrowded apartment buildings."

"So you've lived in overcrowded apartment buildings?"

"Sure. When you're young and haven't a lot of money, that's where you end up."

"But you must have married fairly young."

"At twenty-two. Nigel and I didn't have two beans between us. Not that it mattered. We were way too busy to spend much time at home."

"And too much in love to want for material possessions," he suggested with a mild question in his voice.

I wasn't going to tell Jack that Nigel and I had been crazy about each other. The truth was that I had been deeply moved by Nigel, who was extremely handsome and a little lost in those days. And Nigel had seemed quietly loving and genuinely attached to me.

"Mmmm," I murmured, which was neither yes nor no. My pound cake was almost gone, but Jack still had one piece left. When he saw me eying it, he asked, "Do you want this?"

"Certainly not! If I wanted another piece, I'd help myself to it from the kitchen. I rarely have difficulty speaking up when it comes to my food needs."

He cocked his head at me. "Are there other needs you *do* have difficulty speaking up about?"

When I leveled a cool gaze at him, Jack, to my surprise, colored slightly. One hand lifted in a gesture of apology, the other set aside his dessert plate.

"Sorry. I'm feeling really confused." His brows drew down over puzzled eyes. "There's a sexual attraction that's developed between us . . . isn't there?"

I nodded.

"But you're married."

I nodded again.

"So we aren't going to do anything about it."

I didn't nod.

"Are we?"

I moistened my dry lips and said, "I don't know."

He grimaced. "No wonder I'm confused."

"Well, there are lots of reasons you wouldn't want to do anything about it, either. It's not just me."

"What reasons?"

Ticking them off on my fingers, I said, "First, I'm your houseguest and you're not sure it's proper to seduce a houseguest."

"I thought they did it in English country houses all the time."

"That's a myth—I think. Second, it could screw up the friendship we've been developing, which has its own rewards."

He leaned back against the sofa, a warmth suffusing his eyes as he regarded me. "I do like the friendship we're developing, Mandy."

"I do, too." My pulse quickened just from the way he was looking at me. I cleared my throat. "Where was I? Oh, yes, number three. You're not in the market of a 'relationship,' and you know most women don't really want sex without one."

His brows lifted. "Do I know that? You're crediting me with knowledge I probably should have, but . . . You, for instance, wouldn't be interested in sex without a long-term commitment?"

"We weren't talking about me."

"Of course we were talking about you."

Yes, we were, weren't we? "Well, I'm different," I said lamely.

"I know you're different, Mandy."

"And there's my weight. You're not used to thinking of a fat woman as sexy." This was, to me, the crux of the matter. I swallowed hard against the sudden lump in my throat. "It would hurt me if you were turned off by my naked body."

"I wouldn't be," he said, his voice gentle. "I find you very appealing, Mandy."

"Yeah, well, in my clothes looking all cuddly." I sounded gruff and a little contentious. "I'm a realist, Jack. I know the world's perception of weight. Lavinia Hager turns out to be fat phobic."

"Your department chair? Holly hell."

"Right." I lifted his plate from the pillow beside me and rose from the sofa. "Let's just take it easy. The situation is confusing to both of us."

He followed me into the kitchen. "It's my turn to do the dishes. Why don't you find a rain jacket, and we'll go for a walk after I finish?"

"Sort of like a cold shower? Sounds good to me."

CHAPTER TEN

Swathed in a bright yellow slicker like his own, and an old waterproof hat, I was guided by Jack on a vigorous hike around the Oconomowoc area. His house was a distance from the town to begin with, and then he wound us around Fowler Lake and into the center of the old town.

After a hot cup of tea at a quaint cafe, he herded me back along North Main Street. Jack told me stories about the palatial homes and about his childhood. He even told me about a yacht club that had recently burned down and the community debate over whether to rebuild it. He was obviously trying to distract me (or himself) and exhaust us into the bargain. When we arrived back at the house, I told him I was going to take a nap and he said he'd be in the game room working on the puzzle.

Unfortunately, my nap lasted for two hours. I only woke when Jack tapped on my bedroom door, saying, "Are you okay, Mandy? I've made a reservation for dinner for us in an hour. Shall I change it?"

My clock insisted that it was after six. How could I have slept that long? "I'm fine," I called as I climbed off the bed and stumbled toward the door.

Sleeping in the daytime is not something I do very often and it disorients me. I opened the door to find Jack standing solidly in the hall, waiting for a fuller answer from me. In an hour I would be hungry, no doubt, but I'd expected to stay in and fix a meal together.

I rubbed my face to help wake me up. "That's fine, if you're sure you want to go out. I could throw something together from what's in the freezer."

My hair was tousled, my eyes misty and my face soft from sleep. I know what I look like in that state—I've seen myself in the mirror. It's not something to make a man wish to devour me, and yet that is the impression I got when Jack stared at me. I briefly glanced down to make sure I hadn't taken any of my clothes off, but the teal sweatsuit, though disheveled, was entirely in place.

"How should I dress?" I asked. "I didn't bring much."

"Something casually elegant."

"How fortunate! I have several casually elegant outfits with me."

He looked embarrassed, and I wondered if "casually elegant" was a code he and his wife Karen had used. "What you'd wear to work, I guess. I haven't been to the Olympia in years, but I couldn't get a reservation at the Golden Mast because of some reception. It doesn't really matter what you wear."

"Okay. I'll be ready in a few minutes."

When I returned downstairs I found him in a pair of gray slacks, a solid blue button-down shirt with a patterned sweater over it, and loafers. He looked exceptionally attractive, and casually elegant, as it were. My own red dress, with a gold, red and blue scarf and dangling silver earrings, was obviously adequate for the evening. Jack nodded appreciatively, but said only that we should be leaving.

The Olympia turned out to be a resort and conference center, the only one anywhere in the vicinity, and the diners did not come in blue jeans. The dining room was comfortable and stylish, with white tablecloths and a rose-and-baby's-breath bouquet at the center of our table. Before the menus came, I said, "Maybe we should establish right at the start that I'm paying."

"Nonsense," he said irritably. "This is my treat."

"Your treat was bringing me along for the weekend, Jack. Please let me take care of dinner."

He was torn. I don't suppose Jack had had many occasions to let a woman pick up the tab. A long marriage, a position near the top of the hierarchy at the University hospital, how could he have? To help him decide, I put on my haughty British expression.

He smiled and relented. "Okay, you pay. But I warn you I'm going to order an expensive bottle of wine and the best steak they have."

"*I* get to order the wine because I'm paying," I informed him, adding graciously, "But I'll let you advise me, since I'm not all that familiar with American wines."

We had automatically slipped back into the teasing vein which lay dangerously close to the attraction artery. Both of us knew it, but it seemed so natural, and so enjoyable, that we allowed it to play itself out. I felt like an unmarried woman on a date with an especially desirable man. For the time being I could flirt with him as though it were perfectly permissible. Jack, after all, knew what the situation was.

Surprisingly, I remember little of the food, except that we spent a long time over our meal, relishing the conversation. As I finished the last bite of dessert, Jack leaned toward me with a challenging light in his eyes and said, "There's dancing here Saturday nights. Why don't we try it, Mandy?"

Nothing would have pleased me more, but the prospect was alarming. Dancing was one of my favorite activities, yet it had been ages since Nigel and I had gone dancing. At department parties I tried to make up for this lack, but not all the men were ready for my energetic style and I usually had to curb my zeal. Considering Jack's decorous presentation to the world, I wasn't at all sure he would appreciate my enthusiasm, either. I didn't want to be an embarrassment to him.

But that was the lesser of the two problems. The second one, of course, was the physical proximity which would generate even more heat than we were experiencing between us, which was quite enough to be fighting off already. Was agreeing to stay and dance like provoking him sexually? Would he expect me to make love with him? Actually, that wasn't nearly as distressing a question as whether I would be able to resist the temptation myself.

His question still hung in the air, though I had let quite a time pass without answering. "Maybe one or two dances," I said, hesitant. "My feet will probably give out after that long walk this afternoon."

The check came then, and naturally was placed in front of Jack. Though his gaze followed my hand with nervous energy, he allowed me to move it toward me and place a credit card in the folder. Very good, Jack, I told him silently, smiling. He returned the smile with a glint of wry amusement in his eyes and laid a hand over mine to squeeze it briefly. Probably my instant, intense reaction should have warned me that the dancing wasn't such a terrific idea.

Our waiter assured us, as he brought the credit card receipt, that the Olympia had the Midwest's most exciting new dance lounge. "It's very romantic," he said.

Jack nodded, as if that were exactly what we wanted. I trailed along on the way to the lounge, worrying that I was getting myself into a hole from which I would not be able to free myself. My marriage had lasted almost twenty-three years. People remarked on how rare that was, often congratulating you as though you'd pulled off some magic trick. And maybe we had. Though I had come to America planning to take a hard look at my marriage, that didn't mean I should be ready to jump into bed with the first man who turned me on. Granting Jack any more status than that was beyond my sensibilities at the moment.

There were only a few people in the contemporary-looking room, but most of them were dancing. My guess was that the room would fill as diners left the restaurants and chose between the piano bar and the dancing lounge for their evening's entertainment. Soft jazz was complemented by blue and pink spots shining on the dance floor. Jack asked me where I wished to sit, and I told him, a little stiffly, that it didn't matter. He chose a place between the dance floor and the bar and ordered us Grand Marnier, my favorite liqueur.

When our drinks arrived, we toasted one another, our eyes never leaving each other's face. Almost immediately, Jack stood up and held his hand out to me. The music was soft and slow, and I came to him a little nervously.

No wonder. He pulled me against his body, gently but firmly, and proceeded to lead me through a remarkable series of steps where I floated, and swung, and was generally held close enough that I could feel what he intended to do next. For all that I love dancing, I'd never found a partner with such incredible grace and skill. When the music sighed to a close, I lifted my head from his shoulder and said, "You didn't mention that you were an expert."

"I've had a lot of experience. And a few lessons, early on. Karen was appalled at how little I understood about movement to music."

The next piece was fast-paced, with a strong almost sexy beat. I grinned at Jack. "This is my forte. Just tell me if I mortify you. I'm accustomed to cutting back my flamboyance."

My experience is that many men of our generation simply cannot loosen up enough to truly enjoy fast, sensual dancing. I expected Jack to be one of those awkward, dutifully trying souls who look like they'd rather be driving race cars. His proficiency at slow dancing would not be any sign that he could become fluid to the quick strains that pounded the air around us. But he was.

Watching him was a pleasure. He was in perfect synchrony with the music. His whole body moved with rich, sexy energy. Jack danced the way I expected he might make love, with generous abandonment.

He seemed delighted by my own performance, which I could tell was even more sensual than I usually allowed it to be. His eyes and smile encouraged me. His body called to mine.

Neither of us was aware of anyone else in the room.

Sometimes his hand caught mine in a frankly possessive way that made me catch my breath. Sometimes he touched my cheek, or drew a finger down my nose—all playful but astonishingly intimate actions. My throat tightened each time, and desire flowed through me.

Hadn't I said just one or two dances? The music faded and I stood mesmerized in front of him. It would probably have been a good thing to leave then, before further contact could destabilize my rationality. But I said nothing, knowing that more than anything I wished to be pressed tightly against his body again.

Which was exactly what happened when the next song began. He tried nothing fancy this time around. We circled the dance floor slowly, no doubt looking cool and self-possessed, but in actuality clinging to each other for dear life. His heart beat under my ear with a speeded up rhythm. His body felt firm, almost taut against mine. My own flesh felt soft and yielding, lush with possibility and with the hunger I had denied for so long.

Jack bent his head and kissed my forehead. When I looked up, he stared into my eyes and then lowered his lips to mine. His kiss was deliberately sweet, light as a dream, but my body nonetheless trembled from a swirling flash of desire. Jack felt it and drew me closer to him, sighing into my hair. We swayed to the music more or less in place for some time, making no further attempts to kiss or touch, but I at least was growing more and more aroused by simply being in his arms.

Through another slow song we moved languidly around the floor. Jack said nothing, but his eyes continued to speak to me of need, and of an almost playful wish that this could indeed lead somewhere. But there was a reserve, too. He was holding back to see what would happen. Had I indicated yet that I was willing? Was I? This was a whole new kettle of fish, as my mother would have said. And why bring her into this, like a moralizing character erupting on stage? This was something I would have to decide for myself.

When the music changed abruptly to a fast rhythm, Jack stepped back from me and said, "Perhaps it's time to go home."

"Yes."

He left a large tip on the table and took hold of my hand. "We could stay if you really wanted to."

"No."

His smile hardly lightened the intensity of those midnight blue eyes. As we walked to the car he spoke of living in Oconomowoc when he was young. But he was really talking to me about his body.

"When I was a boy here, I thought the most exciting thing you could do was sail a boat on Lac la Belle, or ski in the mountains or compete in a tennis tournament. It was delicious to feel your muscles respond, to experience your body adapting to a sport's demands. You could *feel it* when your body did something really exquisite."

"I've never regarded sports in quite that way," I admitted. "My body hasn't always been a particular source of satisfaction to me."

Jack stopped where he was, about to unlock the passenger door for me, and encircled my waist with his arms. Gently he drew me against him, holding me there tightly for several minutes. I could feel his hardness and once again my breathing faltered. That was when I knew I had decided, irrevocably, to make love with him.

"You'll freeze if I keep you standing here," he said at last, reaching around to unlock the car door. As though I were something precious, he helped me into the car and closed the door. Once seated in the driver's seat, he turned to me and traced the line of my lips with his thumb. I thought he would kiss me then, but instead he started the car.

The rain had completely stopped but there was no moon and the trees still dripped moisture as we drove through town. Lac la Belle and Fowler Lake looked dark and mysterious, and the lights glowing from houses across the water were friendly beacons. Neither of us spoke until we reached the house.

"I thought we could have a nightcap in the living room," Jack said as he opened the front door. He'd left a light on in the room, an imitation Tiffany (or perhaps the real thing, for all I knew), which gave a charming glow to the wood-trimmed room. "I'll start a fire. Why don't you get us some Grand Marnier?"

"Sure." I walked directly into the kitchen where I'd previously found a liquor cupboard and lifted down the liqueur. There were miniature brandy snifters into which I poured a very little of the Grand Marnier.

Jack turned to smile at me when I returned but continued to work on the fire. I watched his deft movements, the fine shape of his surgeon's hands. Squatted down before the hearth, his buttocks looked tight, his back straight, his arms powerful. As the flames began to leap, he drew the sweater over his head, saying, "It will get a little too warm for this."

The room was actually cool where I sat on the sofa, but from earlier experience I knew the fireplace gave off a considerable amount of heat. Wanting to tuck my feet up under me, I kicked off my pumps. Jack noticed and nodded. "Great. Get comfortable. I'll join you in a moment."

Anticipation was making my throat dry, and I took a tiny sip of the Grand Marnier. Firelight flickered on his strong face, giving him an almost austere look. I was a little frightened, if truth were told, because it had been so long, and I felt curiously naive, even after years of explaining sexuality to dozens of patients who knew so much less than I. No one had touched me—except myself—for many years.

Shortly Jack joined me on the sofa, much closer than he had earlier in the day, and raised his glass in salute, "To us."

"To us."

After one sip he removed the glass from my nervous fingers and set it on the coffee table alongside his. He gazed steadily into my eyes, running his fingers through my short springy hair. Then he slowly unknotted the colorful scarf at my neck and drew it off, leaving me feeling oddly exposed. His lips descended to mine, but this time it was not with a gentle pressure. The hunger that had been rising in him spoke through his mouth. Seduction, not playfulness, was his intent.

He tasted my lips with his tongue, and allowed me only a moment to do the same before his tongue slipped in, persuasively searching for pleasure spots. My mouth had turned into a sensuous receptor, yielding to his gentle urgings. A shiver of expectation raced through me.

"Are you warm enough?" he asked.

"I think so."

"Will you be warm enough if I take off your clothes?" ·

There was plain speaking. Suddenly I felt shy of my body, not yet ready for him to see it. "In a little while."

"Mmm."

His hands had moved to my back, where they massaged my flesh through the cotton dress. Yes, I thought, I want you to get to know the feel of me before you see me. Know me by touch, let the shape of my body be a part of your arousal, so that you come to accept me. His hands were gradually moving down to span my hips while his tongue continued to tantalize the surfaces of my mouth. I was already almost giddy with desire. It had been so very, very long.

Perhaps he himself needed to cool down a bit. For some time he simply held me against him then, murmuring pleasure against my hair. I took the opportunity to run my hands along his head and shoulders and back. He felt so substantial, so real. The night before, when I had watched him sleeping in the car, and felt the tide of desire, I had not thought this moment possible.

"What are you thinking about?" he whispered.

"How very unlikely this is."

His abdominal muscles contracted with a laugh. "But it's what you want, isn't it?"

"Most decidedly."

Jack kissed me then, his lips gentle on mine. "Me, too." His hands moved to cup my breasts, which made my body tremble again. "I'm glad that feels good," he said. "I want to give you pleasure."

Almost more pleasure than I could bear, when his thumbs rubbed against my sensitive nipples. My sigh was practically a moan. Jack began to unbutton my dress. With my eyes shut I could feel his progress down to my waist. And then his hands were inside the dress, but my breasts were still protected by a lacy bra. My hands slid down to grasp his buttocks. Sensations rioted through my body; Jack groaned.

One of his hands slipped inside my bra, the other traced the path of my left leg up to its joining with my trunk. The pair of pantyhose were a more impressive barrier than the bra, but the response his fingers created was hardly less than it would have been on flesh. My whole body writhed with reaction to his touch.

"Maybe it's time to get some of these clothes off," he said.

My body was so warm by this point that I wasn't alarmed about the chill of the room. But was I ready for him to see me? His expression was part agony/part whimsy, his brows lifted questioningly. Most bodies don't look like model bodies, I know very well from my medical practice. But it would be just my luck if Jack had been married to a gorgeous creature all these years. When I hesitated he turned up the heat by lowering his mouth to my freed breast.

"The pantyhose and underpants can go," I agreed unsteadily.

He laughed. "I feel like a teenager," he teased, but with surprising efficiency removed the items. "You wouldn't be shocked if I took off my clothes, would you?"

Because he deserved it, I gave him my haughty British look. "We expect you to remove your clothes," I declared with regal aplomb. "We are not in the habit of removing our clothes until others have done so."

He planted a kiss on my nose and tweaked my chin. Then he disrobed, with no shyness at all, of course, and looking directly at me the whole time. He had a good physique, a little more sturdy than he looked in clothes. His shoulders were broad, his waist narrow, but his arms and legs were surprisingly muscular.

"Wow!" The word slipped out of me without my agreement. His penis was erect and I confess to being a little startled by its size. Nigel was not so well endowed.

"I'm pleased that I meet with your majesty's approval," he said, his eyes alight with humor. "I am, of course, at your service."

"God, I hope so."

My fingers itched to wander over his naked flesh but I felt a little foolish now, in my dress. Hesitantly, I stood up and began to lift the cotton fabric above my head. The bra came with it and both pieces dropped to the floor with a soft sigh. Totally bare, I could not quite meet Jack's gaze, which seemed to me to perhaps be just the tiniest bit . . . appreciative. But that might have been wishful thinking. His erection certainly didn't plummet.

He held out his arms to me. "Forget the sweatsuit. This is the way you ought to be cuddled."

Jack drew me down to him, his hands sensuously stroking my arms, his lips seeking my breasts. New waves of desire swirled through me. I clung to him, my fingers digging into his back. He slipped one leg between mine, and I could feel the throb of his penis against my thigh. Our pace had speeded considerably with the disrobing, and I touched a shaking finger to his cheek.

"You'll need to use a condom, Jack."

"My dear, I'm a very cautious man. I promise you don't need to worry about my health."

"But I need to worry about pregnancy."

He frowned. "Pregnancy. You don't use birth control?"

"No." I wanted to say more, but couldn't manage to find the right words. "I wasn't expecting this. I didn't bring anything."

"Mandy, I've been celibate for the better part of a year. I didn't expect this either, and I don't *have* a condom."

"I thought men always expected this," I grumbled. "How old is your son?"

"Luke? Seventeen."

"Look in his room."

"That's ridic..." he started to say, and then he nodded. "Right. I remember seventeen. Always hopeful." He rose and admonished me, "Don't go away."

"I'm not going anywhere."

CHAPTER ELEVEN

Watching him cross the room and take the stairs two at a time was a rare treat. When he glanced over the balcony, he blew me a kiss. My throat contracted with an ache entirely different from the pounding one in the rest of my body. That was the way it should be between a man and a woman, that playful, loving sense of happiness and expectancy. Did other couples really have that in long marriages? Or did their desire for each other mostly dwindle and finally die?

My eyes filled with tears which I desperately fought back. This was not the time or place for mourning my marriage. Right now I was being offered pleasure that I hadn't experienced in so long I'd forgotten how it felt. A man to hold me, to stroke me, to excite me and satisfy me. A willing man, a generous man.

"What is it?" Jack asked gently, crouching in front of me. "Why are you crying?"

"It's nothing," I said, angrily rubbing away the moisture with my fists. "Did you find one?"

He held a foil package out on the palm of his hand. "But you've changed your mind, haven't you?"

"No!"

The word came out too loud and desperate, and Jack cocked his head at me. "I've been thinking about it, too, Mandy. You're married. Do you and your husband have some understanding about while you're away for so long?"

I sighed miserably. "Maybe. He offered me a separation. I don't know. It was confusing. But we don't have a real marriage anymore, either. I promise you, this is my decision. This is my body, and I'm in a position to decide what's right for me."

"You told me earlier that you've never committed adultery."

"Yes, but this is different."

"Is it?" He brushed the hair back from my eyes, gently running his fingers around my face. "I don't think I'd have found you here crying if you were certain about what you wanted."

"But I am. The tears have nothing to do with you."

"They have to do with Nigel. I heard you tell him you loved him this morning."

"And he told me to have a nice weekend."

Not quite grasping my meaning, Jack said, "I don't think that meant he was giving you permission to have sex with some other man."

"I don't need his permission," I replied stubbornly. This was a bizarre conversation to be having, me naked on the sofa and him crouching in front of me. Time to come to the crux of the matter. "Would you rather not make love with me, Jack?"

He groaned and shifted onto the sofa. Lying down the length of it, he pulled me tightly against his body. "I don't want to do anything you'll regret, Mandy. Maybe you're just doing this to prove something to him or to yourself. Maybe you'd regret it later. I don't want to be responsible for that."

So why had he moved us into this incredibly provocative position? Every part of me seemed to be touching some interesting part of him. My face nestled against the roughness of his shadow beard. My breasts pressed against the tingly hair on his chest. My arms and legs wrapped around the firm length of him. His penis, fully rigid, strained against my belly.

"Hold me," I whispered.

But he drew back slightly, his hands leaving my buttocks. When I realized he was putting on the condom, I thought he had decided for both of us. Elation filled my heart. My body, held in check until then, burst forth into a tempest of desire. Every nerve ending seemed to acknowledge an intransigent need. Every part of me felt gloriously lush with longing. Jack drew me back down to him, his penis poking between my legs.

And that is where it stayed. He never tried to enter me, but thrust in a manner that rubbed back and forth against my clitoris, bringing me perilously close to climax. "It's all right," I said.

He merely smiled and lowered his lips to my breast. The combination was too much for me. All hell let loose in my body, as though I were ricocheting between bursts of startlingly bright lights and exotic, exquisite sensations of pleasure. Jack held me tightly but continued to thrust between my legs until his own release came. His face was a marvel of open enjoyment. He kissed my cheeks and my nose and my lips.

"Heavy petting," he said, with a touch of irony. "I told you I was feeling like a teenager."

"And a very responsible one at that." I felt the tears sting at my eyes again. "We are pleased, Dr. Hunter."

"Thank you, ma'am. I'm delighted to have been of service to you."

Contrary to my expectation, I slept soundly, alone in my own bed. In the morning Jack knocked on the door and I told him to come in. Too sleepy still to know what to expect from his being there, I was neither surprised nor disappointed when he asked if I'd like to go canoeing.

"If you want to come, you'll have to get up now," he said, standing at the end of my bed in khaki shorts with cargo pockets on his thighs and a red and green plaid shirt. "This is the best time of day. It isn't raining, but it's going to be overcast."

Propping myself up on one elbow I said, "I like canoeing, but I'm hungry, Jack."

He grinned. "I'll pack us food. You won't starve."

"They all say that," I muttered. "I can be ready in ten minutes. Is there some hot coffee?"

"Already in the thermos, but I'll pour you a cup."

"Thanks." When he didn't turn to leave, I asked, "Was there something else?"

He shook his head but said, "I don't want there to be any awkwardness about last night."

"We'll manage."

As I passed through the living room in what I hoped were appropriate beige pants and a green turtleneck jumper, I couldn't help but grin at the memory of the previous evening. Only by a strong effort of will did I resist picking up the pair of underpants I could see peeking out from under the sofa. They must have been Jack's because I'd made it to my room with everything we'd removed from me, including the scarf.

Jack glanced up from the oilcloth-covered table where he was making sandwiches with the lunch meats he'd bought the previous day. "Sandwiches okay? I'm making a whole stack of them."

"Sure."

He poured a cup of coffee from the large thermos and handed it across, a little careful not to make too much contact with me.

And I'd hoped he'd give me a good morning kiss, even if it was platonic. "How about a slice of toast and jam before we leave?" he suggested.

"Good idea." I fixed it myself and as I was happily crunching the toast, I couldn't help asking, "Did you eat anything?"

"Cereal, toast, coffee, yogurt and a piece of fruit."

"Well, that should keep you."

"Sarcasm becomes you."

I sighed. "So I've been told."

He placed a mountain of food in his knapsack and put his arms through the straps. Though he wasn't particularly tall, he seemed to tower over me there in the kitchen. For a long moment he stared down at me, his eyes alight with warmth. Now, I thought, he's going to kiss me, and it isn't going to be platonic. But all he said was, "You're going to need a jacket until it warms up."

Because he considered my jacket "too good" for this expedition, he handed me one of his own and I burrowed into it as we walked out into the cool morning air. His pace was a little fast for me, but I hurried to keep up, not saying anything. In the boathouse there were also a windsurf board, a kayak, waterskis, and life jackets hanging on the wall, but we concerned ourselves only with the canoe. Together we carried it to the dock and lowered it into the water.

Jack stopped to size me up. "How well do you swim? Do we need a life jacket for you? I always bring flotation pillows."

"I swim extremely well, though I'd hate to have to do it this early in May in an ice-cold lake. The flotation pillows will be adequate."

There was no way for him to avoid helping me into the canoe. With one hand he gripped the canoe to the dock and with the other he steadied me by the arm. Fortunately, I had significantly improved my sense of balance recently and gaining my seat was no problem. He handed in his backpack and then carefully lowered himself into the space at the rear of the canoe. We each picked up a paddle and I set our pace by stroking smoothly along the port side.

For some time we said nothing, merely learning the strength of each other's strokes and the rhythm we set up together. Docks and houses were scattered at intervals along the lake, though the houses appeared to be set back farther on the other side. The entire perimeter was lined with newly leafed trees, and the scene looked particularly sparkling fresh after the previous day's rain. The lake water was cold and I asked, "Is there good fishing here?"

"Not bad. I've never been much of a fisherman, but we have the equipment if you'd like to try your hand."

"No, thanks. I was just curious."

Birdsong burst gloriously from a tree close by on the shore as we paddled along. I laughed out loud. "That's how it is where we vacation in the Lake District."

"You and Nigel."

"Yes, both Nigel and Cass usually go."

"Tell me about Cass. You've said very little."

As we progressed around the lake we discussed our children, the things we worried about and the things that made us proud. Jack was remarkably frank about the privileged traits his children had acquired that were unpalatable to him. He never blamed his former wife, in fact only mentioned positive things about her, but it seemed likely that the kids had acquired more of those mannerisms from her than from him.

When we reached the other side of the lake, Jack explained that there was a road between the houses and the docks, which was the reason the houses had seemed farther back. Many of the docks had the same kind of pontoon-like boat, and I asked him what they were.

"I call them martini boats. Or floaters. People have their after-noon cocktails on them while they cruise around the lake, talking to other groups and generally enjoying the sun."

"Very patrician of them."

"Yeah. I've never had the least desire to get one." He paused and added, "Want to talk about last night, Mandy?"

His jacket had begun to seem too warm. As I shrugged myself out of it, I felt him lift it away from me. "Actually," I said, "I wouldn't mind having a sandwich first."

"Sure."

This unfortunately required my rearranging myself so that I faced him. He'd rolled up the sleeves of his plaid shirt and looked very sporty. The backpack rested against the port side of the canoe where we could each reach into it. "After you," he said.

The first sandwich I removed was salami and I decided to keep it. Before I took a bite, however, I looked Jack straight in the eyes and said, "First of all, I'm the one who's responsible for last night. Not you, not our forced proximity, nothing but me. I wanted to sleep with you, oh, maybe not for sure until we were in the car coming up, but once I'd decided, I made sure you knew it."

If I'd expected him to find this an astonishing statement, I appeared to be far off the mark. Jack merely regarded me with a lazy smile. "And why do you think you decided in the car that you wanted to sleep with me?"

"Well, not because you did anything to entice me."

"Didn't I?"

"Of course not. You were sound asleep."

"I did sleep," he admitted. "I've been told I look very vulner-able when I'm asleep."

"I don't decide to sleep with someone because he looks vul-nerable, Jack."

He pursed his lips, shook his head. "You're wrong, you know. There's something very enticing to a woman about a man who momentarily looks vulnerable. They want to protect him, and that's exciting."

"Nonsense. You're making that up."

"Well, it may not be part of my own experience, but it's true."

I finished chewing a bite of the sandwich before saying, "Well, you didn't fall asleep on purpose."

"Didn't I?"

"Stop that! You were exhausted, and sad, and under stress. That's why you fell asleep."

Jack reached across and touched my lips with a fingertip. "But those are the reasons you wanted to protect me, my dear, because I was tired and depressed. If I'd been a totally honorable man, I would have pretended to be in good spirits, so you wouldn't have had to worry about me."

"That's ridiculous," I complained, taking another bite of my sandwich. He continued regarding me with *sympathy*, for God's sake, so I said, "You just like to take the blame for things, don't you? Even though your wife asked for a divorce, you decided you were *really* the one responsible. This is exactly the same thing."

"You're quite right. It is. Because in both cases I was, consciously or unconsciously, the cause."

Now I had him. Like a lawyer at trial, I pounced. "But you had no reason to wish to entice me," I said silkily. "You may have unconsciously wanted to be out of your marriage. I have no way of knowing. But you had no reason on earth to wish to fill me with desire for you. Even if you were some nut case who enjoyed turning people on, there would have been the embarrassment of having to refuse me."

"Did I refuse you?"

"No, of course not. You were far too polite."

He scoffed at my reasoning. "You think I'd make love to you out of courtesy? Think again, Mandy."

"Well, it wasn't like that, exactly. I seduced you. Not just last night, but by flirting with you the night before, and being provocative during the day. You won't deny I did that, will you?"

His eyes danced. "No, I won't deny that. You were a perfect delight. I especially liked it when you'd decide to behave yourself."

"See? And sometimes I did. But . . . but by evening I didn't seem to have any choice."

"Neither did I."

"Then I was successful," I insisted. "Surely you can see that."

He shook his head. "It didn't happen that way, Mandy."

"Then how did it happen?"

He sat on the bottom of the canoe, his legs on either side of mine, his hands along the gunwales. "My guess is that we were attracted to each other the morning we met, and the attraction simply grew during the week. But I knew you were married, and I could have kicked Cliff for doing what he did. I knew it wouldn't be smart to put the two of us alone together."

"You're making this up."

"You wish. True, I was going to ignore the attraction if I could. You are, after all, married. But I managed to convince myself that you and Nigel had some arrangement, because you were going to be away for so long. Talk about wishful thinking."

My shoulders lifted in a shrug more of embarrassment than indifference. "Maybe you thought I wouldn't be making a pass at you unless I had a temporary release from my marital vows."

"*Would* it be all right with Nigel?"

That stumped me. For all the years he hadn't made love with me, he'd never indicated one way or the other whether he'd approve of my taking a lover. And asking him had seemed tantamount to asking for a divorce. Since no attraction I'd felt in all those years was as strong as my desire to maintain our family, the question hadn't arisen.

"I don't know," I admitted frankly. "It might be. But due to the odd circumstances of our marriage, I feel justified in being the one to decide what I do."

His expression had turned serious. "Mandy, the world isn't like it was when we were kids and followed in the wake of the 'sexual revolution.' Now there's AIDS. I don't even sleep with Karen anymore."

"I beg your pardon?"

He looked a little sheepish. "Well, we did for a while. Don't ask me why she wanted to, because I don't know. *I* still did. But then she started seeing other men, and that was the end of any physical relationship."

I stared at him. "Let me understand this, Jack. You and your wife both wanted a divorce, and she filed for one. And you lived separately?"

"Right. But sometimes when we were talking on the phone about the kids, we'd kind of revert to the way we'd been, you know?"

"I don't think so."

"Oh, divorce doesn't have to be all or nothing, Mandy. Here's a person you've loved, and you're still fond of, except that things have changed and you can't really live together anymore. Sometimes one of us, not always me, would make reference to a time when things had been good between us, and that would occasionally lead to our seeing each other."

The thought of it made me want to giggle, and to hug him. "So you'd have a rendezvous at your apartment?"

"Usually. Once or twice the kids were away and I'd go back to the house."

"Did you ever bring her here?" I asked, gesturing across the lake to his retreat.

"No, not after we decided to divorce."

Somehow that made me feel better. "But you don't do this anymore?"

He shook his head. "I've been celibate for months. You can't just sleep with anyone."

My eyebrows rose. "No? You were prepared to sleep with me."

"That's different."

"How?"

"I'm not sure. Your long-term marriage, my special attraction to you, our being here together."

Though I didn't find this a completely satisfactory answer, I decided not to press him any harder. For a while I nibbled at my sandwich while he poured each of us a cup of coffee. When he handed it to me, he asked, "Why were you going to sleep with me?"

"Because I wanted to. I'd felt turned on since the drive up and . . . I was just going to do it."

"But you couldn't."

"Of course I could have," I contradicted him, feeling indignant. "It was you who misunderstood my tears and changed the outcome."

"So what were your tears about?"

He had been extremely open with me, but I found that I could not equal his honesty. "It's hard for me to explain."

"Try, Mandy."

Instead of finding a way to explain the circumstances without making Nigel and me look ridiculous, my eyes welled up with those stupid tears again. I waved aside his look of concern. "I'm fine, I'm fine. I shouldn't . . . My tears don't mean anything. You must think I'm trying to manipulate you or something. I don't mean to. Just give me a minute. I'll be fine."

Which was true enough. While I finished the sandwich I stared across at the row of docks and the attractive houses beyond them, thinking only of the setting and the weather and the birdsong. After a while I said, "It has to do with my weight."

"What about your weight?"

"Nigel finds it unattractive."

"Weren't you overweight when you met?"

"Yes, but I've gained more over the years—childbirth, aging, eating too much, not enough exercise, the usual."

"And Nigel hasn't aged, or suffered from lack of exercise?"

My shoulders rose and fell. I wasn't quite able to meet Jack's gaze. "He's naturally thin, and he's one of these people who believe that all you have to do is exert a little willpower and you can be as thin as he is. Well, I guess most people believe that, especially doctors. And it's bullshit, Jack."

"How do you know?"

Never in my life have I been able to discuss this issue with someone close to me without feeling devastated. Any hint of criticism feels like a veritable avalanche to me. I can discuss weight rationally, even professionally, with other people, but not with people whose opinion means a great deal to me. Jack was beginning to fall in that category.

"Will you really hear me if I tell you?"

"Of course."

I grunted. "Of course, nothing. People have their minds made up about this. They don't really hear what you say. Have you ever told a patient to lose weight?"

"That's hardly my province, Mandy. Their weight has nothing to do with their need for brain surgery."

"So would you if you were a pediatrician, or an internist?"

"I don't know. There are some conditions that are exacerbated by weight. I'd encourage patients with those conditions to lose, I suppose."

"But your average, healthy patient who was overweight, would you talk about it with her? Or don't you think a patient can be healthy if she's fat?"

He shook his head and laughed. "You're spoiling for a fight, Mandy. You're just waiting for me to take one wrong step so you can decide I'm full of it, and you don't have to pay any attention to my opinion."

I glared at him. "You didn't express an opinion."

"I think overweight people can be healthy." He regarded me intently, then, with his brows slightly raised. "But you aren't really interested in my opinion as a doctor. You're interested in my opinion as a man, and not about health so much as attractiveness."

That was partially true. Right now my main concern was whether Jack could possibly find me attractive. And was there a difference between sexual attractiveness and just general gosh-you're-pretty attractiveness? Hell, what did I want him to say?

When I didn't say anything, Jack added, "I'm betting you know you're desirable. You've as good as said other men have found you sexy and have come on to you. You radiate some kind of excitement, this special glow, that announces you're a woman with vigor and passion." His eyes traveled the length of my body, and his lips twisted ruefully. "And you are definitely voluptuous."

My heart pounded uncomfortably when he said that. If we'd been at the house . . . Well, we weren't. "Thank you," I said. "I'm glad you think so. But I'll bet you've never found a heavy woman sexually attractive before. It's just because you're depressed."

"An interesting assumption," he mused, leaning back against the seat. "Now Karen is certainly on the thin side. Mmm, let's see. Have any of the 'see but don't touch' attractions to other women been to larger women?" He seemed to consider this point for some time, squinting against the sunlight that had decided to pour down on the lake. "I don't think so. Does it matter?"

"Of course not." I stared at the forest of newly-leafing trees at the curve of land ahead. "Were you always faithful to your wife?"

There was a short pause before he answered. "Yes, but I admit to a couple of flirtations the last few years. Nothing adulterous, just a few stolen kisses and lunches. Another reason why I consider myself to blame for the divorce. I had just gotten so restless, so disappointed and frustrated. I thought the flirtations might let some steam off."

"Did they?"

"Not really, because they didn't solve any problems." He shifted irritably on the wooden boards, a frown darkening his face. "Even though I'd chosen women who seemed to enjoy the spice of that kind of relationship, I couldn't justify it to myself. I kept thinking I might hurt one of them."

"Well, you might have," I said, feeling very defensive.

"Not with the women I chose, apparently."

I could feel my chin stiffen. "I'm not like that."

"Mandy, you've got to stop intertwining subjects here. We weren't talking about you, were we?"

"No, but I'm another one of these women you've chosen to have a flirtation with."

"But I'm not married anymore, and we also didn't have *sex* sex."

"We would have."

He smiled a lazy smile at me. "Yes."

"So what was that all about?"

"Pure and simple sexual attraction, between you and me, consenting adults. We chose to play with fire and I don't think it's burnt us. The real question isn't why we did it, but whether we're going to do it again."

My chest had begun to ache. "Are we?"

His brow wrinkled in a perplexed frown. "I'd guess you have a lot to think about before that question gets answered, Mandy. Not that I don't have some thinking of my own to do—about this depression and other things—but the way I'm feeling right now, there's no question that I'd rather be in bed with you than out in this canoe."

My sentiments exactly, but I knew from the set look on his face that he wasn't going to pursue that desire until I made an assessment of my situation. He was a forty-three year old man with a great deal of sexual experience, not a teenager fumbling his way toward his first achievement of intercourse. If I told him right then that I had no conflicts about sex with him, and that we could simply go back to the house, he wouldn't believe me. And obviously, considering my tears, it wasn't true, as much as I wished it was.

"Okay," I sighed. "I'll do some heavy-duty thinking."

"I'm off for a week's trip on Tuesday. That might be a useful separation." Jack shifted back onto his seat, retrieved his paddle and winked at me. "Let's move this baby along a little faster, Mandy, and get some real exercise."

CHAPTER TWELVE

J ack and I became pals. God, I hate being buddies with a man. At least Nigel and I weren't buddies. We were sort of friends, but not buddies. What buddies do is hang out together fairly often, and tease one another, and not have any serious or sexy exchanges. They keep it light. Women have more sense than to maintain the emotional distance men do with their buddies.

From the time we left Oconomowoc until Jack departed for his trip to Seattle, and then after he returned a week later, we spent time together, but it was carefully regulated time. We rode bikes, we often sat beside each other in the dining room, we spent time in the living room with the other boarders, pontificating on topics we wished to impress each other with. But we spent no time alone in any situation where we could possibly become intimate, accidentally or on purpose.

This was not my choice, and yet I suppose it was what had to happen. I was finding it difficult to think about my relationship with Nigel. We didn't actually have a marital relationship. Being married was something different. Though we were technically married, we might have been reasonably compatible roommates, sharing an interest in this child we had created a long time ago.

When I had called home the week following my trip with Jack, Nigel was there but he was distant. Abstractedly he asked about my work at the University and inquired about my enjoyment of my trip, but he had little to say for himself. Everything was okay. The house was okay, the garden was okay, London was okay. He hadn't accepted any invitations to dinner from neighbors; he was much too busy.

Trying to elicit a personal remark from him, I said, "Sounds like you don't even have time to miss me."

"It's turning out to be a very good time for you to be away," he said earnestly. "I'm getting an incredible amount of work done, just an amazing amount."

"I wanted you to tell me you missed me, Nigel."

"Well, of course I do. You know that."

But I didn't know it. In fact I suspected quite the reverse. His life went a great deal more smoothly when he didn't have to be home to share dinner with me, when he didn't have to hear about my day, when he didn't even have to explain about his own. Nigel had probably been meant to be a loner. He would have popped some frozen dinner in the oven and let it burn while he read a report, or lingered over his meal considering some problem until every bite of his food was stone cold.

Earlier, when Cass was a child, Nigel and I had joined forces to do our best for her. We had, to the extent we could, planned our lives around her. That goal had held us together. Our relationship to each other had disappeared somewhere along the way, without explosions of anger or noisy recriminations.

But I had felt anger, and shame.

Because the earliest and most noticeable change in our relationship was that Nigel no longer touched me, no longer made love with me. I had thought he must be having an affair. What other excuse was there for such behavior? Never one to keep my thoughts to myself, I had accused him of having a mistress, and he had laughed. His laughter had devastated me.

Not only was he obviously telling the truth, but my impeccable logic insisted that if the problem wasn't another woman, then it was me. Nigel was still living with me, and assured me he had no intention of ending our marriage. So the logical conclusion I had to reach was that my body no longer appealed to him.

Gradually I came to believe it was my weight that had sapped any desire from him, though he would half-heartedly deny it when I asked. He insinuated that he no longer felt much sexual desire at all, but I found this argument unconvincing. We were young and healthy, and I certainly had lost none of my sexual desire. Obviously it was my size that repulsed him.

For a while I hated my body, which I had never previously paid much attention to. In my family having a hearty appetite was considered a healthy attribute, even if one became rounded and overweight. Somehow my full limbs and breasts and hips and buttocks had seemed lush to me. This was the size my body was intended to be, and I always thought of myself as having the courage to satisfy my appetites, both for food and for life.

Denying myself the food my body seemed to require had never occurred to me, but in the desperate desire to win back Nigel's ardor, I decided I would lose the extra weight. Nigel was unfailingly encouraging, urging me to lose more and more, delighted as the pounds fell away. And he was patently disappointed when I never reached the chart weight for my height.

"But you look so much more attractive this way," he'd said as he stood behind me one morning, surveying me in the mirror. "You're wearing more elegant clothes. You look healthier."

"And am I more desirable?" I'd asked.

He'd turned away, adjusting his tie. "That's not the issue, Mandy. You're losing the weight for yourself—for your health and your appearance."

The weight loss changed nothing between us physically.

And soon, my weight increased. I watched in dismay as pound by pound it returned.

Maybe if I'd never tried to lose weight and then to keep it off, I would never have felt the shame. But there was something mortifying about failing in such an important (and seemingly simple) undertaking. My marriage and my future happiness were at stake, weren't they? Obviously I didn't have the necessary willpower, or the determination, to succeed.

The issue of weight, which had previously been a non-issue with me, became an open wound in my marriage. Professionally I espoused the view that I was the size I was intended to be, and I could cite studies like the ones Sarah's folder was full of, to prove it. But at home I was always vulnerable to that shoulder-tingling, face-burning mortification of being a woman whose weight, and whose personal life, were out of control.

Like unfinished, and unfinishable, business, I seemed tied to Nigel by my failure. I knew it made no sense. I knew it was contradictory to my whole rational insistence that I was a perfectly acceptable person in my round body.

But that drastic emotional split existed in me. I had lived with it for many years. And even for the joy of being in Jack's arms I could see no way of resolving it. So I remained buddies with Jack, giving him the companionship and support he needed while he worked to reestablish his equilibrium—and I longed to establish a more intimate relationship with him.

One day when Jack and I were having lunch together at the hospital cafeteria, he left his pasta salad to answer a page. Standing by the wall with the phone in one hand, his expression became intense and distant. When he frowned, the dark line of one eyebrow came down lower than the other. I found this asymmetry as endearing as his lopsided smile.

"Sorry," he said as he returned to the table. "Nastor's got food poisoning or something. I'm going to have to fill in for him. They already have the patient prepped in the O.R."

He began to lift his tray and I motioned him away. "Don't worry about that. I'll take care of it."

"Thanks. See you later, Mandy." Jack took two or three steps away from our table, then suddenly turned. "Would you like to observe?"

"The operation?"

He nodded. "This is a pregnant woman with a spina bifida fetus. We're doing in utero surgery to see if we can repair the problem."

I wasn't even sure they were doing that in England. Of course I wanted to observe. "You're on," I agreed, jumping to my feet.

"Good thing no one's depending on you to be in your office this afternoon," he teased as he grabbed up both of our trays, with all that uneaten food, and delivered them to the tray return window.

"Yeah, I'm really lucky."

Apparently there were often observers at neurosurgery operations. No one questioned my being there. Jack handed me over to the circulating nurse when we arrived, and she saw that I had the appropriate scrubs. I joined two medical students who were already there.

The neurosurgery operating room was much like the OB/GYN ones. Smaller, perhaps, but even with the extra observers it didn't feel crowded. Bright light bathed the sterile surfaces of metal and tile. There were glass-fronted cabinets with shelves and shelves of supplies. The surgical tray being overseen by the scrub nurse had wildly different tools than those I was accustomed to.

Jack spoke with the patient, a pregnant woman in her early thirties, before allowing the anesthesiologist to put her under. Then he began to recite the facts of the case, for the medical students and resident as well as for me. His voice, deep and unmuffled by the surgical mask, quietly filled the small chamber. He worked as he talked, explaining everything as he went along.

My eyes were glued to his hands, hands that seemed amazingly adept as he got into the real work of the operation. On a routine ultrasound, he explained, the developing fetus had been identified as suffering from spina bifida. God, I remembered the first time I'd delivered a child with that unfinished spinal cord. My heart still trips when I think of it. In those days it was a surprise, and we hadn't the options we have now.

Though the operation was a tense one, Jack never lost his easy calm. He described for his audience what the problems were and how he was attempting to solve them. "If we're lucky," he said at one point, "this will sufficiently repair the defect that the child will develop normally. In any case, there will be no scar."

That's one of the fascinating things about in utero surgery. The incisions heal perfectly, as if they never occurred, like a miracle. Nothing after birth leaves so little mark of its happening.

"Dr. Potter," Jack said suddenly, out of the blue.

"Yes, Dr. Hunter?"

"Can you recall the incidence of spina bifida in England?"

"Not with any precision," I admitted. "Is it different from in the States?"

"I believe it's slightly lower, but I'd have to check the record. Have you delivered children with spina bifida?"

"Oh, yes. One just last year. Unlike most of my patients, this one had had no antenatal care and the spinal defect came as a complete surprise."

Jack nodded as he continued to work on the deformed spine of the developing fetus. "Dr. Potter practices OB/GYN in England," he explained. "When almost every pregnant woman receives prenatal care, there's a greater chance of recognizing problems soon enough to deal with them effectively."

Then he resumed describing what he was doing, and after a while called me over for a closer look. Standing beside him in front of the opened womb, with the repairs now completed, I felt a stirring inside me that I couldn't quite pinpoint. Perhaps it was the wonder of seeing a child before he was born, or the marvel of scientific accomplishment. More likely it was the knowledge that this man beside me was every inch the humane, skilled man I'd believed him to be. If it wouldn't have broken sterility, I swear I'd have stood on tiptoe and kissed him.

The skin around Jack's eyes crinkled and I could tell he was smiling at me. I gave him a sassy wink before stepping back to join the medical students. It was a moment I knew I'd treasure — especially when I returned to England in the fall.

Dr. Hager continued to keep my clinical participation to a minimum, though other department members worked to include me. And on several occasions I volunteered at Angel's clinic way outside of Madison. This required my renting a car, but it felt good to be doing something worthwhile. The clinic was a little scruffy and lacking in the latest gadgets, but its patients were needy and grateful. It was a pleasure to work there.

It turned out that Angel and Cliff actually owned a house somewhere midway between Madison and her clinic, so that neither of them would have an impossibly long commute.

"But Cliff still found himself getting home late so much that we decided to buy a small place in Madison as a pied-á-terre," Angel explained as we had lunch one day. "And you know how it is, Amanda. There weren't any simple little places at reasonable prices for sale, and Cliff saw Mayfield House and it reminded him of San Francisco, and suddenly we owned it."

I laughed. " Keeping it simple is never as easy as it sounds. Did he find Sherri, or did you?"

"I did. Without Sherri the whole thing would be impossible," she admitted. "But it's easy to find tenants for the units because of the university. I usually interview them by phone, and Sherri checks them out when they come to see the place."

Naturally Cliff took no part in this process, I thought. Seeing my skeptical reaction, Angel shook her head and said, "You have to remember, Amanda, that I only work part-time."

"Yes, but it's always three or four days a week. And then you take care of a baby and a house and a husband. Considerably more than you husband does," I offered pungently.

She grinned. "Hey, this is what I asked for when we decided to get married. My family lives close by and they help. And speaking of them, Amanda, I wonder if I could ask a favor of you."

"Anything," I said.

"My mom is having a little difficulty with menopause. She doesn't like to talk about it with me, and she doesn't have a GYN of her own, but I'm sure she'd talk with you one day at the clinic if I arranged it."

"Well, of course. I'd be more than happy to do that."

Mrs. Crawford's problem turned out to be more than menopause, but less than the cancer I think she had unconsciously feared. Eventually I operated on her for a twisted ovarian cyst at the University, ably assisted by Sarah. Everything went well, as it should have, but I seemed to have earned a special measure of respect from both Angel and Cliff.

Cliff admitted one evening at Mayfield House that he'd never seen his mother-in-law so complaisant about a medical procedure. "Maybe Angel didn't tell you," he said, "but her mother is actually almost allergic to doctors. It's a wonder Angel got into medicine at all."

And Angel could scarcely thank me enough for the way I'd managed to keep her mother both fully informed and astonishingly calm. "I've never seen any other doctor do that," she admitted. "Lavinia Hager is nuts not to make use of your obvious talents."

But it was almost a month after the trip to Oconomowoc before Dr. Hager paged me to ask me to attend a delivery. Mystified by her change of heart, I showed up in L&D just as Dr. Hager was conducting board rounds on a patient about to be taken to the delivery room.

Ms. Stremler was an obese woman of perhaps 350 pounds. Dr. Hager was telling the group of medical students and residents, who stood well within earshot of the patient, that this woman would probably have to have a caesarean section because of her "enormous weight."

Lavinia nodded curtly to me as I joined the group, continuing, "Because of her refusal to lose weight, her condition has become very shaky." This brought on giggles from some of the group, one murmuring loud enough for me to hear, "Shakes like a bowlful of jelly."

"For that kind of behavior," I said to him, giving my coldest stare, "you'd be put back six months in your medical progress at my university."

Dr. Hager ignored my interruption. "Ms. Stremler has evolving preeclampsia, so we have to move toward delivery. Women of her size seldom manage a normal vaginal delivery. Perhaps Dr. Potter would enlighten us on some of the problems morbid obesity has for a pregnant woman."

Ah, she'd brought me here to humiliate myself, despite the fact that I couldn't claim "extreme" obesity for my very own. Fat was fat to Lavinia Hager. Didn't she realize I'd performed this teaching service in my university for years with doctors, nurses, midwives, students? I proceeded to cover as many of the difficulties as I could think of without actually seeing Ms. Stremler's chart.

"It's difficult to get a decent ultrasound of the fetus because of the fat layers, so we generally don't have as good an indication of the baby's health when it comes time to deliver. Sometimes primigravidas of Ms. Stremler's size develop gestational diabetes." Here I looked toward Dr. Hager for an indication if this was true in the patient's case. Hager nodded.

"This often produces a larger baby, which could make vaginal delivery more difficult. I imagine her doctors are considering the risks of a caesarean section, which are a surgical challenge in cases of obesity, so they have attempted to induce labor. Is that correct, Dr. Hager?"

"Yes, we're doing what we can to offset the consequences of her obesity. Tell the group about the risks of caesarean section for such women, Dr. Potter."

There was a snicker from the back of the group. If I had been sure who'd done it, I would have dismissed him or her. As I wasn't, I proceeded to explain about poor blood supply to the fat layer, the difficulty of choosing an incision site, anesthesia problems, multiple drains, postoperative complications, etc.

I launched into this discussion in my usual enthusiastic way, trying to make these youngsters understand that these were problems which called for making careful decisions. Frequently there was no *right* answer, just one with a better chance of success.

As I began to comment on the subject of training doctors to handle such situations, since obviously there were many obese patients in our society, Dr. Hager interrupted me to say, "That's all we'll need to cover for the present, Dr. Potter."

The board rounds group wasn't having any of that, however. By my passion for the subject they knew I would be able to answer questions that other OB/GYNs weren't always willing to address, and queries popped up from all over the group. Hager could not very well deny them the opportunity to learn, so she drifted toward the back of the group, impatient to leave, but not willing to do anything which would lessen her authority.

For a good ten minutes I supplied answers to interested questions in my usual frank and comfortable way. When a resident asked me something I didn't know because I hadn't examined the woman, I led the way to her bed, introduced myself and asked if I might satisfy our curiosity. She was a friendly woman who had probably been examined in front of dozens of training doctors and merely shrugged her shoulders with a big smile.

"No, I'd guess the baby isn't terribly large," I said, after exploring with my fingers. "Eight pounds tops."

"Dr. Hager thought from the ultrasound that it would be much bigger," someone said. "Because of her gestational diabetes."

"Well, of course I haven't seen the ultrasound, though we don't usually get a truly accurate one in these cases. Thanks, Ms. Stremler. I think they'll be wanting you soon in the delivery room. Best of luck."

Dr. Hager had appeared at my side. "I'm offering you the opportunity to act as Ms. Stremler's obstetrician, Dr. Potter. In the event she cannot deliver vaginally, I'm sure you'll be able to teach us something useful about British methods of c-sectioning an obese patient to avoid postoperative complications."

"I'd be delighted," I said, smiling down at my first really challenging American patient since I'd come to Madison. "Will that be all right with you, Ms. Stremler?"

"I love your accent," the woman replied. "It'll be a pleasure to hear you saying, 'Push, push, push.' And my name's Brenda," she added shyly.

"Okay, Brenda. Let me get rid of all these innocent bystanders and you'll fill me in on your pregnancy before we trundle you off to deliver."

The unnecessary shift in obstetrician was highly irregular, but I believed the patient would be none the worse for having me, so I jumped right into the breech, as it were. Brenda was a thirty-two year old woman in reasonably good health and whether she delivered vaginally or by c-section, I was determined to do what I could to see an outcome of good baby and good mother.

When her cervix was totally effaced, we took her to the delivery room and set things up for a natural birth, with all the necessary equipment for an emergency c-section within easy reach. Brenda's husband had left her when she insisted on continuing her pregnancy. Her sister was supposed to have attended her delivery, but was in bed with the flu. So those of us in the delivery room became her family and her support system.

The nurse, the waiting pediatric resident, and I gave her mountains of encouragement. In the end we didn't even have to use the Mityvac suction device. Brenda had learned her lessons well in antenatal class, and used her breathing to help her push the little girl out before any distress occurred.

It was a beautiful birth.

CHAPTER THIRTEEN

Though I arrived back at Mayfield House quite late that evening, and exhausted, I felt magnificent.

Apparently it showed. Jack was seated alone in the living room, doing a crossword puzzle. When he looked up to see who had come in, he smiled. "You look like you just won the Nobel."

"That's how I feel, but it was just a successful high risk birth."

"I thought Hager wasn't letting you do any of those."

"This patient was extremely obese, and Hager thought it would be a good lesson for me to present her blind and then attend her delivery."

Jack looked appalled. "The woman is losing it. Someone should have a talk with her."

"Well, it's not going to be me." I took a seat across the room and curled my legs up under me. "That's the problem with putting someone in power who has a nasty blind spot. Sarah told me Lavinia has never let an overweight resident into the program. As though weight had anything to do with capability."

"Actually," he said, regarding me with his head cocked to one side, "you'd be the best person to talk to her. People who don't get into the program—well, who's to say whether it was because of their weight or because of a personality conflict or their evaluations? With you, it's obvious what's going on. Everyone in the department has probably recognized it."

"Oh, great. Just the kind of notoriety I've always craved."

Jack patted the seat beside him on the sofa. "Come sit here, Mandy. It will be all right."

I knew it wouldn't; he probably knew it wouldn't. But the intoxication of the delivery and the desire for some reassurance after Hager's attempt to embarrass me moved me to the sofa. We were, after all, in the main room of a large and well-populated building. Obviously nothing *really* important was going to happen. Not here, at any rate.

It was a long sofa, with comfortable fluffy back pillows and firmer seat cushions that supported you. I sat a foot or so away from Jack, but he inched over until his hip and shoulder were pressing against me. He took one of my hands and twined his fingers through mine. And we sat there looking at each other in a way that reminded me of dancing together at Oconomowoc.

When he cleared his throat, I raised my brows inquiringly. "Have you given any thought to what we talked about at the lake?" he asked.

"A lot, but I never get past a certain point."

"What point is that?"

"Where I can see that Nigel and I haven't had much of a relationship for a long time."

He frowned. "Then why haven't you done something about it?"

This was tricky. I shifted slightly away from him. "For a couple of reasons. I thought it was best for Cass that we were both there for her."

"She's twenty, Mandy. Almost on her own." He glanced at our twined hands, then looked across at me. "So it's more than that. On the phone you told Nigel you loved him."

"Well, I do," I admitted uneasily. "I just don't know *how* I love him anymore. A long time ago . . . Well, that's sort of personal."

"It was pretty personal my telling you Karen and I slept together after we were separated. Help me understand your situation, Mandy."

Though I attempted to withdraw my hand from his, he kept a good grip on it and I smiled ruefully. "I'm not used to revealing stuff like this, Jack. It's hard for me."

"Oh, really?" he said, laying on the sarcasm. "I do it all the time. I stop strangers on the street and beg them to listen to my story."

"All right, so it's not what you regularly do, either. But I've never told anyone some of this stuff, even my best friends."

The line of Jack's mouth softened. "So I'd be the first person you told. Wouldn't that be okay?"

My cheeks flushed unexpectedly. "But it's like a betrayal, Jack. Nigel would hate it if he knew I'd said anything."

"But it's your life, too, and I'm not going to understand unless you tell me. There's something odd about your situation, or you wouldn't be considering having an affair with me."

Suddenly I was very hungry. "I haven't had dinner yet, Jack."

He shook his head in mock despair. "We'll go back and raid the kitchen. Sherri put something aside for you. Meatloaf, probably. You could make a sandwich."

He followed me back through the TV room, the dining room and into the kitchen. No one was around. Sherri had obviously finished cleaning up because the counter tiles were clean and only a wall lamp was on to give a warm glow to the room.

Cobalt blue tile and polished wood graced the room, with fabric touches here and there—the lamp shade, the seats of two kitchen chairs, a window covering. And over the cooktop a sparkling copper exhaust tube, with copper pans hanging from a cast iron rack. Cliff's sister, who was apparently responsible, was obviously talented at this interior decorating business.

Jack pulled up a chair and sat down backwards on it, motioning with his chin to the bread box. "We had a sourdough bread with dinner that would make a great sandwich."

God, I thought you had to go to San Francisco for real sourdough, but Sherri had either found or made a tangy round loaf. While I sliced bread, searched out the meatloaf and mayonnaise, and poured myself a glass of fruit juice, Jack filled me in on the other boarders' dinner conversation. "Sophia is teaching reading to an illiterate adult. She's delighted that she thought of doing it."

"Humph," I said. "I remember suggesting that to her practically the first day I got here."

"Crissy and Mark are arguing about the least expensive place to spend the summer."

"Are they going to do it together?" I asked, curious.

"It's hard to tell. They can't stop sniping at each other, but they also seem to rely on one another."

The paper napkins were in a blue plastic box that matched the counter, and the dinner plates on a nearby open shelf. I helped myself and sat down at the small oak table across from Jack. While he speculated on our Australian co-guests, I bit into my sandwich. Actually, I was even hungrier than I'd thought and pretty well worked my way through it before I made any comment on his tales.

"Have you seen any of his work?" I asked, referring to the sculptor, Rob Sharpe, who lived in the unit next to mine.

"Oh, yes. Before you came he had all of us to his studio to see his sculptures. He works with woods and does female figures. Usually nude but very artistic. Sophia was shocked."

"Naturally." I prowled around looking for something to finish off my meal. The coconut cookies in the jar were not one of my favorite kinds. There was fruit on the counter and more in the fridge, but that didn't appeal to me. "I want something sweet."

If I'd been paying attention, I would have noticed that Jack had gotten up from his chair, but my back was to him. I felt his hands on my shoulders, turning me around. The look in his eyes made me swallow hard. Astonishing how quickly one's body can respond to that kind of message. He wrapped his arms around me and bent his head to kiss my lips in the sweetest, most provocative way.

After a long time, we drew apart for air and I said, "So I've decided on a different dessert. A woman is allowed to change her mind."

He shook his head. "We still have to talk this through, Mandy. I just wanted to remind you that we have a good reason for sorting it out."

"Then I'll have dessert," I whined, rubbing my forehead briskly to dispel the haze. "A bowl of ice cream."

"Why not bring a piece of fruit and we'll talk in the garden?"

"Fruit is healthy. I don't want anything healthy," I complained as I picked up an apple and followed him out the back door.

There wasn't a lot of light left in the sky, but it was warm enough to sit on the wooden bench where I'd first run into him. It occurred to me that he didn't look as depressed anymore. "The Prozac is working, isn't it?"

"Yeah. Thanks. Even the kids have noticed."

"I'm glad, Jack. I should have noticed the change sooner."

He shrugged. "Around you I've never felt as depressed as I did at other times. You make me feel good."

Embarrassed, I quipped, "I'm an angel of mercy."

"You're a beguiling woman who's having trouble resolving a sticky situation, Mandy. We don't have to resolve it, of course. We can go on exactly as we are. But I don't think that's what either of us really wants. I know it's not what *I* want."

Just his voice made me ache inside. I wrapped my fingers around the apple, trying to still the shiver that passed through me. "Look, Jack. I don't have any qualms about sleeping with you. My marriage is mostly a convenience now. But I feel as if you've sent me digging in hazardous emotional mine fields, expecting me to resolve everything in order to make the way clear for us to go to bed together. Trust me, I don't need that."

As earnest as I sounded, he merely laid his hand over mine and replied, "I don't want you to be crying when we make love."

"I won't be! That was just an aberration. Probably jet lag."

He shook his head. "You haven't slept with anyone else, Mandy, in spite of opportunity."

"There hasn't been anyone I was attracted to strongly enough to make it worthwhile."

Jack considered this briefly, gazing out over the wildly blooming garden. "But you thought being away from your husband, being in America, would make a difference."

"I thought, I *knew*, that *you* would make a difference, Jack. Not Wisconsin. Not being away for six months. If I'd run into you in London, my reaction would have been the same."

"I like to think so," he said.

That flare of desire sparked in his eyes again, brightly, and he leaned over to kiss me. His lips urged mine to meld with his, to join with his yearning. He nudged my mouth open with his tongue, gently but persistently tracing the hungry recesses. His hands traced warm, tingling paths on my back. He pressed my body against his chest for several minutes and then let me go. Moved back on the slatted bench and sat still, his eyes pleading with me to open up to him.

"Nigel and I haven't had sex in years," I whispered.

This was not, I think, what he'd expected.

"Years? Like two or three years?"

"Much longer than that."

"How much longer?"

"Jack, you don't need to know that."

"Why don't you want to tell me?"

I had to fight hard to keep the moisture from my eyes. "Because it makes me feel ashamed," I said fiercely.

His brows pulled down. "Ashamed of what, Mandy?"

"Of myself, of course. Of my body, this stupid, great, unattractive body of mine. How can I accept my body when my own husband rejects it? When through years of marriage he's been so repulsed by it that not once has he reached out to touch me? Don't you think that's something to feel ashamed of?"

"For Nigel, maybe. Not for you."

"You simply don't understand." Distressed, I rose from the bench. I hadn't given him a chance to understand, I knew, but I couldn't say anything more. I'd said too much, betraying myself and my husband. All for what? For the excitement and comfort of sex. Trusting to a man I hardly knew, the knowledge I'd lived with every day but buried deep from other eyes. "I need to go in now. I need to be alone."

"Not a good idea," Jack protested, but he allowed me to pull free of his supportive hand. "Let me stay with you for a while. Let me hold you."

I shook my head. "You can't help me now, Jack. I shouldn't have told you. This is something I've always known I had to handle on my own. Please forget I said it."

"You know I won't be able to do that." It was so dark now that I couldn't make out his expression from the distance I'd put between us. As I retreated farther, backing up the brick path, he called, "You have nothing to be ashamed of, Mandy. Try to believe that."

"Sure," I said, and fled.

A light tap had come at my door half an hour later, but I'd told Jack I still needed to be alone. He slipped a Hershey's candy bar (with almonds) under the door. The gesture moved me profoundly. Here was a man saying my weight was okay with him, that I should have something sweet if I wanted it. And I wanted it.

Though I'd told Jack I wasn't going to be the one to speak to Lavinia Hager about her prejudice, I changed my mind overnight. As Jack said, I was precisely the person who should talk to her, and should agitate within her department if I didn't receive some assurance that this sort of behavior wouldn't be repeated.

Vaguely I was aware that I was allowing myself to get so exercised over this situation to avoid facing the issue with regard to Nigel, but energy in a good cause is worthwhile wherever it comes from. When Jack sat down beside me at breakfast, I said, "Thanks for the candy bar. That was very dear of you. And I've decided I'm going to speak to Dr. Hager after all."

He looked surprised, and studied my face for a moment. "If you're sure, Amanda." (He was always careful to call me Amanda when other people were around.) "She could use it against you, if you became . . . emotional."

That was very good counsel, and I nodded. "God save us from emotional women! Don't worry, Jack. I'll be very professional—full of righteous indignation, but with my anger well under control."

Under the table he squeezed my hand.

Lavinia Hager's administrative assistant got me into her office at 2:00. The department chair looked both irritable and harassed. "What was it, Dr. Potter?" she asked, waving me to a chair opposite her desk. "Carol said you insisted on seeing me, but I have a really full calendar."

"This is a matter that needs to be dealt with immediately," I said, squeezing into that narrow chair once again. "Your behavior toward me yesterday was inexcusable."

She sat with hands folded in her lap and a frosty smile. "You've been insisting that I let you see high risk patients, Dr. Potter, and I allowed you the opportunity. It was a pity you weren't able to show us your expertise by doing a c-section on the woman."

"Not a pity for her." I matched her frosty smile with one of my own. "Yesterday you attempted to humiliate me by making me present a morbidly obese woman on rounds. This apparently was my punishment for being fat myself and having the temerity to wish to be active in obstetrics here. It's demeaning to your whole department, Dr. Hager, when you attempt to pass on your own fat phobia to students and residents."

"I'm not fat phobic, Dr. Potter."

My brows rose. "You have a prejudice against obese people, patients as well as colleagues. It's as insupportable a prejudice as a racial or ethnic one. Every patient has the right to be treated with dignity. And frankly, I believe every colleague does as well."

Lavinia Hager, as Cliff had pointed out, had a reputation for being an accommodating woman. I had seen her myself facilitating compromises between staff members and between staff and patients. Ordinarily she showed a real respect for our patients and for her colleagues. Apparently on this issue of weight alone her vision was completely skewed.

She regarded me with unflappable calm. "You're quite mistaken, Dr. Potter. I have no prejudice against obesity, other than my very natural concern for an individual's health."

"Photos from years of residents show there hasn't been one large man or woman in your training program. There are almost no nurses on staff who are overweight. I think that reflects your attitude."

"My attitude is that we choose health-conscious healthcare personnel, Dr. Potter. They provide a good example to our patient population." She shifted papers impatiently on her desk. "My guess would be that you feel a trifle uncomfortable in such an atmosphere because of your own weight difficulties. I can recommend a staff psychiatrist who has had good success with obese patients."

Both a flash of anger and a jolt of shame rushed through me. But I struggled to remembered Jack's warning. "You don't seem to have kept current with the literature about obesity, Dr. Hager. It becomes clearer daily that people are pre-programmed with regard to their weight."

"Thousands upon thousands of people lose weight on diets."

"And almost no one keeps it off. Perhaps I could send you a recent editorial from the *New England Journal of Medicine*," I suggested helpfully.

"That won't be necessary. I'm well versed in the subject." She glanced significantly at her watch. "I'm way behind today, Dr. Potter, if you will excuse me."

"What I won't excuse is any more demeaning behavior with regard to my weight, Dr. Hager." I rose, careful to leave the narrow chair as gracefully as possible. "I have an agreement with your university which I intend to carry out. I expect your cooperation and your recognition of my position. My weight has nothing to do with my capability, nor should it cause a lack of respect from you."

Lavinia Hager shook her head as though bewildered by my tirade. "I'm very much afraid it's your perception on the subject that's distorted, Dr. Potter. I'll have a word with Dr. Lattimore. He may have some insight into why you'd react so strongly to a simple change of attending on a high risk patient. Dr. Lattimore, as I recall, had some reservations about your taking his place. Perhaps he'll feel you should return."

Dr. Lattimore is an asshole, I informed her mentally. Aloud, I said, "You must do as you see fit, Dr. Hager. I've been perfectly clear about where I stand."

She kept a dignified, dismissive silence and I left her office, carefully closing the door behind me so there was no whisper of a slam. I smiled at her secretary, thanked her for her assistance, and left the office. Rage is not too excessive a word for how I was feeling. Always, when people threaten to damage my career because I stand up to them, I feel the same white-hot anger burning in my gut.

It's not that I'm particularly vulnerable to that kind of tactic, but the abuse of power makes me crazy. How about people who can't combat such a threat? What do they do? Lie down and take it? The academic system is uniquely designed for such abuses. Similar things have happened in England. Look at Wendy Savage, a fellow OB/GYN who was only reinstated in her position after an inquiry cleared her of charges lodged by a superior who simply wanted to get rid of her.

The training in America, too, was of such a hierarchical nature that the whole time you were in the system you had to bite your tongue even when you knew you were right. Well, I wasn't in training, and I had no investment in Dr. Hager or her university. I didn't even much care what she said to Lattimore, because we already had our difficulties.

I just wished I'd been more successful in impressing on Lavinia Hager the magnitude of her prejudice.

CHAPTER FOURTEEN

So how did it go?" Jack asked when I found him waiting at the bike rack.

As I unlocked the purple bike, I shrugged my shoulders. "About as I expected. She denied that she had a prejudice against fat people, threatened to talk with my London boss about my behavior and offered to recommend a psychiatrist for my weight problem."

Jack laughed. "*Exactly* as expected. Are you glad you did it?"

"Yes. I've made a policy during my medical career of speaking up."

"But not in your home life."

I tried to give him my haughty look, but I wasn't particularly successful. "No, not in my home life."

We were riding along the road between the hospital and the Veterans Administration and it was uphill, so I didn't have to say more. Then there was a downhill and a levelish stretch before we had to ride up the next hill, where Mayfield House was perched amidst some charming older, larger buildings. The ten speed bike made it possible for me to manage this last great exertion, though when I was riding alone I sometimes took a more devious zigzag route to make the ride easier.

Jack hooked his helmet on the garage wall and reached for mine. Only then did I notice how deeply troubled he looked. "What's the matter, Jack? Did something happen today?"

He nodded. "It's not something I can talk about."

"But it has to do with work? You haven't had any bad news about your family?"

He lifted first his and then my bike up onto the wall hooks. His face had a drained quality about it. How could I have missed this when we met? I must have been so full of my own concerns that I wasn't paying much attention. And he'd been doing well with the Prozac lately, looking more relaxed and happier.

"No, it was work," he said. "Not just one thing, a series. You know how you have days like that."

"Yes, very well."

Though it was apparent he wanted to drop the subject, he seemed compelled to add, "A little girl came in with her parents. She was the most adorable, lively child and it was obvious they doted on her. But the MRI showed a grade IV astrocytoma, Mandy. There was really nothing I or anyone else could do for her. It breaks your heart."

"I know it does." I took hold of his hand, squeezing it hard. "I hate feeling helpless in the face of disease. It must be even more difficult for you with kids."

His hand tightened convulsively on mine. "And then scans came back from two patients I'd operated on just a year or two ago and both of them showed new growths. Two of them. What are the odds of that happening? They were both malignant, and I hadn't been able to debulk them more than sixty or eighty percent, but, hell, that should have given them more time."

I was silent, just holding firmly to his hand. He stood looking out the open doorway into the garden, pretending, I think, that I wasn't there. Because he had even more to say.

"I can stand it when they die. Usually they've had more time than they might have, their parents have started to accept that their kids won't always be there, and the kids somehow absorb that knowledge. Or their handicaps are so desperate that they need the release. But what I can't stand is an operation going wrong, for no discernible reason."

His shoulders slumped as though under a great burden, and he kept his eyes focused on the gravel garden path. "This was the second time I'd operated on Kevin for a tumor. Everything went perfectly the first time. He was back playing baseball in a couple of months. But this time . . . "

For a long moment I didn't think he was going to continue. Then he shifted toward me, drawing my hand into both of his, and said softly, "Everything went perfectly in the O.R. Nothing looked wrong. Nothing. There was no abnormal delay in the transmissions. The electrical activity between the tumor and the normal tissue wasn't disturbed. We didn't have to back off with the Cavitron or loosen up on the retractors. The operation went perfectly."

Jack let out a long, ragged breath that tugged at my heart. "He's paralyzed. Walt called me from the recovery room and I went straight over. There's no reflex movement at all."

"Couldn't things get better?"

"They could, but I don't think they will. This has happened once or twice before and we've ended up with quadriplegic kids. In some ways I think it's worse than their dying. For them, for their parents. These poor parents will watch for every sign of movement, for the smallest hope, and I don't think they'll get it."

I wanted to take him in my arms and comfort him, but he was maintaining an emotional distance that warned me off. "I'm so sorry, Jack. How terribly sad for everyone."

"Yes." He met my sympathetic gaze with a pained one of his own. "When you know what went wrong, at least you can learn something. But today, there wasn't even that solace."

"No."

We remained standing there, my hand crushed in his. Eventually, to my relief, he put his arms around me, and held me tightly against him, so that I could hug him back with all the empathy I felt. There was nothing more that needed to be said. From my own professional experiences with death and disability, I had some idea of the pain and loss he was feeling.

But we're each alone at times like that. No one else can know exactly how we feel. Jack might be blaming himself, or he might be cursing fate, or he might be reevaluating whether pediatric neurosurgery had sufficient rewards for him. I could only hold onto him and hope he knew how much I wanted to offer the support and healing balm he needed.

When he eventually drew back from me he said, "You know, Mandy, one of the things I was concerned about in taking an antidepressant was that I'd lose my ability to feel deeply about something like this." He mouth twisted mournfully. "I needn't have worried."

A car drove up outside the garage and its horn tooted shortly. Jack brushed the hair on my forehead with his lips and moved farther away from me. "Cliff said Angel was picking him up this evening. I'm sure she'd like to say hi to you."

I frowned. "But, Jack, I'd rather stay right here with you if I can help you."

"I could use some time alone. Thanks, Mandy."

By now I could hear Angel talking with Sherri. Jack slipped out the back way and I distracted attention from him by erupting out onto the gravel drive. Angel, looking wonderfully attractive in a green silk suit with a cream-colored blouse, had stepped out of her car to greet Sherri.

Sherri was delivering the news that Cliff had been held up at the hospital. "He asked me to tell you he wasn't sure when he'd be finished," Sherri admitted, her voice sympathetic.

"Damn." Angel heard me and turned to smile. "Amanda. How great to see you. I've been very lax about getting you out to the house for dinner, haven't I?"

"Not to worry," I said, giving her a warm hug. "You look gorgeous. Planning on a big evening?"

She gave a moue of disappointment. "I *was*. A favorite artist's gallery opening and then dinner at L'Etoile. We've had this planned for a month."

"Well, maybe he'll still get here."

Sherri shook her head. "It didn't really sound like he'd be done any time soon. He suggested that you go on ahead and he'd catch up."

"Oh, right," Angel snorted. "He'll come here and look at the clock and say to himself, 'Well, it's too late now,' no matter what time it is."

She imitated Cliff so perfectly that both Sherri and I laughed. But there was a somewhat drawn look to her face. Suddenly she turned to me and asked, "Why not come with me, Amanda? I think you'd enjoy the opening. Gail does remarkably good photography. And Sherri could save your dinner for poor Cliff when he eventually gets in. You haven't been to L'Etoile yet, have you?"

"No." Being out the whole evening wasn't what I wanted, but she seemed so eager, with almost a note of entreaty in her voice, that I agreed. "Let me just run upstairs to freshen up. Okay?"

Jack didn't answer my knock. From my window I noticed that he was in the garden, so I slipped a note under his door explaining where I was going. When I rejoined Angel, she held the passenger door open for me and I climbed in. After she had seated herself, fastened her seatbelt and put the car in reverse, she turned to me and said, "I really need to talk to someone about Cliff, Amanda. I hope you won't mind."

Naturally talking with other women about their marital problems is difficult for me, considering my own. But since Angel needed someone to talk to, my curiosity was aroused and my wish to be of help ignited. "Of course I won't mind," I assured her.

She flashed a smile at me as she headed toward University Avenue. "It's so difficult for me to confide in anyone here, especially my family. They're very supportive, but this is something I can't drop on them. It would color their view of Cliff, and I don't want that."

I was instantly alert. "You'd better tell me what the problem is first, so I understand what you're talking about. Why, for instance, would their view of Cliff be colored?"

"I suspect that Cliff is having an affair."

"Cliff? But my dear young woman, it's perfectly obvious that he's dotty about you."

"Well, yes," she agreed, flashing me an ironic glance, "I think he is. But he's feeling so trapped here that he needs an outlet to release his spleen. You see, Amanda, coming to Wisconsin was a real sacrifice for Cliff. He loved being at Fielding, being in San Francisco, living in his delightful house."

"So why did he come?"

Angel grimaced. "Because he wanted to prove to me that he was capable of compromise, that he didn't consider his own career more important than mine, or his wishes more significant.

It was how he managed to win me over to marrying him. I loved him, but he seemed such a sexist that I didn't think there was any way we could live together."

"And now you think he's getting back at you by sleeping with another woman?"

"Not exactly getting back at me." She rubbed her forehead, frowning. "It's not as simple as that. As I said, Cliff is feeling trapped. I think he believed having Mayfield House would make him feel more in control of his life again. And it did, for a while. But it hasn't solved anything. He's still in Wisconsin and that's not where he wants to be."

"Well, for God's sake, probably half the people in the world are somewhere they'd rather not be," I said, exasperated. "It seems to me the man wants everything, without being able to see how difficult he's making life for you."

She regarded me warily before the light turned green and she had to pay attention to traffic. "But he thinks I *have* everything. I'm married to him, I'm living near my family in Wisconsin, I'm practicing where I want to—out in the boonies, and I have an adorable baby. What more could I want?"

"Cliff isn't stupid."

"No, but he has a limited ability to envision things through someone else's eyes. I knew that when I married him. He has a lot of wonderful qualities, but that isn't one of them."

Cliff was a charming man. He was a handsome man. He had a good sense of humor and a sharp mind and real surgical talent. He was also, I felt certain, deeply in love with his wife. That didn't mean he could understand how she felt.

"But what makes you think he's having an affair?"

"Oh, little things. Sometimes he isn't in when I call Mayfield House late. Once I found a notepad on the passenger seat of his car. It had very feminine writing in it and when I asked he shrugged and said, 'It must be Claire's. I gave her a ride home the other day.' Claire is a very sharp, and very pretty, woman in medical records at the University."

Angel's face flushed slightly. "And he's not as interested in sex. His desire used to outstrip mine, and now it's almost the other way around. Cliff, who's just about the sexiest man on earth."

I decided I'd skip that subject if at all possible. "None of those things adds up to an affair, Angel."

"I know. But there's something the matter."

"Have you asked him if he has some problem?"

"Sure, and he just blows me off. Would it be like spying if I asked you if you've ever seen him with a woman?"

That made me laugh. "My dear, I'd be glad to be a spy in a good cause, but I haven't seen him with a woman, and I don't expect that I will. Angel, he's not that kind of man. At least I don't think so."

"Every man is capable of infidelity."

Angel hardly seemed the cynical type, and I touched her arm as she managed to squeeze the car into a small parking space. "Every man and every woman is undoubtedly capable of it, but that doesn't mean they'll necessarily be tempted to do it, or accept the guilt of doing it. Cliff is very proud of you and his son. And he's proud of his own integrity. It would take a lot more than being stuck in Wisconsin—which I, by the way, am finding quite delightful—to tempt him to break his marriage vows and disrupt his life with you. I sincerely believe that, Angel."

She stared at her hands on the steering wheel. "Then what is it, Amanda? He was so excited when Roger was born. But for the last few months he's been restless and on edge. We try to get away, but his work interferes, or mine does, or we can't find someone to stay with Roger. I don't know what more I can do."

"Perhaps that's the problem," I said briskly as I pushed open my door. "You're doing too much."

"Beg pardon?" Angel climbed out and locked the car, looking at me over the top. "I have to do this much. Cliff can't seem to manage. He's all thumbs with Roger, and always overestimating what a child that age is capable of. Cliff hates organizing and can't seem to handle the least detail of family life without screwing things up. I'd love to have him take more responsibility, but he refuses."

I gave her my "doctor-in-charge" steely look. "Don't let him refuse. Part of his restlessness is that he feels helpless, and he's not going to feel capable until you force him to be. I know you shouldn't have to do that, Angel. It's just one more burden for you, but in the long run it pays off. I had to do it, most of my friends had to do it, and I think you'll have to do it, too."

She sighed and tucked her purse under her arm. "You know what I picture? I picture making Cliff responsible for picking up Roger from the sitter and he gets tied up at the hospital and doesn't remember to call and the babysitter *has* to be somewhere, so Cliff permanently screws up an arrangement that I've worked really hard on."

"The more responsible he becomes for the child, the more it will be impossible for him to let things like that happen." I fell into step beside her walking down the sidewalk toward the gallery. "I had some very touchy moments with Nigel when Cass was small. He *assumed* the baby was basically my responsibility, and I had to teach him that simply wouldn't work. In the long run he was glad, Angel, and Cliff will be, too."

"Maybe." She paused before we reached the cheerily lighted entrance of the photography opening. "There's one other thing. He wants me to have another baby."

After the various tensions of my day, I simply couldn't help it. I burst out laughing. And, as serious as the matter was, Angel saw the ludicrousness of a husband who couldn't even help with one child insisting on another, and started to shake with amusement. Eventually we stood like two idiots on the sidewalk, howling with the absurdity of it all.

There was a light on in Cliff's room when Angel brought me back to Mayfield House. She thanked me for coming with her as we entered the building and let herself into his suite, closing the door instantly behind herself.

We had stayed out a long time, lingering over our meal at the French restaurant. The advice I could give her was simple, and extremely difficult to put into practice. But Angel was a determined woman, a woman deeply in love, and she absorbed it all. If it felt a little hypocritical to be giving marital advice, at least what I had to offer was from my own past experience. I would have been loath to tackle more current issues.

The living room and telly room were deserted, so I climbed the stairs to the second floor. No light showed under Jack's door across the hall from my unit. Nevertheless, I went to stand there, listening for the sounds of movement. The silence was complete, so I knocked very lightly, not enough to awaken him if he'd already fallen asleep. When he didn't respond, I went across to my temporary home and turned in for the night.

Angel was long gone by the time I arrived at breakfast the next morning. Cliff was already at the table, and he regarded me suspiciously, but he only said good morning. Jack came down a few minutes later, looking better than he had the night before, but still a little tense. As usual he took a seat beside me.

"Did you and Angel have a good time?" he asked as he poured himself a glass of orange juice.

"Delightful. The photography opening was fascinating and the meal was delicious." I didn't want to say anything the others would understand about his difficulties, so I added, "We got back a little late."

"You certainly did," Cliff muttered. "I thought you'd had an accident or something."

"Isn't that sweet?" My tone was unreservedly mocking. This from the man who'd stood his wife up and wasn't pulling down his weight in the family. "I'm surprised you didn't come out looking for us."

"I almost did," he retorted. A brief look passed between him and Jack, and then he commented, "And I would have if you'd been any later. Or at least I'd have called the restaurant."

"If you'd remembered what restaurant we were going to."

Cliff's hand paused in pouring milk over his Cream of Wheat. "Of course I remember. Angel had it all arranged. We were going to L'Etoile, or maybe the Ivy Inn. I don't think Angel ever told me which. But I'd have called both."

"He's a charmer, isn't he?" I asked Jack.

Jack shook his head in wonder, at my audacity I suppose, but said, "You shouldn't hold Cliff entirely responsible. I got him talking and the time passed before we knew it."

That put an entirely different light on the matter. Cliff had obviously acted as confidante to Jack and been supportive of him, which had apparently done Jack a lot of good. On the other hand, I couldn't help but wish I'd been the one who lifted his spirits and underpinned his self-confidence.

Cliff had raised a brow at me, as though I should be impressed by this pass, and I smiled wryly at him. "All right. I suppose that's understandable. But I still detect a trace of passive-aggressive behavior tucked somewhere in here."

"Hey, I don't have a drop of passive-aggressive blood in my whole body," Cliff protested. "It was an emergency, and I was the only one who could handle it."

"Strange how that happens," I murmured. "In such a large university medical center, too. You'd think there would be any number of people to handle emergencies. Maybe your American system isn't designed as well as ours to manage crises."

Cliff glowered at me, not wishing to consider the possibility that our English system fared better than his (since it probably didn't), but unwilling to retract his statement that only he could have dealt with the situation. In actual fact, Angel and I knew that in all probability he could have gotten away if he'd really wanted to, but his need to be indispensable was strong, especially in this unfamiliar world of Wisconsin.

"I think the best policy here is silence, Cliff," Jack advised. "Amanda is very good at this sort of verbal skirmish, and I'd hate to see you dealt a punishing blow. She's still annoyed with you for suggesting that I take her to Oconomowoc."

The others at the table weren't paying much attention to our conversation up until that point, but Crissy Newman, from the attic, frowned at this. "Sometimes I think men are totally insensitive to a woman's situation," she said to the table at large. "You may think things have changed so massively that a woman doesn't need to protect her reputation these days, but it's not necessarily true."

Mark, of course, disagreed with her, and Cliff allowed them to bicker for the duration of his meal because he wasn't especially keen on challenging me. Not that he thought I could best him. Heaven forfend. But because I might just bring up some uncomfortable truth that he'd rather not face at that hour, or any hour.

When Jack was lifting the purple bike down from its rack for me, he said, "You know, Mandy, Cliff's not as bad as you seem to think he is."

"Cliff is charming. He just needs a little help in figuring out how to be a decent husband and father." I turned to meet Jack's gaze. "I'm glad if he was helpful to you last night."

Jack sighed. "He was, in some ways—the macho 'You-can-do-it-because-you're-really-good' ways. He assured me that everyone has disasters. Maybe I needed that. But you wouldn't have handled it that way."

My heart pounded uncomfortably. "How would I have handled it?"

He handed me my helmet and stood looking down at his own. "You'd have let me grieve. You wouldn't have tried to jolly me along. You'd have sat with me, just been there for me. You wouldn't have talked much and you wouldn't have tried to hurry up the healing process."

"That's what you would have wanted me to do. I'm not sure I'd have been able to."

Jack looked directly into my eyes. "Oh, you would have, Mandy. That's the kind of person you are."

"But I wasn't there for you," I pointed out, feeling a little sick at heart. "I could have stayed and done those things. Did I misunderstand? I thought you wanted to be alone."

"I did. Until I was alone up there in my room. Then I wanted you to be with me."

We were moving now, pushing our bicycles out into the morning sunshine, the grass still wet with dew. Jack's deep blue eyes held a hint of humor. "You'd have slept with me," he said. "To comfort me."

"Yes, I know I would. Is that what you wanted?"

He lifted one shoulder dismissively. "Just for a while I did. But then Cliff came along, trying to find out where you and Angel had gone, and he'd heard about my patient, and we talked. He was very encouraging, very sympathetic, but also very much the proud surgeon. He thinks it's weakness to entertain feelings of helplessness or sadness. To him keeping those emotions at bay is part of the image."

"Which is one of the reasons patients think doctors are such jerks." We were about to climb on our bikes but I wanted to say one more thing before we weren't able to hold a decent conversation. "I'm glad you feel all those things, Jack. I hope you'll let me try to help you."

"Count on it," he said, reaching out to tuck a wisp of my hair under the helmet. "But it won't be by sleeping with me, Mandy. That wouldn't be fair to either of us."

Oh, I don't know, I thought as we pedaled down the hill and turned the corner. He looked so solid there in front of me. But his wiry hair curled down on his neck, making him look oddly vulnerable. He was right: if I'd stayed home the previous night we would most likely have become lovers. *I* had no objections to comforting him physically. Too bad he was too honorable to take advantage of me.

But having a lover wasn't exactly what Jack needed right now. He needed someone solidly supporting him, preferably making no emotional demands. Unlike Cliff, he didn't shy from emotions, but he was currently overloaded. My own needs, for the time being, would have to be put aside so that I could concentrate on helping Jack regain his equilibrium.

Just as we reached the bicycle-parking area, Jack was hailed by a colleague. "He's going to help you with your stiff upper lip," I teased, locking my purple vehicle to the metal rack. "It's done wonders for the British."

"You'll have to tell me about that," he said. "See you later, Mandy."

Then he allowed me to wander off so his fellow neurosurgeon could engage him in uplifting dialogue.

CHAPTER FIFTEEN

It wasn't Jack but Cliff I found waiting for me in the living room when I came home. I could tell he'd been waiting for me because as soon as I closed the front door he trotted over and offered me a glass of sherry "in his room." Since there was no way this was a come-on, it was obviously his way of obtaining a private chat with me. I shrugged and followed him.

Unlike most of us, his living area was spacious to the point of looking almost spartan with his few furnishings. The turret part of the room had nothing in it but a window seat, and there was a simple burgundy-colored sofa with two matching overstuffed chairs. He waved me to one of the chairs and ask, "Dry or sweet sherry?"

"Dry, please."

Either he always had a tray set up with two glasses and several bottles of sherry, or he'd prepared for me, and I suspected the latter. As he poured the drinks, he frowned in concentration, wild eyebrows bristling above his eyes. It was easy to imagine him being intimidating to residents and even patients if he forgot to display his ready charm and intense interest.

As he handed me my glass he said, "Angel's annoyed with me and I think it's your fault."

"Do you?" I laughed, genuinely amused. "You'd rather blame anyone than yourself, wouldn't you, Cliff?"

He took the chair opposite me and glowered at me in his most formidable manner. "Talking to you seems to bring out the worst in her. You must egg her on to push for changes. Most of the time she's not like that."

"Most of the time she's probably too tired to do anything but give in to you, Cliff."

"On what?" he demanded, looking perplexed. "What do I do that's so wrong?"

The sherry was very good, and I was particularly fond of sherry. I took another sip, gathering my thoughts together. "We discussed this some time ago. You don't do your share of the child care. You don't take any responsibility for organizing a very demanding schedule for your family. You expect your wife to handle everything."

"She's good at it."

"She's exhausted from it. She's so discouraged and confused that she thinks you're having an affair."

"An affair!" Cliff roared this so loud I feared someone would rush in to rescue him. "What the devil do you mean? Angel knows I'm not having an affair."

"No, she doesn't. And basically it's easier for her to think you're having an affair than that you're so selfish you won't take on your share of the responsibility for your family."

Cliff hadn't gotten past the idea of his wife believing he was having an affair. Discarding his sherry on a side table, he considered in a very physical way, grasping his knees with his powerful hands and lowering his head into a bull-like battering stance.

"That's ridiculous. Who would I be having an affair with? You must have put the idea into her head."

"Hardly. I told her she was wrong."

"You did? How do you know I'm not?" he asked crossly.

"Because you're so obviously in love with her that you'd have to be nuts to be seeing someone else. Besides, you don't have the time."

That made him chuckle. "Damned straight I don't. Who does she think I'm having this affair with?"

"Claire somebody."

"Claire?" he asked blankly. It took him almost a minute to drum up a Claire in his life. "Oh, for God's sake! Because of the stupid notebook in the car? Angel couldn't possibly be that absurd. What's gotten into her?"

"As I said, it's easier for her to believe that than what's really bothering her—that you're not carrying your weight. She has pretty much the whole burden of your son and your household and your restless moodiness."

"I'm not moody."

I glared at him. "You're moody and you're selfish and you're taking advantage of your wife."

Realizing it was useless to deny all these charges, because I wouldn't believe him, he took a different tack. "Amanda, we're here in Wisconsin because Angel wanted to practice family medicine in an underserved area. We have a kid because she wanted to have one right away. We're here because her family is here."

"You're here, as I understand it, because you wanted to prove that you could compromise."

He looked flabbergasted. "Angel told you that?"

"But instead of proving you can compromise," I said, ignoring his astonishment, "you're using it as a weapon to justify why Angel should carry all the burdens. She's got what she wants, so she should have to pay for it. You're suffering, so you should get special treatment—a house in town where you can lay your head when you're too tired to go home to your wife and son, exclusion from child care duty and arrangements, freedom to conduct your life in the way you did before those obligations descended on you. That's not the way it works, Cliff."

His face was red. I'd never seen it like that before, and I wasn't sure if it was from anger or embarrassment or just a surfeit of emotion. He seemed literally unable to say anything. Giving him a chance to recover, I sipped my sherry and looked out the side window to the garden. From this level you saw more vines and looked up into the thickly-leaved branches of the trees from underneath.

After rather a long time Cliff said, "I can't believe she told you that."

"Well, some of it I merely surmised," I admitted. "Angel didn't call you selfish or say you got special treatment. I can see that for myself."

"But the compromise. That's a personal thing, between the two of us. Not something to share with other people."

I nodded, knowing from my very own personal experience how he felt about this. "That's the stunning thing about personal matters, isn't it, Cliff? If you're not allowed to talk about them with other people, you can't ever really share your disappointment and disillusion, can you? And if you can't share them, then you just have to live with them, don't you?"

But he hadn't heard me, at least not clearly. Cliff was feeling shocked and betrayed. Oh, hell, I thought, now I've done it. Angel didn't ask me to stomp around in her marriage; she just asked me for some advice. And I'd given it, so I should just have stayed out of the business after that.

I might have, too, if Cliff hadn't invited me in for a drink and instantly tried to put the blame on me for his problems. And if I hadn't known so intimately how the revelation of personal matters could shake one to one's core.

Cliff came to dinner, but he said little. Sherri had made a chicken salad which suited the hot weather perfectly. There was an assortment of grainy rolls and muffins, along with trays full of raw vegetables. A very healthy meal, if one ignored the sour cream dip, which of course I didn't.

Jack suggested we take a long walk after our meal, and when I went upstairs to put on walking shoes, the phone rang. It was Angel, naturally, and I cringed when I heard her voice. But she pooh-poohed my worries about interfering.

"Don't think a thing of it. I know how Cliff is, and it hasn't done him any harm to realize that we've talked about the marriage." Her sigh drifted over the line. "He's acting as if I've betrayed some sacred trust. Really, I wish he could hear himself. As though the way he's been behaving isn't a betrayal of our arrangement! Please, Amanda, don't give it another thought."

Though her reassurances relieved me, I was still mulling over their problems when I returned downstairs to find Jack. He'd wandered outside, leaving the front door open for me. A breath of cooler air wafted along the hallway. My gray slacks and yellow oxford cloth shirt would still be plenty comfortable without a sweater. Jack wore jeans and a University T-shirt, looking energetic as usual.

"How did it go today?" I asked as I fell in beside him.

"No change in the paralysis. His parents are still hopeful, though, which makes it almost unendurable to talk with them."

"They'll come to accept. They almost always do."

He ran a hand through his hair. "No matter how many times you stress the things that can go wrong, parents are only really hearing what they want to hear—that their son is going to be well. Sometimes, when I'm afraid they're in Never-never land, I make them repeat the possible catastrophes. And I always insist that they look at the rehabilitation center before we do anything. Maybe I shouldn't, but I want them to understand from the start what comes after the surgery."

We turned the corner past a large red brick house, but I was picturing the rehab ward. "I don't think you can really do less if you want fully informed consent. But it must be upsetting for them."

Jack nodded. "I send our nurse practitioner along. She knows most of the patients, and she can make those desperately handicapped kids become real people to the new parents. They're always impressed with the drive those kids have to get better. Rehab scares them, but it makes them realize their child could end up there, too."

We had come to an architecturally distinctive wooden house, the second story cantilevered out over the first, with intriguing details and unusual rows of windows. "Frank Lloyd Wright?" I asked.

"I don't think so, but he did buildings in Madison. Taliesin is in Spring Green, not far from here. We'll drive over there one day."

As tour guide or friend, I liked Jack's way of assuming that the two of us would do things together. His suggestions weren't just throw-away ideas, either. He'd remember them and leave a note suggesting we go to Baraboo or Cave of the Mounds. We'd been to the Madison zoo and the Milwaukee Public Museum. As friends, of course. Buddies.

"I'd love to see Taliesin," I said, turning away from the house and matching my pace to his.

"I can't do it this weekend, or next. I'm taking the kids to Colorado for the whole week. They wanted to go whitewater rafting on the Colorado and this is the only week we could all manage to get away."

"Is it dangerous, whitewater rafting?"

He touched the tip of my nose with a teasing finger. "Will you worry about me?"

"That depends on how hazardous it is. And it can't be too difficult if you're taking the kids."

"Little you know. My kids are daredevils. Well, half the time they are. The other half they can be stuffy little prigs," he admitted, laughing.

I loved the way he seemed to see his kids so clearly, and to accept all their qualities. "Lucky you get to take them when they're being daredevils."

"Very true. Karen takes them to New York and Chicago for special musical events." He wrinkled his nose. "I used to fall asleep. My background, Karen says. I'm culturally deprived."

"Poor Jack."

For some time we walked along the sidewalks in silence, passing charming midwestern homes with graceful trees shading their windows. After London, everything seemed rather spread out to me. The house on Netherhall Gardens had a tight little garden and the look of being barely squeezed onto its lot. Of course, where I'd grown up there weren't any other houses at all, in that distant past. Those summer days had seemed idyllic, with their freedom to roam as I wished and very little parental supervision. The world had seemed a safer place then. It probably had been.

"Penny for your thoughts," Jack said.

"Oh, just thinking of England and where I grew up. There weren't many other kids around. I could loll away a whole afternoon just lying on some hill, chewing on a blade of grass and thinking about what I was going to do when I grew up."

"You mean, being a doctor?"

"Well, I had rather a romantic idea of what a doctor did," I admitted with a grin. "I thought they were all surgeons and rushed about saving people's lives."

"Don't they?" he teased.

"That's how I was going to be. I had a rather old-fashioned picture of how I'd practice, from a surgery in my house. And people would rush their dying children and injured old women to me. Naturally I saved them, right there, in the nick of time, and everyone congratulated me and brought me chocolate cakes and trifles. I had a sweet tooth even then."

He surprised me by saying, "You have a sweet mouth now," and bent to brush my lips with his. No more. As though it were a mere gesture of friendship.

But it didn't feel like friendship to my body. For weeks I'd protected against erotic feelings for Jack by stoutly reminding myself that I was married, that he had called for a soul-searching by me that I couldn't quite do, and that having an affair was a "common" thing for us aristocrats to do. I wasn't going to let the touch of his lips ruin all my hard work.

We had strayed rather far afield and I said, "Maybe we should head back toward Mayfield House. I have a few cases I have to read up on for tomorrow. Hager has loosened the reins somewhat, but I'd hate to have her watching if I stumbled."

"You aren't going to stumble, Mandy. Don't let her rattle you."

What rattled me was the way Jack was looking at me. There was hunger in his eyes, and need. The sorrow had been pushed back to a mere shadow in the deep blue depths.

"Um, and you probably need some time alone," I said.

"Yes."

But he didn't look like he wanted time alone. His hand came to clasp mine, his fingers twining tightly against my flesh. "All right, Jack. Let's talk about this."

"I want you."

"All of a sudden? Just like that?"

"Hardly," he said with a snort. "As though I've forgotten our weekend at Oconomowoc. But I've said I wouldn't use you to comfort me, and I won't. So we'll forget it."

"I don't remember agreeing to that."

He cocked his head at me and pursed his lips. "No, you didn't. And it's not exactly comfort I want tonight, is it? Still, there were other reasons we weren't going to make love."

A shiver rippled through me. I had told him more than I'd meant to the other night. Please don't bring it up, I begged him silently. He was watching me very closely, ready to say more, but he closed his lips and waited.

"I'm a grown up," I said. "I know what I want, and what I can handle. Making love with you won't destroy me with guilt. As far as the other stuff goes, believe me, I'm working on it. It's not going to be resolved tomorrow, and I'm ready to make love with you today. Besides, I started taking birth control pills after that weekend in Oconomowoc."

He laughed. "I bought some condoms of my own—and had a talk with Luke."

"So it would be all right, wouldn't it? Neither of us would be breaking our own code, unless you suddenly decided you needed sexual comfort. It *was* a rather rapid shift you made from conversation to desire."

"It was that image of you lying on a hill, chewing on a blade of grass. I could see you there, and then I could see me there. We were young and hesitant. Maybe neither of us had made love before. We were just lying in the sun, naked and touching each other, exploring. It was a very erotic image."

Tell me. There is something extremely titillating about the discovery of one's body by the opposite sex. I could feel the sensations his hands would have evoked in me, cupping my young breasts, tentatively tasting my newly adult nipples with his tongue.

He would be aroused and a little concerned about my reaction to his erection. Would it frighten me away? Would I be brave enough to touch him? Oh, God, please let her touch me! he'd pray.

And I would be both curious and slightly worried about that swollen penis bumping against my crotch. I wouldn't be familiar with young men's penises, either slack or erect. This would be the first time we'd touched without heavy clothing in the way, open to each other's critical view. He would be golden from working alongside his father in the fields, or pale from a winter of rain and snow, newly released from school to sunlight and me.

We would be worried that someone might discover us there, out in view of only the valley below and the hill opposite. What if someone should come along? This was not the place to be, lying on the rough grass and the lichened stones. But the feelings were too good for us to be willing to stop. And that touch of danger added spice to the already chaotic maelstrom inside each body.

"God, Jack," I said, trying to shut down the racing tape in my mind. "If it's all the same to you, I'd prefer continuing this discussion back in my room."

"Or mine," he suggested. "My bed's bigger."

"Now how do you know that? Was there someone interesting living in my unit before me?"

"A literature assistant professor with an Edgar Allan Poe complex," he informed me succinctly. "No, it's because I was moving in from the start and Cliff promised me a king size bed. You'll like it."

His eyes were so delightfully warm and tempting that I could feel my body's arousal rising another notch. "I'm sure I will," I said primly, casting my eyes down in mock shyness. "So long as I can wear my old flannel nightgown."

"Well," he drawled, "I wouldn't mind at all having to remove it, but I'd be just as happy to dispense with this shirt you have on now."

We were making rather good progress in the direction of Mayfield House. Though I wanted very much to keep holding his hand, I now withdrew mine. No sense in letting someone from the house see us and put two and two together. This was a matter between just the two of us.

But when we came hurriedly through the front door, Cliff pounced on me immediately. "I need to talk to you, Amanda," he said.

"Not now, Cliff. I have something I have to do."

"But this is important. Urgent."

Not as urgent as my business, I very nearly informed him. "Tomorrow, Cliff. I simply can't do it right now."

"Why not?"

Jack caught his eye and said, "She really can't talk with you now, Cliff." Whether his firm words or his determined expression convinced Cliff, I don't know. Cliff frowned, said, "Oh, all right," and watched with a puzzled look in his eyes until we'd disappeared upstairs.

CHAPTER SIXTEEN

Like a spy Jack narrowed his eyes and surveyed the area, cocking his head to listen for intruders. Then he motioned me toward his room with one imperative hand, with the other placing his finger on his lips to silence me. He looked so provocatively playful that I only managed to resist giggling until we got inside his door. My laughter felt like bubbles of champagne. Suddenly I was as light as air, as free as a woman with no past at all. I might very well have newly invented myself from that girl lying on the hill.

Jack pulled me close to him, holding me tight. "I love to hear you laugh. You have the most erotic laugh in the whole world."

"There is no such thing as an erotic laugh," I insisted, kissing his nose and laughing.

"Oh, yes, there is. Listen to that throaty undertone, and the dancing higher notes. That's a sensuous laugh, a provocative laugh. Only people licensed to seduce should be allowed to laugh a laugh like that."

"And are you giving me a license to seduce?" I asked, my finger running from his chin down his neck to the hollow beneath.

"God, yes."

"Very well then. I think we should see this king size bed of yours."

Jack led me into his bedroom, where the bed took up a fair amount of the floor space. There were clever touches, presumably arranged by Cliff's sister, which attempted to make the room look more spacious—a rocking chair instead of an upholstered armchair, a tall, narrow chest of drawers, window curtains pulled all the way back to the wall. But the most prominent feature in the room was, without doubt, the king size bed, made up with an antique quilt and cream-colored linen.

"Very attractive," I said. "Is it comfortable?"

"You'll have to judge that for yourself." He walked around me and turned down the quilt and sheet. "This is our very best model, marked down because it's a floor sample. If you were to decide on it today, I could give you a *very* special deal on it."

I moistened my lips suggestively. "What kind of a deal?"

He patted the left side of the bed. "Sit here, ma'am, and I'll take off your shoes so you can test it. What charming feet you have, so small and delicate. Sometimes it's a good idea to massage one's toes before lying down at night. Did you know that?"

"I had no idea. Imagine. That feels . . . quite nice. I'm not at all sure I could manage to do that for myself. The bottoms of my feet are usually ticklish! Well, perhaps not when they're stroked in that very . . . appealing way. Oh, are you finished?"

Jack gave me a sardonic look and moved to the other side of the bed, kicking off his shoes as he sat down. "We have many more areas to cover, and you're not going to be able to experience the real comfort of this bed if you're in all those restricting clothes. Perhaps I could relieve you of some of them."

"If you think it's really necessary," I said eagerly.

"Oh, I do."

The buttons of my lemon-colored shirt were rather small, and Jack was marginally patient with them. When he tugged the shirttails out of my slacks he put his hands on my waist, massaging the exposed flesh with strong, inviting hands. He considered my bra for a moment, and shook his head. "Slacks first, I think."

I thought it would be awkward, his getting the slacks down, but nothing he did made me feel gauche. He kneeled in front of me on the bed, lowered the front zipper slowly with curious fingers, and proceeded to work the slacks over my bottom and down my legs. "You'll be able to experience the bed now," he said.

"Like this?" I asked, astonished. "In my underclothing?"

"Definitely. The bed is, after all, just a solid support when you think of it. Here, slide down full length against the mattress and you'll see what I mean."

He nodded as I positioned myself flat against the creamy sheet. "Excellent. Now let me point out some features that may surprise you. You feel the way your buttocks press against the mattress?"

To illustrate he slid his hands under me, stroking my bottom and then down my legs. "That kind of pressure is perfect," he said, drawing his hands up the inside of my thighs until they met at the apex. My flesh quivered with anticipation.

"The amount of pressure is important. Say, for instance, that someone were to be lying on top of you." He moved to half cover me with his body. "The mattress needs to give sufficiently for you to be comfortable. Are you?"

I swallowed with difficulty. "Yes. Except there seems to be something pressing into me. Perhaps it's your clothing."

"I doubt it," he said, bending to kiss me. "But perhaps I'm wearing too much for you to get the hang of this."

"You're definitely wearing too much for me to get the hang of it."

Jack knelt between my legs, and while he watched me he removed everything but his boxer shorts. "For modesty," he explained.

"Oh, I'm all for modesty. For a very short while."

His boxer shorts strained with modesty, or whatever. "Excellent. Sometimes one arches one's back when in bed." He lowered his mouth to my bra and nudged the soft fabric out of his way. The touch of his tongue sent my whole body into an arch. "Precisely," he said. "And you'll note how supportive the bed is during such a movement."

I groaned. He continued to draw on my breast, with the same effect. Obviously we'd lost track of who was seducing whom, but it was so delicious having him arouse me that I scarcely had the will to do anything except enjoy it. He made a terrific bed salesman.

"Maybe you went into the wrong line of work," I suggested, before I remembered, in my distracted state, that he was in the throes of a career disappointment with which I'd meant to help him. I ran my hands down his back, slipping them into his shorts and over his firm buttocks. His penis strained against me. I loved the feel of him butting insistently at my groin. "Are you sure we need these pieces of cloth between us?"

He lifted his head from my breast and smiled slowly. "Now that you mention it, I believe they *are* a little superfluous." Reaching behind me, he unhooked my bra and slid it off. "That's what I like," he murmured. "A woman whose breasts don't disappear when she's lying on her back. But you probably have some objection to their size."

Frankly, I had no objection to them at all when he was cupping and nuzzling them that way. It made my throat tighten and need race through my body. Oh, God, how could I have lived without a man's touch for so long? Or without touching a man. I tugged at his boxer shorts, managing to get them down to the point of his erection. With a tsk of pretended annoyance I said, "You're going to have to help me here, big boy. Something's in the way."

Jack chuckled and abandoned my breasts to roll away from me. He didn't actually attempt to remove the boxers himself, just gave me enough assistance to make it possible for me to work them over his erection. Seeing him so ready to make love to me, I could have wept with joy, but I was afraid he'd misunderstand. I was also a little afraid to touch him, not out of innocence or embarrassment, but because it might be too much for him to control his ejaculation.

His quizzical look decided me. I brushed my fingers tentatively along the shaft, feeling its wild dance, and then over the smooth, silky head. His body trembled and his smile widened, but there was no adverse effect. For several minutes he allowed me to explore and tempt him, but eventually he whispered, "My turn now, Mandy."

My cotton underpants weren't long in place. Jack's fingers were like magic, touching spots I'd almost forgotten a partner could stimulate. The rhythm of his stroking—on my inner thighs, my buttocks, between my legs—left me breathless with urgency. Every part of my body felt luscious and desirable. That had never happened before in my life.

Jack spent generous amounts of time lovingly urging my swollen flesh to greater heights of arousal. If my breathing speeded up too much, showing I was right at the edge, he backed off and kissed me lightly, working his fingers through my hair, massaging my scalp, whispering sweet words of encouragement. "Oh, yes, enjoy every moment, Mandy. Don't you feel like you could explode? That's how I feel. Would you do one more thing for me?"

"Anything."

He laughed. "I'd like you to put the condom on me. I'd like you to touch me again—but not too much. Let's see if we can't work this so we're both at our heights."

The condom seemed to appear from nowhere. Perhaps he'd put it under his pillow to bring him sweet dreams. I had shown so many women how a condom worked that I had become an expert in application of them—to a plastic male model, at least. His warm, urgent flesh was much more rewarding. When the sheath was in place, I stroked him while he closed his eyes and drew a ragged breath.

And then he drew me close to him, my breasts pressed against his chest, and his hand once again tracing the line of my inner thigh and the recesses of my body that awaited him. Banked fire leaped again into roaring flame. He positioned himself so that as we rocked together he rubbed against me in a way that took my breath away, and quickly propelled me over the edge. "Oh, Mandy," he sighed as he slipped into me.

Jack filled me in a way that made me feel complete, that made me feel whole, as though a part of me had been missing. I clung to him, simultaneously experiencing both a tranquil solidity and an amazingly effervescent release.

And all the while I gloried in the pleasure he seemed to take from being in me, and how simply he gave himself over to his own satisfaction. As he came he stared straight into my eyes, an exquisite look of pleasure on his face. We held tightly to each other as our bodies gradually quieted. I could feel an enormous grin on my face.

"I'll take it," I said.

Sleepily he nuzzled me with his nose. "Take what?"

"The bed, silly. Everything you said was true. It's the perfect bed."

"Ah. Well, you know, Mandy, I don't think it had anything to do with the bed. It had to do with us."

If the appropriate answer to that was a kiss, I gave him the appropriate answer. We lay together side by side, still merged. Jack brushed the hair off my forehead and kissed me right where my brows met. "You have the most delightful eyebrows," he said. "Did you know that one hair just dances off by itself in the most charming way? All the others are quite respectable and re-strained, but this one has a mind of its own."

I knew the hair. It had resisted all efforts to smooth it down with the others. No one had ever referred to it as charming before. "And did you know that your eyes are the color of midnight when you're making love?"

He laughed. I could feel his laugh ripple through my own body. "Will you stay all night with me?" he asked.

"If you want me to. But I should get back to my own room at a reasonable hour. Cliff is likely to knock me up at the crack of dawn."

"That's a great British phrase, knock you up. We mean get someone pregnant when we use it."

"I remember. Angel says Cliff wants to knock her up. Well, she didn't put it that way. Apparently he wants another child."

"And you think he has a lot to get sorted out before they do that."

My eyebrows reached their haughty best. "You don't?" I inquired in my starchiest voice.

"It's none of my business."

"And none of mine, either, you're pointing out. But it won't do. Angel has asked for my advice and anyone who does that is hopelessly caught in my toils."

"Have I ever asked you for advice?" he asked, sounding both amused and alarmed.

"I don't think so, but it's possible. I'd watch my step if I were you."

"Thanks for the warning."

We lay silently for a while, then shifted into positions in preparation for sleep. He had his arm around my waist and I kept a hand on his thigh. The first mists of slumber were starting to fog my mind when he asked, "How many years, Mandy?"

Could I answer that? No tide of shame engulfed me this time. There was a deep sadness, true, and a quiver of anxiety, but no throat-tightening feeling of making myself too vulnerable. "Twelve," I said.

"Oh, God." Jack held me even more tightly against him. His lips brushed my hair. "I'm so sorry."

"So am I." Which was all I found to say before I drifted off to sleep, secure in his arms.

We overslept, having forgotten to set an alarm. By the time I noticed the clock two feet from my head, it was already seven. I yelped and leaped out of bed, then bent down to give Jack a good-morning kiss. But we both had to hurry, so I just pulled on my outer layer of clothing, not completely sure where my bra and underpants had ended up. I had barely made it back to my quarters when Cliff was pounding on the door.

"I'm not dressed," I called. "I'll meet you in the living room in ten minutes."

He grumbled, shuffled a bit to speed me up, and eventually wandered off. This was certainly going to cost me breakfast, and I was starved. But I was also feeling absolutely intoxicated. No, no, I wasn't falling in love with Jack. That would be foolish.

But this was an interlude that each of us needed because of where we were in our lives. He had made me feel enormously desirable last night, and I would always bless him for that. And

I hoped that he knew he had my total emotional and intellectual support during the trying times he was going through.

Still, above and beyond all that, it had been terrific sex. Playful and lush and powerful. And it had been all right to tell him how long I had been without a partner. I trusted him never to use that against me. And he had trusted me enough to allow himself to be vulnerable with me, too. We certainly were a pair of emotionally shaky middle-aged folks. But maybe everyone our age was like that, if they acknowledged how they really felt.

Cliff was chomping at the bit when I reached the living room, which meant he didn't appreciate the speed with which I'd showered, dressed and more or less put myself together for the day. "My room," he said.

With a shrug I followed him, and my brows rose at the sight of two trays of breakfast on the sidetables. "Very well done, Cliff," I praised him.

"I figured you wouldn't be able to concentrate if you were hungry," he growled.

I laughed. "Good thinking. That's perfectly true."

"But you have to pay attention to me," he insisted, following my lead and placing his tray on his lap. "I've got to be out of here in half an hour, and I have to tell you something before I go."

"I'm listening." I took a spoonful of yogurt with fresh blueberries on it. Very tasty.

"You and Angel think I'm just some jerk who can't be counted on to take care of Roger properly."

"I think the idea was that we don't think you do your share."

He frowned at the banana nut bread he'd picked up, then set it down again. "I've never told Angel what I'm going to tell you. That doesn't mean I'm saying you can't tell her. I just need to get this off my chest. Probably I should have called Jerry when it happened. Jerry's a psychiatrist friend back in San Francisco.

He'd have given me sensible advice. But I didn't even want him to know."

If Cliff needed to walk around this issue, I wasn't going to hurry him. I listened and ate my blackberry muffin.

He lifted his gaze to mine. There were sad lines creasing what was ordinarily an aggressively strong face. "This happened when Roger was about two months old," he said. "Really little, hopelessly helpless. He'd been crying a lot at nights, so that sometimes during the day he slept more than we'd expected. You know how that is."

I nodded my understanding.

"So Angel went out to do some errands. I didn't expect her back for a couple of hours. It was a Saturday. One of the rare ones when neither of us had been called out. Since Roger was asleep I put on the headphones to listen to some music. And I fell asleep, too, only waking when the phone rang."

Cliff ground his teeth at that juncture, and stopped talking. His head was turned slightly away. Maybe he was forcing back tears. It was impossible to tell.

"One of my patients was losing ground fast and the residents weren't able to figure out what was happening. The surgeon on call was caught up in a multiple emergency operation situation and said he'd be with them as soon as he could. So it was really up to me, you see?"

"Yes, I see."

"All the possibilities were racing through my mind. Was he bleeding internally, did he have an infection? Maybe we'd missed something really important when we operated. I grabbed my coat and ran out of the house. I jumped in the car and drove off. I forgot Roger."

Tears pricked at my eyes, for him, for the baby. I didn't say anything.

"I was halfway to the medical center when I remembered. I don't know why I remembered then. Maybe I caught a glimpse of the car seat out of the corner of my eye. I used my car phone to call home, in case Angel was back, but I only got our answering machine. I called the hospital and told them I couldn't make it, no explanations, just find someone else."

The lines of sorrow on his face had deepened. "And you know what I kept praying the whole way home?"

"Yes," I said. "That Angel wouldn't be back before you got there."

He blinked at me. "How would you know? I mean, I should have been worried that there might have been a fire or something awful happening. And all I worried about was whether Angel would find out how irresponsible I'd been."

"Was Roger all right?"

"What's all right?" he asked, looking down at his large impotent hands. "He was screaming. I could hear him before I even got in the house. But I'd been so relieved that Angel's car wasn't there that it came as kind of a shock to me. He must have been crying for a long time, because his little voice was giving out and his body was shaking with sobs. I hadn't fed him because he was asleep the last I knew. And he was wet and dirty and I didn't think I'd ever be able to calm him down."

Cliff continued to detail what he'd done, winding up telling me that by the time Angel had returned Roger had been asleep once again. "I couldn't tell her," he said. "I've told patients when I've made mistakes, they have the right to know. Angel had the right, too, but I couldn't do it. I couldn't bear for her to know that I *couldn't* be trusted to take care of Roger properly. I found the words would stick in my throat if I tried to say anything, and I tried for weeks. Eventually I simply avoided situations where I had to take care of him. It seemed safer for our child."

Cliff wasn't looking for absolution from me, as some men telling this story might have been. But he delivered his narrative in a way that told me he'd gone over it in his mind innumerable times, wishing he could make it different. And wishing that, at the very least, he'd been able to tell his wife, to share the burden. He'd been terrified that she would not have been able to forgive him, of course.

"You're going to have to tell Angel," I said gently. "She'll be able to handle it, I think. Mostly you're going to have to forgive yourself, Cliff. I know it was an awful thing to do, but it wasn't done intentionally. You're going to have to build up some faith in yourself, too. Are you afraid Roger is going to hate you forever because of what you did?"

Cliff didn't answer me. His face indicated that there didn't seem to be any other possibility. No wonder the poor man wanted another child—so he could do it right with the next one.

"Talk to a pediatrician or your psychiatrist friend about that. Children are traumatized by a lot of things, but it doesn't have to screw up their lives. And he certainly isn't going to hate you. It probably took him a little while to trust that someone would come when he needed help, but Angel says he's not a clingy baby. And, frankly, Cliff, I should think what he most needs is to see that *you* will come sometimes to answer his cries. I think you owe him that."

"But what if I do it again? And why should Angel ever trust me with him?"

"I don't think you'll do it again, with this horrendous example in your mind. Whether Angel will be able to trust you . . . " I shrugged my shoulders. "That's something you'll have to find out. But Roger's your son, Cliff. You have to be a part of his life."

There was a knock at the door and Jack called, "Are you ready to go, Amanda? I have to leave."

Cliff nodded and rose. "Go. Thanks. It's helped to talk with you."

I gave him a hug as I left. "We all mess up sometimes, Cliff. You'll work things out."

Jack had already gotten our bikes down and come back to get me. When we were climbing on them, he lifted his eyebrows in a semi-questioning, but-don't-tell-me-if-it's-none-of-my-business look. "You don't want to know," I told him. "But I'm glad *I* know," I added, winking at him.

His eyes gleamed with amusement. "*I'm* glad we finally managed to make love last night, Mandy. I'd begun to think it wasn't going to happen, and I really wanted it to."

"Me, too." I looked up at him with a tentative smile. "I kind of hoped we'd do it again—sometime soon."

"The kids and I fly out to Colorado this evening. But it's only a little over a week before I'm back." He reached over to touch my cheek. "Of course, you'll probably have found someone else by then. You're a pushover for bed salesmen."

"Oh, I am, am I? And what about you? All I had to do was mention lying on a hill when I was growing up. What if some woman on this whitewater rafting trip decides to discourse on her early years of whitewater rafting, and how they'd all lie on the beach in their bikinis with the sun streaming down on them and . . . ?"

He laughed and climbed onto his ten-speed. "If she does, I'll be thinking of you."

I tried to mock him by saying, Nice line, doctor, but the words wouldn't come. In actuality I felt terrific. This warm, erotic man had made love with me last night, after all those years, and there was no way I could scoff at that. "You're a sweetheart, Jack," was all I said, and rode off ahead of him on my bike.

CHAPTER SEVENTEEN

If I'd known Jack was bringing his kids to dinner that night, I'd have worn something different, or not been there, or something. It wasn't entirely unusual for one of us to bring a guest—Sherri encouraged it. There was always plenty of food, and I think she and Cliff might have arranged that she got the extra fee.

In any case, when I arrived in the dining room Jack was standing with two of the most attractive teenagers I'd ever seen. And I'm not given to hyperbole. Everything isn't "the best" or "the funniest" or "the saddest" thing I've seen in my life. These kids were really good-looking. Jack saw me come in and waved me over.

"This is my friend Amanda Potter," he told the two of them. "She's an OB/GYN from England."

They both said how-do-you-do politely and shook hands. The girl asked me if I lived in London and why I was in the United States. When I had answered, the boy asked a more in-depth question about the Effective Care in Pregnancy and Childbirth concept. When other people joined us and the discussion became more wide-ranging, I paid attention as these golden children interacted with the adults.

Sandra (pronounced Sondra by her, but not by Jack) had long blond hair in a sassy ponytail. Even in her sporting clothes she looked elegant. The blue jeans flatteringly hugged her fifteen-year-old figure, and her light cotton shirt highlighted both her tan and her emerging womanhood. Her blue eyes sparkled when she talked. She was gracious with adults, showing no sign of intimidation or nervousness.

Rob Sharpe, our resident sculptor, considered her with a mildly detached, moderately artistic eye, and a severely male manner. Even Sophia Granger seemed impressed with Sandra's intelligent conversation. Crissy Newman watched her from across the room, while Mark Bird approached in the name of congeniality.

Cliff was talking with Luke. At seventeen you could see that Luke would be an extraordinarily handsome man. Though he bore a resemblance to Jack, he had been put together on a different scale. He was taller, fairer, more classically good-looking. Jack's wiry hair had become pleasantly waved on Luke, and his deep blue eyes lightened to an unusual shade of aqua. What was most striking, however, was Luke's poise. When combined with an athletic build, an intelligent mind and a privileged background, the kid looked like a real winner.

I'm not sure how he did it, but Jack managed to seat me between the two of them. Forewarned, I suppose, Sherri served fried chicken and corn on the cob with a lovely salad full of all the greenery so readily available in early July. I worried, momentarily, whether the teenagers would be so sophisticated as to scorn fried chicken for its cholesterol (as most adults did these days), but basically they were still young and certain of their invulnerability. They ate the chicken with gusto.

Rob was seated on Sandra's other side and he drew her attention by discussing his sculpting, but Luke had his father on his right, so he turned to me as we ate, continuing the discussion of ECPC we'd started before sitting down. He sounded so genuinely interested in it that I asked, "Are you thinking of going into the medical field?"

"Oh, no. My dad and my granddad are doctors, so there's some pressure on me, but that's not where my interests lie."

I had a sneaking suspicion where his interests focused from comments Jack had made, and from seeing Luke's room in Oconomowoc, but I was curious to hear Luke talk about them himself. "What would you like to do?"

"Be a baseball player," he said immediately. "I'm on my high school team; I'm a pitcher. People tell me I could go all the way to the majors."

With an effort, I kept my gaze from wandering off to his father's, because I knew the subject distressed Jack. "And how does that work? I mean, where do you start?"

Luke narrowed his aqua eyes. "First, I'll need to get into a college with a good baseball team. My folks won't let me skip college, and that's okay because you get a lot of great experience there. The majors scout you and everything."

"Is it as difficult to become a professional baseball player here as it is to become a professional cricket player in England?"

"Oh, tons harder," he scoffed. "Cricket doesn't call for as many skills as baseball does. And it's so slow!" Afraid this might have offended me, he hastened to add, "Of course, it might not seem like that to someone who's seen it all his life."

"I think it's a colossal bore," I admitted, "but I don't know much about your baseball either. It certainly seems to move faster."

"There's no comparison. I've already been to half a dozen Brewers' games this summer."

"So if you become a professional ball player, how long does that kind of career last?"

He looked at me suspiciously, and I could see Jack grinning behind him, but Luke shrugged and said, "Some guys are still playing when they're forty, but that's pretty old."

"And what do they do afterwards?"

His face took on a stubborn look. "By that time they've made a lot of money. They can pretty much do what they want. They don't have to go to an office every day, or to the hospital," he added with a touch of disdain. "If they've made a big name for themselves, they endorse products or become sports announcers. That kind of thing. But I think I'd want to become a novelist, like Jim Dodge or Ken Kesey or Po Bronson. You'd have the inside knowledge of baseball to use as a background."

Seventeen, huh? I would have expected a son of Jack's to be more realistic than this and I was sorely tempted to offer Luke a few solid tips about life, but I managed to keep my mouth shut. Fortunately, just then Sophia Granger, seated across the table and listening to this conversation, felt an urgent need to inform Luke that Dodge and Kesey were scarcely her idea of literary giants, and she'd never heard of Po Bronson.

After a while Sandra turned her lively face to me and began pelting me with questions about London. "I want to work there the summer after high school. My dad could probably find me something to do at a hospital, don't you think?"

Behind this question I could see the opportunistic mind working that if he couldn't, surely I could. As adults we call this networking, but seeing a fifteen-year-old capitalizing on an advantage rather startled me. Not that Cass didn't know the propitious time to ask Nigel or me for a favor, but we were her parents.

I didn't think I'd seen her do it with other adults, but maybe she did.

"I'm sure he could. Jack probably has lots of contacts among his colleagues in England. And of course most of them are in London."

She frowned slightly, but retained the rueful twist Jack often got to his mouth. "I wouldn't want to do anything gross. Like cut open mice in a lab or something." Her pert nose wrinkled prettily. "But I'd work hard and I catch onto things quickly. I'd work in France but my French isn't nearly good enough. Maybe I'll do my junior year of college abroad there, though. By then I'll have improved."

"That sounds like a good plan. Do you have some idea what you'll major in at university?"

She offered a radiant, fresh-faced smile. "Not yet. There are lots of things I'm interested in—business and sociology and history. Sometimes I think I'll be a lawyer. You can't get much more powerful than that as a woman."

"And you're interested in power?"

"Oh, not really. I just want to be where it's obvious I'm in charge and that I know what I'm doing. Like Marcia Clark. She's cool."

"So you'd be more interested in criminal law than civil?"

Sandra looked at me a little blankly, and I realized she was young to understand the differences. Law was law, and it was exciting. Somehow both of Jack's children seemed to have adopted the idea that medicine was not an appropriate career for them. Too much work, maybe. Now, Mandy, I warned myself, these are bright, enthusiastic and self-assured youngsters. That's what every family wants to raise. They're naive and a little over-optimistic now, but they'll learn.

Someone else had caught Sandra's attention, and I listened to her eager explanation of what would happen on their whitewater trip. She sounded like a kid now, with none of the pseudo-sophistication she'd shown earlier. When Luke joined in, he sounded just as young and artless as Sandra.

Obviously Jack knew his children very well. Though he thoroughly loved them, he wasn't blind to their faults. Not every parent could manage that. I wasn't sure I could always be objective, even when I needed to be, with Cass. Which made me wonder if Karen could, and whether indeed Jack's ex-wife would see certain things as faults in her children. All very interesting, but, as Jack would no doubt tell me, none of my business.

When dinner was finished, there was a general shuffle toward the front door. The three travelers had already stowed away their luggage in Jack's car, which he was leaving at the Milwaukee Airport while they were away. Everyone wished them a good trip and commented on how good it had been to see the kids, and then the travelers were out the door.

Not wishing to get caught in another discussion with Cliff, or with my fellow guests on how extraordinary Jack's kids were, I hurried up the stairs and into my room. Not two minutes later there was a light tap on the door and Jack's voice saying, "It's me, Mandy."

When I let him in, he caught me in his arms and squeezed me against him. "I couldn't leave without kissing you good-bye," he said, and proceeded to do so very nicely. After a moment he sighed, drew back and asked, "What did you think of the kids?"

"They're about the most attractive teenagers I've ever seen, they're positively charming, and they have a great deal to learn about the big, bad world."

Jack laughed and kissed the tip of my nose. "I knew you'd see it. Yeah, they're great, and I do my best to keep them reality-based."

"I bet you do. Now go, they're waiting. Have a wonderful trip."

He pressed my hand. "Thanks. I'll miss you."

"Me, too," I said, and hoped I didn't sound as forlorn as I felt.

Saturday was my regular day to call Nigel. Though I dropped notes to him now and again, the phone call was my major method of keeping in touch. By now he had to know that I would call him Saturday afternoon his time, but it never seemed to occur to him to call me first if he wasn't going to be at the house or at his lab. Generally I persisted until I reached him.

This Saturday I sat for a long time on the window seat, looking out into the wildly growing garden, debating what I would say to him. I could say nothing about Jack, or I could tell Nigel the bare bones of the truth. It wouldn't be exactly lying if I said nothing at all, but it certainly wouldn't be particularly open of me, either.

Actually, I don't think I ever really considered not telling Nigel. For years, we had never gotten further in our discussions about our marriage than my saying, "I don't want to live this way indefinitely, Nigel," and his saying, "Mandy, if you want to divorce me, that's your decision. I'd like to keep our family together for Cass's sake."

If Nigel had thought at twenty-two that what he wanted was a family, over the years I think he'd changed his mind. Not that he didn't love Cass. But given his druthers, he would have lived alone, so he could have come and gone as he wished, and not had to spend so much time accommodating other people. I had found it sad beyond words to be the person he had to accommodate the most, as though I were an enormous drain on his energies, when all I wanted was to be his partner.

Down below in the garden sunlight dappled the bench where Jack had been sitting when I'd first run into him. His depression had lifted considerably since then, no doubt because of the medication. And, maybe, a little, because of our relationship. He wasn't a lone wolf like Nigel. Jack thrived on having someone to talk with, to spend time with, even, I suppose, to make love with. Though he also treasured time alone, he seemed as refreshed by interaction as by reflection.

Pulling the phone over to me, I dialed the London house number first. Nigel didn't bother to put on the answering machine anymore; that would only mean he'd have to return calls. When I got no answer at Netherhall Gardens, I tried the lab, where I let the phone ring and ring. Sometimes he was there, but wandering around, or caught up in his own thoughts. Just as I was about to give up, with something of a sense of relief, he answered.

"Hi, Nigel. It's Mandy."

"Hi, dear. How are things going? Any more trouble from the department head?"

Tust Nigel to finally take an interest in my life here when I'd given up on him. I tried to concentrate on answering the questions. "The early part of the week was distressing, but things seem to have taken a turn for the better now. I've begun a schedule of surgery, and I'm deep into the ECPC research. Dr. Hager has backed off considerably."

"Good. I ran into Lattimore the other day. He was looking rather fit, considering. He asked me how you were enjoying yourself. Don't you keep them informed at the hospital?"

"Oh, yes. I send regular reports. He probably doesn't bother to read them."

Nigel laughed. "No, he wouldn't. He's still really annoyed that he didn't get to go."

"He hasn't written me at all, though I know he's written Hager. How are things going with you?"

He spent some time filling me in on his research work and how the office politics were playing out. Cass had called him during the week to complain about the food at the holiday camp where she was working, which didn't come anywhere near satisfying her vegetarian appetites.

"Well, that's about it," he said, sounding like he was ready to say goodbye.

"Wait, I have another matter to discuss."

There must have been something in my tone of voice that alerted him. "Oh, what's that? A problem?"

"Sort of. When I left London, I intended to give a lot of thought to our relationship. I've tried over these last years to make you understand that I'm not satisfied with our marriage."

"Mandy, no one's satisfied with their marriage. We do very well together."

"But we haven't had sex for a dozen years, Nigel. In my mind marriage includes sex."

He was silent, so I went on. "The other night I slept with a man here. Had sex, intercourse, whatever. I'd never done that before, Nigel."

"No?" He sounded disbelieving. "I'm sure you've had the opportunity."

His coldness and disbelief put my back up. "Of course I have, but I haven't done it. This time I did."

"You'll have to excuse me if I don't believe you," he said. "One instance in particular stands out in my mind, Mandy. You offered me no explanation of why you didn't come home Easter a year ago. Remember?"

I remembered. And what I remembered was that I'd offered him the choice between my silence, or my explanation if he would be willing to sit down and discuss our non-existent sex life with me. Since he hadn't chosen the latter, I'd not satisfied his curiosity. "And you suspect that I've had any number of affairs during these years?"

Nigel hesitated, then said, "I suspect you've had a few, not a lot. Since you were discreet, I never said anything."

You didn't say anything because you didn't care, I thought, angry. Aloud, I said, "That was very thoughtful of you, very avant garde. But there was no need to restrain yourself, because I didn't have any."

"Mandy," he said sternly, "Lattimore practically gloated over me, he was so obvious about what was going on."

My voice hardened. "Doug Lattimore? Surely you jest."

"Not at all. He's acted this way for years, every time I've seen him at one of your department functions. That's why I won't go anymore."

"Well, I guess old Doug and I will have to take this up between us," I finally managed to say. My blood was on fire: the hypocrite, the dirty snake. Doug Lattimore, who had made my life a misery for years, had also convinced my husband we were lovers. "But, if you'd been concerned, Nigel, you should have discussed it with me. Then I could have assured you it wasn't true, which it isn't."

"He wouldn't have hinted at it if it weren't true."

"Can you hear yourself, Nigel? You're saying that you believe Doug and not me. You've been married to me for more than twenty years and know me extraordinarily well, yet you're willing to believe that I'm lying to you about this. Why would I? I've just told you I slept with someone this week. If I'd slept with Doug—a disgusting thought—I'd be more than willing to tell you."

There was a long silence on his end of the phone. His voice came stiffly when I was about to say something. "Are you telling me that this is the first time you've made love with someone since . . . other than me?"

That was a good catch. Nigel was in fact the first man I'd made love with, some time before we were married. Except for Jack now, he was the only one. "That's what I'm telling you, Nigel."

"I find it hard to believe."

"Why? We've been married all this time."

"But you were insistently sexual, Mandy."

What did that mean, insistently sexual? That I wanted my own husband to make love to me, that I'd tried innumerable times to seduce him? All to no avail. The sadness and anger warred, as they always did. But I said, as coolly as I could, "I've perfected the art of masturbation. It has several advantages over lovers."

"And as many disadvantages, I should think."

His voice held a note that I couldn't identify. He seemed to be saying that none of this had anything to do with him, but somewhere in his tone that didn't ring true. Had I been wrong all this time? Was his absorption in his work not as total as I'd assumed?

"Perhaps you've had experience of lovers?" I was tentative, attempting a nonjudgmental tone of my own. "This might be a good time to clear the air on that subject, Nigel."

"It's not a subject I'm willing to discuss."

That, after all he'd had to say about my supposed infidelities. "We'll have to discuss it if we're to resolve anything."

"No, Mandy, we won't. I think I've made myself clear about that. If you want a divorce, fine. Is that why you called?"

"I called to let you know where things stand. That this turns out to really be a separation, as you suggested when I left. I haven't decided about a divorce yet, but it may be the only resolution."

"When you come back, we could go to counseling."

"Would you be willing to discuss our sexual situation there?"

"Certainly not."

"Then I can't see the point. We both may need some time to think about this." My head had begun to ache. A huge feeling of emptiness, too, was invading me. To have reached this point after twenty-two years of marriage seemed impossible, unthinkable. "Let's not discuss the matter with Cass yet, okay?"

"As you wish."

"I won't call you for a while. I hate the feeling of having to track you down and forcing you to talk with me. But I'll be here if you want to call."

Nigel cleared his throat. "Mandy, it's all right about this affair. I mean, you're away in America for six months, lonely, susceptible. We won't worry about it when you come back, if you decide to come back to me. Think about it."

"Goodbye, Nigel."

Is that what I wanted—absolution from Nigel? Hardly. I had always wanted a marriage that included sex and open discussion of the problems that arose. On many subjects, and on many levels, Nigel and I had done very well. But there's no way to overcome the obstacle of someone stonewalling you. It's a deadend.

And this revelation that Doug Lattimore had hinted to Nigel that we were lovers, where did that come from? To my certain knowledge, Doug cheated on his wife regularly, but he hadn't done so with me. Nor had he hit on me in any way. Which was all to the good, since I found him repulsive in a sleek, sleazy way.

Some men used their position in OB/GYN to seduce women, and Doug was one of them. He charmed attractive patients into thinking he was so taken by them, and only them, that he was breaking his own ethical code to have a short affair with them.

After which his "guilt" took over, and he very sorrowfully ended the affair. Usually on the phone, which is where I'd heard him, more than once.

Early on, I had tried to do something about it, quietly, by giving a hint to the woman involved, whom I had met under social circumstances. Apparently she repeated the conversation to Doug, which earned his undying enmity toward me. I told him he should be grateful I hadn't gone to the behavioral ethics committee at our hospital, and he had laughed at me. "Who's going to take your word against mine?" he'd asked.

Who, indeed? The women he chose were not unsophisticated. They basically knew what they were doing. And some of the other men on the behavioral ethics committee had indiscretions of their own to hide, or hospital political debts they owed. Doug wasn't going to be censured by them. The only fallout would probably have been my own dismissal under some false pretext.

It had never occurred to me that Doug would try to take revenge on me by hinting to Nigel that he was my lover. What would the purpose be? To get me in trouble with my husband? Poor Doug, he couldn't have picked a worse object for his sordid innuendo. Presumably Nigel wouldn't have cared much, in the first place, and would have been unable to bring the subject up because he wasn't willing to discuss our own sexual distance.

Doug must have been frustrated by the lack of success of his ploy, but obviously he'd continued working it. Really, the man had a lot to answer for. On the other hand, he was in London and I was in Madison, which pleased me and irritated him. There was something to be said for that.

And Nigel? Well, his response—aside from his thinking I'd been having affairs for some time—was pretty much what I'd expected: We could keep on the way we have been. But I couldn't, and I'd known that since I came here. My fear was that when I returned it would seem the easiest thing to do, keeping on. My "fling" would be over, I'd still have to face a stressful work situation, and my daughter, even at twenty, would still benefit from having an intact family.

The whole picture depressed me. I decided to get on one of the bike trails Jack had introduced me to. The ride to Paoli and back would exhaust me physically—and built up a good supply of endorphins to carry me through the weekend.

CHAPTER EIGHTEEN

Cliff was gone for the whole weekend, not even returning Sunday evening as he sometimes did. I was worried about him and Angel, especially when he didn't show up for dinner on Monday. Later that evening, when I was going over a report I'd written on my progress with the ECPC materials, there was a knock at my door. Cliff stood there looking almost haggard, his face drawn and his eyes tired. I invited him in and offered a glass of sherry, which he accepted.

For a long time he simply sat in the easy chair, staring into the amber liquid, not saying anything. I considered leafing through a magazine I'd bought earlier, so as not to seem to be waiting for him to tell me why he'd come, but he eventually shook off his silence and said, "It didn't go well."

Angel is such a compassionate woman that I was surprised. I'd worried that she would be too easy on him. Despite Cliff's obvious distress, I was glad she hadn't. These lessons in life sometimes have to be hard won if they're going to be lasting.

He raked a hand through his disordered hair and focused somber eyes on me. "Have you talked with her recently?"

I shook my head. "Not since last week."

"I told her about what happened with Roger that day, and she cried."

He didn't go on for a while but I said nothing.

"Angel doesn't cry much. At least not in front of me," he admitted, as though perhaps that was his fault, too.

His face underwent an even more profound deterioration. One of his eyes twitched. "She said, 'You should have had the courage to tell me at the time, instead of behaving like you'd gotten away with something.'" He ground his teeth and grimaced. "That wasn't exactly how it was and I tried to explain, but she didn't seem to hear me."

"I'm sure she did," I said. "Just give her a little time to assimilate everything, Cliff."

He shrugged helplessly. "But what if she doesn't get over it, Amanda? What if she thinks I've disappointed her one too many times? What will happen then?"

I felt surprisingly sympathetic to Cliff. "Whatever happens, you'll deal with it. The two of you love each other. That's a solid foundation to work from."

He clasped his hands between his knees, not looking at me. "I don't know what to do now."

"Careful," I cautioned him. "You're coming very close to asking for my advice, and you know I'm likely to give it."

Cliff offered the ghost of a smile. "Tell me what you'd do in my place."

"Right now your problems look a lot clearer to me than my own," I confessed. "I guess I'd suggest professional help. You and Angel could go for counseling."

Those wild eyebrows lowered stubbornly. "I couldn't do that."

"Why not?"

"I hate the thought of someone else knowing there's a problem. Besides you, anyhow." He glared at me and stuffed one hand in his pants pocket. "I only want people to see the good side of me."

Didn't we all? I said, "Hell, Cliff, do you think your facade fools everyone? Do you think your colleagues sit around and say, 'Hey, that Lenzini, he really has it together'? More likely they think something like: Gee, I wonder why he spends half his time in town when he has that beautiful wife and adorable child. I wonder why he isn't adapting to Wisconsin like most newcomers do. I wonder why he thinks he's such a hot shot, when half a dozen general surgeons around here can do the same things he does, pretty much. I wonder why . . . ?"

"All right, all right!" he interrupted me, only half amused. "So people gossip. That's never bothered me."

"People notice things. And they probably find some of your behavior troubling."

"Well, it's none of their business."

Feeling suddenly overwhelmingly sad, I nodded. "No, but it *is* Angel's. She needs to hear you talk about the problems, and maybe you couldn't do that without outside help."

When he said nothing, I continued. "Otherwise, maybe you'll convince yourself that Angel should forgive you and forget all about this incident. After all, it wasn't intentional, and you're sorry. Maybe, eventually, you'll convince yourself that your marriage didn't work out because Angel expected too much of you."

His lips tightened. "My marriage is going to work out."

"I hope so, but I don't want it to be at Angel's expense." I leaned toward him, feeling a real compassion for his situation. "Marriage is a tough proposition, Cliff. No two people want the same things all the time."

He sighed. "It's a constant question of compromising, Amanda. It wears you down."

"Look at it from a different perspective. In some ways marriage is exactly like medicine. In every situation you have to ask yourself what's important—not to you, but to the patient. You may have completely different priorities than the patient does. A marriage has different priorities than a single career person does. It's that simple, and that difficult. Are you more important, or is your marriage, and your family?"

Cliff regarded me with troubled eyes. He made no attempt to answer, but shrugged his huge, helpless shoulders. "I'm exhausted, Amanda. I can't think straight. I know you're trying to help, but I can't seem to put it all together."

"I know what you mean." I'd had a lot longer to put it all together, and I didn't seem to have done such a sterling job of it. "You just need time to think. When you decide what's important, you'll come up with a way to make it happen."

Which sounded like very good advice to me. I hoped I'd be able to put it into practice.

During the early part of the week I accomplished a great deal because I was intent on keeping all personal matters out of my mind. I concentrated the majority of my attention on the Effective Care in Pregnancy and Childbirth data, and what I was learning about the practice of obstetrics at the University.

In England we'd learned that it was difficult to get practitioners to change the way they practiced, even when some of their practices were proved ineffective, or worse. In America the Agency for Health Care Policy and Research had devoted time, energy and funds to increasing awareness, but with no more success than we'd had in getting doctors to change, so far as I could see.

Doug Lattimore was on a Royal College of Obstetricians and Gynaecologists audit committee which had recommended

ECPC, but Doug had his doubts. Even before this trip he'd relegated the whole subject to my sphere. I wasn't at all sure he'd have pursued the matter with any diligence if he'd come to Wisconsin as he was supposed to. Which made it all the more troubling when Dr. Hager called me into her office.

She waved me to the seat opposite her, where only a short time before I'd had to fight for my right to respect in my work here. Since then we had stayed out of each other's way, but she'd allowed me to do the clinical work I'd chosen. Now she offered me a cool smile and leaned back in her chair.

"Today I had a long talk with Dr. Lattimore. He's feeling perfectly restored after his bypass surgery."

"I'm delighted to hear it."

She nodded, as if this were only natural. "In fact, he's feeling so well that he has every intention of finishing off the last three months of the fellowship. He plans to come for August, September and October. That means that you would be able to return to England at the end of the month."

This possibility had never occurred to me. I wasn't even sure it was allowed under the terms I'd agreed to in originally coming. Shaken, I said, "It would be very inconvenient for me to leave at the end of the month. I've only completed part of my report on ECPC."

"Dr. Lattimore realizes that and assures me he would take up where you left off. No harm will be done to the study."

Except that Doug had less than no interest in it, and his own point of view was the opposite of mine. I attempted to remain calm in the face of her subtle delight. "When I accepted the project, it was with the understanding that I would be here for six months."

"But you were only offered the opportunity to come because of Dr. Lattimore's illness." She flicked back a swoop of her silver hair in a startlingly feminine gesture. "Now that he's feeling well again, he has the strongest desire to fulfill his original obligation. The project was specifically designed for him, as you will recall."

Certainly it was put together by the two of them as the most likely project to get funded. Even at the time I'd found it ironic, considering Doug's dismissal of the ECPC conclusions. My belief was that he regarded the stay in America as a six month—now a three month—vacation. But I didn't know if there was anything I could do about it.

"I'll talk with him," I said, as if that's what she'd wanted me to do. "And check the contract I signed."

"Yes, do," she said, rising. "I think you'll find that everything's in order."

Not precisely in order, I found, but with no strong case for my stand, either. The wording was ambivalent. Why hadn't I noticed that at the time? Presumably I was so intent on coming, and on making sure that it was written into the contract that I would practice medicine at the University, that it had never occurred to me that I wouldn't serve out the whole six months. Doug had still been really sick when I left.

By the time I'd gone over my contract Friday evening, I felt thoroughly discouraged. Hager wanted Doug here, Doug wanted to be here, the contract didn't seem to bar that as a possibility. There were less than three weeks until the end of the month. Of course, I could stay a few weeks as vacation time, but then I would have to leave. That thought was incredibly painful.

Back to London. Back to Netherhall Gardens and Nigel. Back to the university hospital where I constantly had to watch my back, after all these years. Back to a home where Cass had flown the nest and started living a life of her own. Back to a crowded city where health care became more and more demanding on its practitioners.

Away from Jack.

All of the other things I could have managed. Certainly I had managed them for years. But I had expected several more months, if I was lucky, of spending time with Jack, of us being lovers. I knew better than to fantasize about an enduring relationship with Jack. We had discovered each other at especially vulnerable times. We had needed each other and been grateful to find just the right combination of friend, colleague and, finally, lover. But you didn't expect a clinically depressed man to make a commitment to you. And you didn't make a commitment to another man when you were already married.

Still, I had wanted to see him come completely out of his depression, to regain his love of his work, to find balance in his life again. For myself, I had hoped to burn down this candle of desire for him to a point where we could both say "Goodbye. It's been wonderful." Three weeks was not going to do that.

But it would have to suffice.

Jack was expected back Sunday evening, late. I hated that he'd be gone two more days, when we had so little time left together. Maybe he would be relieved, though. Maybe a month was just about the right length of time to have an affair, when you were coming alive again.

Mayfield House seemed terribly quiet that night. Cliff was away for the whole weekend, the Australians had gone camping, there was no one in the telly room and very little of interest in the kitchen. I sat in the garden for a long time, watching the light leave the sky, the pinks and oranges and then blues and purples.

My life, in a funny way, seemed to be going backwards. I had come to Wisconsin anticipating that the change would lead me to new ways of thinking, to decisions that would open different paths for me. Now it looked like I would go back to the same old life I'd led for many years. Well, even in London I could make changes, and perhaps I would. But I hadn't done it before, and I was very much afraid I wouldn't do it when I returned.

The light was completely gone from the sky by the time I wandered back into the house. Once again nothing in the kitchen took my fancy. Nonetheless, I helped myself to a bowl of tapioca which I carried up to my room and ate desultorily. Though it wasn't late, I decided to go to bed. If I'd had the key to Jack's room, I'd have slept in his king size bed that night. But I didn't.

Though I stayed up late Sunday night, Jack didn't arrive before I finally fell asleep. The phone rang at seven the next morning, just as my alarm went off. I reached one hand for each of them, knocking the phone onto the floor. "Sorry," I said into the receiver when I finally retrieved it.

"Did I wake you?" Jack asked, sounding amused. "The plane was late. By the time I got the kids home it was the middle of the night. Karen suggested I just stay here."

"Oh. Did you have a good trip?" I asked, trying to sound cheerful.

"You're supposed to ask, did you sleep with her? and then I'd answer, Of course not. Yes, we had a terrific trip. The kids made me book for next year before we left. How's your week been?"

"Up and down. We can talk later. Are you going straight to work from there?"

In the background I could hear faint kitchen noises. He said, "Yeah. I always keep some decent clothes at my office to change into, in case I have to spend the night on the couch there. You don't sound quite right, Mandy. You're not upset that I spent the night here, are you?"

"No, no. I have some other things on my mind. I'm glad the trip was such fun. You'll tell me all about it when I see you this evening, okay?"

"Sure." There was a brief pause, then he said, "I've missed you, Mandy."

"Me, too."

CHAPTER NINETEEN

Because I'd completed a tremendous amount of work over the weekend, even spending many hours in my University office, I felt little pressure to be at the hospital early. Mondays were not days when I did any clinical work, so I was surprised to find Sarah Jamison waiting to pounce on me when I arrived a little late.

"What's this I hear about you going back to England?" she demanded, her voice shaking with outrage. "You were supposed to be here for six months."

Out of the corner of my eye I saw that she wasn't the only one waiting for me. The look on Jack's face would have been comical if he hadn't been so obviously shocked. "England?" he growled.

Sarah was startled by his appearance, and embarrassed that she might have raised a subject she shouldn't have in front of a stranger. I didn't know which of them to answer first, so I waved them both into the office with the great view out over the University campus. Jack hesitated, the frown on his forehead growing. "I have a procedure in half an hour. I just wanted to say hi."

"Sarah Jamison, Jack Hunter," I said by way of introductions, herding them in front of me. I wasn't going to leave that door open for anyone else on the floor to hear. After all, Dr. Hager's office was only around the corner. None of us sat down. I leaned back against the door and explained, "Dr. Hager informed me Friday that Dr. Lattimore feels well enough to finish out the last three months of the project, and that he intends to do it."

"That's ridiculous," Sarah insisted. "They can't just dismiss you like that."

Jack said nothing, but his eyes snapped with anger.

"The contract, unfortunately, doesn't prohibit it. I was so concerned that it be changed to allow me to do clinical practice that I didn't pay much attention to the possibility of not completing the six months. And, of course, Doug was terribly sick when I left. It seemed highly unlikely that he'd *want* to come."

Jack rubbed the bridge of his nose. He'd gotten a wonderful tan from his week outdoors and looked excessively healthy, but the gaze he leveled on me was curiously intense. "Don't you want to fight this, Ma . . . Amanda?"

"I'm a great one for not wasting energy on lost causes, Jack. Life's too short." The major lesson I'd learned was that if you were farther down in the hierarchy than the person you were fighting, you had very little chance of winning. Unless you played hardball, and I wasn't sure I was ready to play hardball.

Jack looked disappointed; Sarah continued to look outraged. "I'm still thinking about it," I promised them, to give myself some time. "It's certainly not what I want to happen, but my options are limited."

"Maybe we can come up with something," Jack said.

I nodded and he reluctantly left. Sarah watched him go, but didn't ask the question that was in her eyes. "Really, this is most unfair, Amanda. Would it help to rabble rouse amongst the natives?"

"I doubt it, and there's no sense forcing people to take sides." I grinned. "Certainly not against the department chair. But thanks for offering."

"Well," she said, moving toward the door, "you know you have my support. Let me know if there's anything I can do."

"I will."

She stopped to ask, "Is he a jerk, this Dr. Lattimore?"

"Yes, but an attractive, courtly jerk. Most women like him."

"I won't."

Probably not, but I felt quite sure that Lavinia Hager did, quite a bit.

The first thing Jack said when I met him back at Mayfield House, sitting at the top of the stairs near my door, was, "Let's go out to dinner, Mandy. We need some privacy."

Dinner was not the main thing on my mind just then, but I agreed. "Somewhere casual," I suggested as I unlocked my door. "I want to get out of these stupid shoes."

He followed me into the living area and pushed the door closed behind him. "Why aren't you fighting this thing?" he demanded, raking at his hair. "Have you reconsidered what happened between us?"

"Not at all." I kicked off the heels and pulled my blouse out from my skirt. Then I began to unbutton the blouse as if he weren't there. "I talked with Nigel over the weekend."

"What did you tell him?"

"That I'd been unfaithful to him. He thought that had happened a long time ago."

Jack's brows drew down in a puzzled frown. "What do you mean?"

"Apparently Doug had led Nigel to believe quite a while ago that he was my lover." I removed my blouse and tossed it on the nearest chair. Then I unzipped my skirt and it slid silently down the half slip I wore. "Naturally Nigel didn't bring this up, because he refuses to talk with me about sex."

"Your husband is nuts," Jack said, trying not to smile.

"Possibly. In any case, he was not easy to convince that this was the first time I'd been unfaithful." I worked the half slip down and off, and then my pantyhose. "Interesting, isn't it? He finds my body so uninviting that he hasn't slept with me for years, but he thinks I've made a practice of sleeping with other men. Go figure."

Instead, carefully regarding my bra and underpants, Jack asked, "Are you going to take off any more?"

"That depends."

He opened his arms and I walked into them. "God, I've missed you," he said, nuzzling against my hair. "During the days it wasn't so bad because of all those rapids and the need to keep from drowning. But at night . . ."

"At night you became a bed salesman without a customer," I teased as I started to unbutton his shirt. "At night you lay there thinking that it would be more comfortable being in that roomy king size bed with a woman's naked body beside yours."

"Not a woman's," he said. "Yours. Hey, the ground was hard. I wanted your soft body there." He ran his hands slowly, lingeringly over my rounded shoulders and down my back to the swell of my buttocks. "Your lush body beside me."

His hands slid inside my underpants and massaged my flesh. I had never felt so abundantly endowed and yet so richly sensual. By this time I had his shirt off, but no more. A need had begun to throb in my body. With unsteady hands I unsnapped his slacks and tugged the zipper down.

There may be no sexier sight on earth than that of a man's pubic hair peeking out through the open V of his pants, his penis urgent against the material below. It's a sight that made me shiver with anticipation and moisten my achingly dry lips. My gaze came up to Jack's. I knew my face was flushed with desire, that my eyes were sultry with yearning.

Jack reached across to slide down one strap of my bra, and then push the fabric down over just one breast. Urgency had already hardened the nipple which he bent to take in his mouth. My hand slipped inside his pants, and found his determined flesh. I wanted him in me *now*.

As though he understood, Jack pushed my underpants down to my knees and gently pressed my buttocks toward his straining penis. With fingers grown urgent I guided him into my body, hearing Jack's and my simultaneous moans of relief at the connection.

Jack shifted me onto the back of the sofa, where I could perch at the perfect height for his thrusting, a height that brought him again and again into contact with my clitoris, building the incredible excitement to a shattering release.

Here in broad daylight, in an amusingly ungainly position, we watched each other climax. There was such warmth, such tenderness and acceptance in Jack's eyes. I was the object of his desire and the fulfillment of it. He held me afterwards as though I were made of the most delicate porcelain, a rare and valued wonder.

And I clasped him to me with all the passion I felt for his appealingly sturdy body, to say nothing of my unacknowledged passion for other, more elusive elements of his soul.

"Damn good thing there was no one in the garden," he said, noticing the open window.

"And a damn good thing the birth control pills should be effective by now."

"Yes, we've been acting like teenagers." He grinned at me. "Only it's a hell of a lot better, knowing what you're doing, isn't it?"

"*You* may know what you're doing," I retorted. "I don't have much recent experience, except with my own body."

"Which is going to make it all the easier for you to show me what you like." With his hands on either side, he rocked my hips in a way that stirred my renewed interest. "You may have noticed that I'm not shy about expressing my own needs."

I laughed. "Yes, I've noticed. Uh, Jack, if you keep doing that, I'm going to have a need of my own again."

"I know," he murmured against my hair. "But you've got a lot of need stored up and it seems to me it wouldn't hurt one bit to help you express a little extra."

His mouth traveled lightly down to my breast, capturing its wanton tip with his lips. Alone, one orgasm always seemed more than sufficient; it served to rid my body of the aches, the urges, the desires that floated through it. Like slaking thirst with wholesome water, I would have my release, and consider myself restored to balance.

Offering myself more had not really occurred to me. The rough edges that remained were acceptable for a woman in my situation. I hadn't sought more than the absolute minimum. There were other ways to disperse the sensuous urgings. Sublimation in work, in friendships, in family. That was the proper course for a middle-aged woman with a body her husband rejected.

Champagne was what Jack was offering. His lips on my nipple conjured bubbles of sheer delight. My whole body felt light as air, floated by a giddy, deep-ranging joy, a laughter that tickled every naughty, greedy nerve in my sensual network.

My hips moved with an urgency I didn't know I could feel, propelling me against Jack's hardness still there in me. His murmurs of encouragement came around the lips that drew on me, tugged me toward a new, generous need. Not the parsimonious satisfaction I'd offered myself all these years, but a big, lush, opulent all-encompassing release. A burst of glorious, magnificently superfluous fireworks.

Since afterwards I found Jack's finger against my lips, I think I must have given vocal expression to my reward, but he did no more than grin like a fool as I attempted to compose myself. "I'm not sure that's entirely fair," I said, somewhat anxiously.

"More than fair, my sweet." He left a trail of kisses across my face. "But my bet is that you're famished, and so am I. Let's get some clothes on and eat here after all."

Not a plan I wished to oppose. Being a seductress and a seductee was hungry-making work. I hoped the aromas drifting up the stairs meant we were having Sherri's fabulous chicken stir-fry.

"You have to at least *try* to throw a wrench into their plans," Jack protested later when we were sitting under a tree looking out over Lake Mendota.

A warm breeze ruffled the collar of my blouse and lifted a wing of my hair. "I can't see why. They're going to win, so anything I do will just make me look foolish. And I'm not fond of looking foolish."

"So you intend to leave Wisconsin in three weeks' time?"

"I didn't say that." I swatted at one of the mosquitoes which were a constant hazard of summer living in Madison. "It would be easy enough for me to extend my stay a few weeks. No one's looking for me back in London."

Jack's expression was grim. "But you couldn't work at the University. Dr. Lattimore would be there. And he'd probably even want your place in Mayfield House."

That was an aspect of it I hadn't considered. Well, he could just find somewhere else to live. But the thought of staying there as a tourist, with no work to do, waiting for Jack to come home each evening, was very unappealing. I said as much.

Jack snorted. "You'd hate it. You could stay in Oconomowoc and have a real vacation—swim, canoe, hike, read, enjoy the peace. It would be easy for me to commute from there."

"That would be great—for about a week. Then I'd feel like some sort of concubine." I sighed as I watched a sailboat dip past the horizon. "Ultimately I'm going to have to go back. It's just a shame this had to happen. The six months would have been perfect. By then we'd have gotten tired of each other and been ready to go our separate ways."

"How the hell do you know that?" Jack demanded, his eyes snapping with annoyance. "Who says we're going to get tired of each other?"

"That's what happens," I insisted, feeling anything but the rational soul I was attempting to portray. "These sexual attractions flare for a while, then die a natural death. We met each other at just the right moment. You were depressed and lonely; I was temporarily free and ready for an adventure. But you live in America, I live in London. We're old enough to know what we're doing, and smart enough not to let anyone get hurt in the process."

Under stormy brows his eyes challenged me. "Are we?"

"Yes, I think we are." Did I? Perhaps it was a matter of degree. Nigel wouldn't be hurt by it, certainly. Jack would have bittersweet memories when he looked back on it after he recovered completely from his depression. If I came out heartsore, well, I knew even now that it was well worth that pain. Life in London would feel different after this, but not worse. Even if I continued my marital facade with Nigel, I'd be richer for having had Jack in my life.

Jack twined his fingers through mine and shook his head. "What a dreamer you are, Mandy. But I don't think you're telling me the whole truth."

I didn't want to come any closer to the truth than I had. "In what way?"

"I suspect you could thwart this nefarious plot by Lavinia and Doug if you really wanted to."

I raised my head, surprised at his acuity. "You mean you think I have something on Doug? I have lots of stuff on Doug, but it's always his word against mine. He sleeps with patients, but only sophisticated patients who should know better. And, of course, he'd been having an affair with Lavinia before his heart attack."

Jack blinked at me. "You're sure of that?"

I shrugged. "Yes, but so what? Their personal morals are their own business. As, I would remind you, are mine, and I'm no longer in a position to be throwing stones, if I ever was."

"I wasn't suggesting you reveal their affair. I'm just surprised you seem so forbearing."

"It's his sleeping with patients that pisses me off," I said, allowing the anger to wash over me for a brief moment. "Any man who takes advantage of his position as an OB/GYN is a shameless cad, so far as I'm concerned. My lack of respect for Doug has made my professional life in London a real adventure."

"A struggle, more likely," Jack muttered. "Well, the one advantage of his coming here would be that I'd have a chance to meet this charmer and see what I could do to make his life miserable."

I laughed. "I like your style, Jack. And the other advantage is that if he's here, I'll have a chance to enjoy my job in London without his breathing down my neck."

"They aren't substantial enough advantages to make it worthwhile," Jack said, squeezing my hand. "Have you told Nigel about the change?"

"I faxed him Saturday, but I haven't heard anything."

His gaze sharpened on my face. "Would you go back to him, Mandy?"

"I don't know. Possibly."

"But you don't have a marriage with him."

"No, but I have a partnership. In some ways, Jack, our having this affair would make it easier for me to continue with Nigel, rather than harder."

His face had become unreadable. "Until someone else came along who tempted you. It will be easier the next time."

Easier, and harder. Stuffing my sexuality back into the narrow confines I'd defined for it wasn't likely to work so well. But I'd met a lot of men in England over the years without discovering someone I had to share it with. Somehow it seemed unlikely to me that another potential partner was sitting around waiting for me to fall into his life. "I'm kind of picky," I said lightly.

"It was my personal magnetism that was irresistible, I suppose."

Though he was teasing, I heard his need for reassurance. "Oh, Jack, you're the most irresistible man I've ever met. But if I'd met you in London, even with all that magnetism, I probably wouldn't have succumbed. Just because of all the reminders there, and the lack of opportunity to spend time with you. And that's how it will be when I get back."

"I don't think so," he said thoughtfully, drawing a line along my arm with his finger. "I think you'll find you've changed. You won't be satisfied to be Nigel's roommate anymore."

Our eyes met briefly before we both looked away. After a while we climbed back on our bikes and returned to Mayfield House.

CHAPTER TWENTY

Jack took me to his retreat at Oconomowoc that weekend. This time we shared his bedroom and generally played house. The thought that we had only three weeks left together made the time seem precious, but even then I insisted that he not spend the whole day with me on Sunday.

"You know very well you want to do something jockish where I wouldn't be able to keep up with you," I said when he suggested a gentle hike around Fowler Lake. "Do it. I believe in only so much togetherness."

"We don't have that much time left," he said, but he was already searching for his biking shorts.

Jack had been gone for almost two hours when the phone rang. I thought he might be calling to let me know he was on his way back, or asking if there was anything I wanted him to pick up at the store. It did occur to me that it might be one of his kids trying to get hold of him, or even someone from the University. So Nigel's voice didn't register with me immediately.

"Mandy? Is that you?" he asked.

"Yes. Nigel? Is something wrong?" A feeling of panic shot through me. Had something happened to Cass? Why would he call me here? I hadn't left the number.

"Everything's fine," he said soothingly. Nigel knows that I'm easily roused to images of family disaster. "Cass said to send her love when I talked to her the other day."

"Good. Does she like the job?"

"Job? Oh, the holiday camp. Not much, but she says she'll survive it."

"How did you get this number?"

"Tony had written it in the address book when you left it with him that time you wanted me to call back. When I couldn't reach you in Madison for two days, I thought I'd try it."

"But there's no emergency?"

"No." There was a long pause. "But I have something to tell you."

"Okay," I said warily. "What?"

Again there was a long pause. When his voice came, it was constricted. "You need to know something about me that I've never told you, Mandy. I'm gay."

My mind felt like it would explode with the dozen different thoughts that tried simultaneously for precedence. Gay. Of course. Oh, you stupid, blind woman. "Are you well, Nigel?"

That surprised a grunt from him. "I'm HIV negative, yes."

"Have you told Cass?"

"No. But I will. You had to know first."

"What made you tell me now?"

I could almost see his wince. "Not your affair," he said. "At least, not directly. But when I told Tony about it, he insisted."

"Tony Growalter." It wasn't a question. "Our" friend of how many years? Blind indeed if you refuse to see. I had even recognized Tony as gay, though he had never declared himself. I had thought how we were in such a good position to be his friends—a straight couple with an almost grown daughter, who had similar interests to Tony's. Too similar, apparently, on Nigel's part.

"Mandy? Are you still there?"

"How long has this . . . ?" But there was really only one important question, wasn't there? "Did you know you were gay when you married me?"

Again one of those unfamiliar pauses. How Nigel hated to be forced to reveal something he preferred to have remain secret. Even now he equivocated. "I'd never been with a man, no."

"But you suspected that you were gay."

" . . . Yes. But I wanted a family. I wanted to be normal. I loved you, Mandy."

Obviously not in the way I had loved him. What did that say about me?

"Mandy, listen to me. I *did* love you. I *do* love you. I thought if you could make me feel that way, I'd be okay. Honestly I did, Mandy. And it worked . . . for a while. I fought it. God, I really tried, Mandy. But it got stronger, that pull. I thought if I went off to Duke and left you in London, I could experiment and get it out of my system and everything would be fine when I got back. But you wouldn't let me go alone."

No, I had been willing to do an American OB/GYN residency rather than let him split up our family. Imagine. Fortunately for him their residencies are so demanding that I scarcely had the energy left to care for Cass, let alone worry that our sex life had declined. Because he was still trying then. I remembered, and my heart ached.

"Oh, Nigel. Couldn't you just have told me?"

"There was so much to lose," he said, his voice strained and rough. "I took a few chances then, before we understood about AIDS. But never again after that. I made sure you were never exposed to even the possibility."

Did he expect me to thank him for that? Maybe I should, but I had no intention of doing it. All those years. Twelve years. He hadn't wanted me, but not because of my oversized body. And despite what he said, he had obviously never really wanted my body, had perhaps even unconsciously chosen me because of my size. Who else was going to want the fat girl?

"And Tony?" I finally forced myself to ask. "Is he your regular partner?"

"My only partner, for a very long time."

"Then you should have lived with him. You should have been open about it."

"And what about Cass? She was still a kid then." Nigel was pleading with me, trying to make me see things from his point of view. "You wanted us to be a family, Mandy. Even after we stopped being intimate, you stayed with me. We made a home for Cass."

We *had* made a home for her, and a loving one. But would I have stayed with Nigel if I'd known? Surely not. Yet here I'd been thinking of going back to him after having an affair with Jack. My head had begun to ache.

"What are you going to do now?" I asked.

He cleared his throat. "Nothing, right away. I wouldn't have told you, except that Tony refused to see me again until I did. So this isn't altruism, and it isn't my way of coming out of the closet, Mandy. I hate the idea of people at work knowing I'm gay. It's none of their business."

"Maybe not, but that's the way things are. You've stayed in the closet at my expense, Nigel. And your coming out will be a good part at my expense, too," I said, realizing it was true. How Doug Lattimore would howl at that one. If Lavinia Hager was fatphobic, Doug was homophobic. Which made it pretty humorous, I supposed, that he'd hinted to Nigel that he was having an affair with me.

"I'm sorry," Nigel said, sounding like he meant it. "I didn't intend for all this to happen, I swear. And I'd have been content to leave things the way they were. Which irritates you, I know, but . . . " I could almost see his shrug. Nigel would feel that he deserved a little reward for sticking with the family all this time, despite the fact that he'd been the one to reap most of the benefits of that situation.

"You got my fax? You know I'll be coming home in August?"

"Yeah, that really tripped Tony. We've been spending a lot of time here."

Don't tell me; I don't want to know. "Well, I have to be grateful to Tony for insisting on your telling me the truth. I only wish he'd done it a great deal sooner."

"Oh, he's tried," Nigel admitted. "He hated deceiving you, Mandy. Not that I didn't. But then when I thought you were having an affair with Lattimore, I sort of felt like I could justify it."

"How convenient." Sarcasm never worked with Nigel, though, so I said, "I don't know how you could have believed him. You knew how I felt about Doug."

"A ruse," he said, "so I wouldn't guess you were having an affair with him. Jesus, the whole thing is such a convoluted mess."

"It wouldn't have been if . . . Never mind. I think I'd prefer you not to be there when I come home, Nigel, all things considered."

"But . . ."

"Look. It's been a hard summer, what with one thing and another. I'm not going to be up for a big drama when I get back. This project is important to me, and I'm not going to be allowed to finish it. Doug will do everything in his power to screw it up. And God knows what kind of booby traps he'll have set for me in the department."

Nigel murmured a not-very-enthusiastic understanding and then asked, "What about the guy you're having an affair with?"

I looked up just then to see Jack standing in the doorway. It was almost too much for me. "He'll be here and I'll be there. I'd like the house to myself, Nigel. Please."

"Okay," he said grudgingly. "But we should talk more about it."

"We'll talk more about it," I promised. "But not now."

"Right. Good-bye, Mandy."

My throat ached unbearably. "'Bye, Nigel."

Jack moved into the room as I cradled the receiver. I found I couldn't look up at him. He moved closer to me, standing a few feet away from the sofa. When I still didn't look up or say anything, he crouched down in front of me.

"What is it?" he asked, his voice gentle.

But I hadn't had time to absorb Nigel's news yet. I needed to think about what this meant before I discussed it with Jack. I needed to think of the times when Nigel's being gay would explain what had happened in our lives—and when it wouldn't.

"Could we talk about it later?" My throat constricted as I spoke. "Right now I have to sort this through, okay?"

"Sure. Want to take the canoe out?"

When he'd pushed me off from the dock, I paddled slowly around the perimeter of the lake, avoiding the other small crafts. The day was pleasant, with a soft breeze and warm sunshine, but I was back in England, skipping wildly over the past twenty-odd years. In the bedroom, in the kitchen, trying to make sense of half of my life through a new prism.

The anger I felt toward Nigel raged through me again and again. And I let it, because when I didn't feel the hot burning of it against him, it was directed at myself. He had lied to me, deceived me, made my life a hell in some ways. All because he wanted a family, didn't want to be recognized as gay. And what about me, married for twenty-two years to a gay man? Nigel, you great prick! You've certainly made me look foolish.

Sometimes I felt hot with shame that I'd not understood, that I'd never recognized the problem. Other times I burned with anger for the waste, for the frustration, for the unhappiness. Not just for me, but for Nigel as well. Instead of the lonely, separate people we'd been, we might have managed a different kind of life. Or maybe I'd have been out of there in a flash, ready to find a "normal" life for myself, to prove I was a "normal" person.

And the weight issues. All the importance I'd given them, was that false? Nigel wouldn't have been any more interested in sleeping with me, presumably, if I'd been a skinny model. Certainly he hadn't on the occasion when I'd lost weight. And the psychological power I'd given him because I thought my weight put me in the wrong.

It was almost two hours before I brought the canoe back to Jack's dock. He was there fishing, a ratty old canvas hat perched on his head, his feet dangling in the water. Seeing him, my eyes burned with unshed tears. He was a remarkable man, a generous man, an understanding man. And he was waiting there for me to unburden myself to him.

When he handed me out of the canoe he held me tightly against him for just a moment. "Feel better?" he asked, cocking his head and examining my face. "I brought a snack for us."

See, that's the kind of thing he did. Nigel had put himself in charge of changing me, seeing that I didn't eat any more than he thought was necessary. Jack had food ready for me and waved me toward it. As he stowed the canoe, I helped myself to the double-decker sandwich he'd prepared. I hadn't realized that I was famished. After a few minutes he joined me, sitting down beside me on the blanket he'd spread with our picnic.

"Want to tell me about it now?" he asked, picking up half a sandwich. "No hurry. When you're ready."

Like my husband, I decided it was easiest to just say it. "Nigel called to tell me he's gay."

Jack just nodded.

"That doesn't surprise you?" I demanded.

"Well, not really, Mandy. I don't know a whole lot of hetero-sexual men who could live with a woman for twelve years and not have sex with her, even if they weren't getting along."

"So you think I should have realized."

At my belligerent tone he grinned, shaking his head. "Not necessarily. Obviously you'd *had* sex with him. You have a daughter. And you have this hangup about your weight, so you could blame it on that."

"It's not a hangup. It's just the reality of how other people see me."

"In any case, it wasn't what kept Nigel from being intimate with you," he pointed out.

"No, apparently not."

"In fact he would probably have slept with you, just to keep up appearances, if it weren't for the dangers of HIV, right?"

"So he says," I grumbled. "Very altruistic of him."

"Well, it's better than dying," he persisted. "And, let's see, there was the man you got on the phone when you called Nigel the first weekend you were here. A family friend. Nigel's lover, right?"

"How could you possibly know that?" I demanded, feeling more indignant than ever.

"I can put two and two together as well as anyone." He regarded me with only partially hidden amusement. "Mandy dear, once you know the missing piece, you can put the whole puzzle together. No one's blaming you for not recognizing the missing piece. It was well disguised."

"I feel so stupid."

Jack pushed a container of corn chips toward me, nudging my knee with it until I reached in and helped myself to a handful. I munched on them for a while and then said, "I still feel stupid."

He laughed. "Well, it's not necessary. Sad, certainly, and angry for the deception and the frustration of all those years. But you had an intact family, and you and Nigel obviously got along well enough to keep it that way. It's had it's advantages."

"I know," I admitted gruffly. "But what's going to happen when I go back, Jack? Eventually Nigel will come out of the closet, and I'll look like a fool, which I have been."

"Knowing my academic colleagues as I do, it's more likely they'll think you were extraordinarily clever to set the whole thing up so that you had maximum freedom sexually while maintaining a traditional-looking marriage." With considerable irony he added, "They'll envy you."

His scenario didn't ring entirely false. I knew a number of people who would have relished that kind of setup. Even I might have taken advantage of it, if I'd known. If I'd met Jack or someone like him in England. Was there someone like Jack in England?

"And it certainly has been a boon for me," Jack said, his grin firmly in place.

"In what way?"

"I feel as if I've been offered this incredibly savvy virgin. That's always been a fantasy of mine. Does that make me a chauvinist?"

I searched his face and found only warmth and caring. "Probably," I said. "We might discuss it further up at the house."

"Good idea. But finish your lunch first. You're going to need your strength."

CHAPTER TWENTY-ONE

Angel called on Monday to invite me to have dinner with them. "Cliff says you're being uprooted to give your boss a chance for a vacation," she said. "I'm really sorry."

"Me, too. Doug doesn't have the same take on the ECPC that I do, and he's not going to be interested in really getting involved with it. But there's nothing I can do, especially since Lavinia and I have never gotten on well."

"Pity." In the background I could hear little Roger let out a howl and Angel call to her husband, "Will you take care of him, Cliff?"

Hesitantly, I asked, "Is everything going okay?"

"Come and see," she said. "Would Wednesday be all right?"

"Um, I don't have a car. Should I come with Cliff?"

"Heavens, no. You're coming with Jack," she said with a laugh.

"You've already talked to him?"

"Sure."

"I didn't think Cliff realized . . ."

"Oh, he doesn't. I thought it would be heartwarming for him to see what he'd started."

"Then how did you know?"

"Intuition. And maybe Jack's mentioning it when I called him about a patient."

Angel and Cliff lived roughly mid-way between Madison and the area in which Angel worked as a family practitioner. Her parents, brothers, sisters-in-law, and various nieces and nephews all resided within easy commuting distance, and provided a strong network of support to each other. If the arrangement disturbed Cliff, I'd never heard him drop so much as a hint of it.

When we pulled into their driveway, we could see Angel in the kitchen, an apron wrapped around her, checking something in the oven. To my delight, Cliff stood in the kitchen doorway with Roger in his arms, letting the child tug cheerfully at his wild hair.

The young couple had bought a modern house designed by a student of Frank Lloyd Wright's. The interior was open to the countryside around it, large windows high and low catching light and view. Though this was probably more to Cliff's taste than Angel's, she looked extraordinarily comfortable in the sleek wood and glass setting. Because of the volume of the music throbbing through the glass walls, they were unaware of our arrival. Jack and I sat for a moment watching them.

"Still," Jack said, as though we'd been talking about the scene, "I'm glad I'm past that stage in my life."

"Me, too." We looked at each other, a wealth of accumulated knowledge in our growing smiles. Then we climbed out of the car.

As usual with such a group, medical talk dominated for a while. It was wonderful to hear Jack talk about his work again with enthusiasm and confidence. As we finished the main course, though, our topics shifted to more domestic issues. Little Roger entertained us with his first attempts at walking as we sat back in our chairs surfeited with a delicious meal of Mexican chicken with the traditional rice and beans. Once, when the child tumbled over a wooden block and hurt himself falling, his little face screwed up in preparation for a howl.

But it never came. Cliff held his arms out to the little boy and Roger, his lips furiously working back and forth in indecision, chose to let his father lift and comfort him without a sound. "Bravo!" I said. "I'm impressed."

"Wait 'til you see me change him," Cliff retorted. "It's given me a new respect for pediatricians."

Jack laughed and put his arm around the back of my chair. "Amanda was telling me on the way out here that she wasn't going to mind anyone else's business any more."

Angel looked at me with mock shock. "Even if we beg you?"

"Certainly not," I said, giving the three of them my haughty English sniff.

Cliff shook his head sorrowfully. "Did I say something rude to make you change your ways?"

"No," I admitted. "I've decided that if I'd paid more attention to my own life and less to other people's, I might have spared myself a lot of . . . trouble."

Angel regarded me seriously. "Really, Amanda, you've been a big help to the two of us. Cliff and I have spent a lot of time deciding what's most important. We're working on a lot of compromises, both of us. First off, I'm only going to work two days a week. While he's young, I want to spend more time with Roger."

"And I'm going to give up the directorship of outpatient surgery," Cliff said gruffly. "There will be a lot less paperwork and academic bullshit."

If Angel's concession surprised me, Cliff's blew my mind. This kind of decision could haunt him all his life, and he knew it. If his ambition played a secondary role to his devotion to Angel and Roger, there was no question in my mind that this was one marriage that was going to stay intact.

"And if you hadn't kicked my butt," Cliff was saying to me, "I'd never have come up with the perfect solution to our childcare problems, either."

"He talked with my brother Tom," Angel explained. "Sally wanted to have a fourth kid because theirs are getting older, and Tom was frantic to find a way to dissuade her. Cliff suggested that they could become our daycare and partial parents to Roger, and maybe another one when it comes along, instead of having any more of their own. They loved the idea, both financially and personally, so we now have a built-in daycare system."

"We probably wouldn't have arrived at this point without your interference," Cliff pointed out, a mischievous light in his eyes. "At least not yet. So maybe you shouldn't give up your penchant so quickly, Amanda."

"I don't actually do it in England," I said.

"Oh, sure," Jack said.

"I don't!"

"You couldn't resist," he taunted. "There's probably always some lovelorn resident in your department who . . ."

"Well, if you're going to count *residents*," I huffed. "And we call them registrars."

"And the woman at the local greengrocer's and the guy who shines shoes at the underground," Jack pressed.

"Never. I've never given advice to a greengrocer, except for maybe Jocelyn, and she asked me if . . ."

Cliff turned helplessly to Angel and asked, "Are they . . . ?"

"Yes," she said, "and it's all *your* fault."

"Mine!"

"You sent them off to Oconomowoc together."

"Ah, so I did. How very clever of me."

Jack humphed. "Little you knew. I probably never mentioned that the first time I met her she suggested I see a psychiatrist."

"And it's done you a world of good," I said, touching his hand where it lay on my thigh under the table. "I should be so successful with everyone."

"But now you're going back to England," Angel reminded me sadly.

"Well, that's always been true."

"Not so soon, though," Cliff said, and frowned. "And aren't you married, Amanda?"

Jack and I looked at each other and burst out laughing. "Sort of," I said. "My husband and I are separated. We suffer from irreconcilable differences."

At that Jack hooted. Little Roger vigorously shook a rattle to add his measure of noise to the gathering. Angel and Cliff looked mystified but content to let us have our joke. When the hubbub had settled down a little, Angel said, "But you'll see each other in London then, won't you?"

I said, "No"; Jack said, "Yes." Our eyes met in surprise.

"It's something we haven't really discussed," I admitted, "but it's not likely Jack will get to London any time soon. I certainly won't get back here."

The lightness of our teasing had instantly disappeared and an obvious tension replaced it. Angel said, "Cliff and I will get dessert," and the two of them disappeared into the kitchen, hauling their protesting son with them.

"I can get to London," Jack said. "It's not that far."

"Don't be silly. It's not only far, it's a world away, Jack. You're going to have to carve yourself out a new life here. You aren't going to want any leftover strings. Face it, you're feeling yourself again, you're ready for life to go on. When I leave, it will all be like a fresh start for you."

He shifted restlessly on the chrome and leather chair. "Mandy, you keep talking like this is some game we're playing, like it had a starting point and it has a predefined end. Like when you step on that plane, the game's over. That's not how people are."

"Well, no, but everything that's happened has been shaped by my coming here, and by your being depressed. Now that I'm leaving, and now that you're not depressed anymore, everything is going to change." That sounded a little harsher than I'd meant it to, and I added, "I don't mean that we won't call each other once we're apart, or write notes or something. That would be only normal."

"And at what point do you see that stopping?" he asked, barely containing his obvious urge to jump up and pace around the room. "After a week, after a month?"

"Maybe we should have this conversation when we're alone," I suggested. "You know me and my dessert."

He scowled at me. "This isn't a laughing matter, Mandy. I don't understand how you got to this point in your thinking."

"Shall I be blunt?"

"Please."

I bit my lip, hard, before taking the plunge. "There is no future for us, Jack. You should be able to see that. You live here; I live in London. If we keep up contact for very long it will only interfere with each of us trying to get on with our lives. And don't fool yourself that down the road we'd meet and continue this idyll. You can't do that. Things change. If it happened that we both were at the right place sometime and wanted to have a fling for old time's sake, there wouldn't be any harm in it."

"Old time's sake!" he exclaimed. "Mandy, we're in the middle of this and you're already looking down the road to a place where we've forgotten each other."

"That time will come, Jack."

"How can you possibly know that? Can't you just let things go where they want to go?"

"Want me to be blunter?"

He frowned at me. "You're being plenty blunt enough, I would have thought."

"I can be more so. I've met your kids, remember. Say you decided you and I had some future and you told that beautiful daughter of yours that you were going to live with me. Do you have some idea of what she'd say?"

Jack flushed. "So what? It's not her concern."

"And your son. I can picture him asking you, oh, very politely, if maybe you could not, you know, bring me to his baseball games, because, well, the other kids would think you were, um, interested in me."

"They're teenagers, for God's sake, Mandy. What do they know?"

"But that's precisely the point, Jack. They *are* teenagers, and they're very vulnerable to appearances. It's not going to be easy for them if their distinguished, athletic father starts appearing around town with an English butterball."

"You are absolutely obsessed with this weight thing, aren't you? No one cares, Mandy! Didn't you just learn that with your husband? All these years you thought he didn't sleep with you because of your weight, didn't you?"

When I didn't answer, he finally gave in to his urge to move and rose from his chair. Looking down at me, steely-eyed like an annoyed neurosurgeon, he asked, "Didn't you? That was the only scenario that went through your mind all those years. And it kept you from seeing the truth, that the man is gay and isn't interested in sleeping with women, even a sexy, attractive woman like you."

"But," I said, glaring with my self-righteous OB/GYN glare, "he chose me originally because he thought no one else would want a fat woman."

"No, he didn't. He chose you because you were the only woman who made him feel interested enough to think he might bring it off."

"That's nonsense. You don't know why he chose me."

"Well, neither do you!"

At this impasse, Angel stuck her head into the room and asked, "Anyone interested in fruit tart for dessert?"

Embarrassed, both Jack and I said, "Yes," and apologized for our uncouth behavior. Cliff returned grinning broadly, with Roger wide-eyed at his side. "Gee, even *we* don't have fights at other people's houses," he said smugly as he placed dessert plates on the table.

"We weren't having a fight," Jack assured him, "just a discussion."

Angel bore in a glazed tart with kiwi, apricots, grapes and pears that looked sensational. "Cliff is exaggerating. Back in San Francisco, when we were trying to figure out what was happening with us, we managed to argue all over the hospital. He proposed to me in the middle of an operation I was doing."

"Really?" I regarded Cliff with renewed respect. "Taking advantage of her even then, were you?"

He turned pathetic eyes on his wife. "I knew she'd manage to turn it around on me. *They* were the ones who were arguing."

Angel shook her head in mock hopelessness. "Having two children already, it's hard to consider acquiring a third," she murmured as she started to slice the tart.

"How unfair," her husband protested, "when I whipped the cream for the tart, which made it impossible to overhear what the two of them were saying."

Jack threw up his hands in despair. "You're all nuts. No wonder Man . . . Amanda so easily slid into your lives."

"And that's another thing," Cliff said. "We seem to be calling her by the wrong name."

Our drive home was naturally the first opportunity we had to continue our personal disagreement. The Lenzinis lived almost an hour's commute from the University hospital, so we were not without time to thrash out the entire subject, but Jack immediately attempted to change the rules.

"You're not telling the truth about all this," he said, even before we'd pulled out of the driveway.

"I'm trying to be as logical, as practical as possible."

"Maybe so, but you're not coming close to being open."

"In what way?"

He turned briefly to look at me before returning his attention to his driving. "You're purposely leaving out any discussion of how you feel."

"What did you want me to say about how I feel?"

"I'd like to know how you feel about me, how you feel about leaving."

"I feel like hell about leaving. I expected to have longer here to do my work, and to enjoy being in America. Mostly, now, I'm bitterly unhappy that I won't get to spend more time with you." I squeezed my hands together, tight, and added in a voice only slightly above a whisper, "I'm excessively fond of you, Jack. In fact, I'm infatuated with you. Is that what you wanted to know?"

Jack pulled over to the side of the road and stopped the car. In one efficient movement he released his seatbelt and mine, taking me into his arms to hug me breathstoppingly against his chest. "Good," he murmured against my hair, very close to my ear. "Yes, that's what I wanted to know. Because that's how I feel about you. I feel enchanted, Mandy, like I've been caught up in a fairy tale."

I kissed the hollow of his neck where a pulse throbbed, and sighed. "But that's the problem, Jack, as well as the joy. We're in a special set of circumstances, like a summer holiday romance. We don't have to deal with the realities, because in a matter of weeks I'll be gone. You've come out of your depression, which in itself should feel like a blessing. Everything is golden right now. And our emotions . . ."

I shook my head, trying to clear it. My head hadn't felt entirely clear for weeks. "Jack, we needed each other. You've been distraught because of your divorce, and because of the drain of some patients not doing well. I've been feeling neglected by my husband and displaced in my work. So we've stolen these very special weeks to escape from those harsh realities. I think that's fair. There's nothing wrong with living out a fantasy when it doesn't impinge on anyone else. But fantasies are naturally limited."

"You see, that's where I think you're not being honest," Jack said, releasing me. "It may be easier for you to believe that than accept the truth. But you and I have endured a fair amount of reality these last few weeks."

I regarded him with a certain amount of wariness. "What do you think the truth is, Jack?"

"That we're falling in love with each other. For real. That it's not some fairy dust that will blow away as easily as it's settled on us. Maybe you're afraid of that."

"Why would I be afraid of it?"

He grimaced. "Because you're not at all sure someone could love you. And because, if someone loved you, you might be forced to make a lot of changes in your life, some of them very difficult. And I'm *not* talking about your weight. Worse, you might find yourself vulnerable to being hurt. What if you ended up loving me, and I didn't end up loving you?"

"Yeah," I said, clearing my throat. "What if that happened?"

"You'd be able to handle it," he said, rubbing his thumb tenderly along my cheek. "But instead of being willing to face that possibility, you've created a scenario where we're both just caught in a kind of temporary insanity that will have a natural end. You're not willing to risk much to see if this is for real."

My fear exhibited itself as stubbornness. "I've told you there's nothing I can do."

"Hmm. I think that's a cop-out." He leaned back against the driver's seat and regarded me with pursed lips. "Though you don't like how short the deadline has become, you're not at all dissatisfied with having a deadline. August, November, really it doesn't matter. You feel sure sometime between now and then we'd naturally drift apart anyhow, so why make a fool of yourself trying to delay the inevitable?"

"And what are *you* doing that's so brave?" I demanded.

"According to you, just having a romance with an 'English butterball' is brave," he said. "Although I prefer to think of you as my English muffin."

I couldn't help laughing, but it was half a sob. "Oh, Jack. You're such a dear."

"Only in this fantasy. In real life I must be entirely different or you'd be considering my potential for the long term."

Even in the darkness of the car I could see his face well enough to know that he was very serious about all this. And he was right, of course, that I had lacked the courage to fight for what I wanted—whether it was my right to another three months here, or for a future with Jack. Why was that?

A mild breeze drifted through the open windows of the car, ruffling Jack's hair. I wanted to run my hands through that wiry brown crop, to sink my face into his chest and hide there. Instead I said, "I need time to think, Jack. Further discussion is going to be pointless until I do some soul-searching. Trust me?"

He lifted each of my hands in turn and kissed them. "I trust you, Mandy. More than you trust yourself."

CHAPTER TWENTY-TWO

At Mayfield House we parted for our own rooms by silent mutual consent. There was too much unsettled between us for me to simply sink into an erotic interlude with Jack. Well, that wasn't precisely true, but Jack probably thought it was. And I did need the space and time to think.

Being with him confused me. So did being alone. But now was the time to sort all this out. I kicked off my shoes and rubbed my feet on the Indian rug, thinking that maybe I'd get one for the Netherhall Gardens house before I left Madison, because, like many things, it would remind me of my stay here.

I made little plans like that all the time, to reassure myself that my life would continue in pleasant ways when I was back in London. Sometimes I'd remember a favorite book, and I'd remind myself that when I got back I'd take the time to read it again. All I was really doing was proving to myself that I expected there to be a huge empty space in my life that I would need to fill when I was no longer with Jack.

So maybe I wasn't being completely honest with myself about him, but how could I possibly admit how I felt? From the beginning I'd assured Jack that I knew what I was doing—that I just wanted a sexual interlude with him. People did it all the time, didn't they? And I had good reason to allow myself room for dalliance. I was a zillion miles away from Nigel, and we hadn't had sex for a zillion years. A brief, adult affair made all the sense in the world.

Honestly, I still believed that. The problem was that that wasn't how it had worked out. Maybe because of those weeks we'd just been buddies, or maybe because I was so sexually needy, but probably because Jack was such a wonderful guy, whatever the reason, I had completely fallen for him.

Nevertheless, I felt almost obligated to pretend that I hadn't. It seemed to me that was the proper position to take. Miss Manners would have approved of that, wouldn't she? If I told Jack it would just be a fling, then I should keep my word and make it just a fling, shouldn't I?

So why was he making such a big deal out of insisting that I admit to the truth? We both knew that under our surface fantasy I was feeling something deeper than sexual attraction. Jack seemed to be saying that perhaps he was, too. But what difference did it make, really? We had totally separate lives, lives that would not mesh.

You don't just walk away from one of the jobs either of us had. There was no more chance of Jack moving to London than there was of me being offered a place in Lavinia's department. We weren't kids. We had families located where we lived. You don't move thousands of miles away from teenagers you're trying to have some influence on. You don't leave your own country just because one summer you fell in love with some guy who maybe loved you, too.

Do you?

What had he said? That I was afraid because I'd have to make a lot of changes in my life. Well, who wouldn't be? I had a daughter in England, to say nothing of a husband. I had a house and a job and friends. Jack wasn't offering to throw over his whole way of life, I noticed. Of course, I didn't know any American doctors who'd ever come to practice in England; the brain drain was always in the opposite direction. And his kids were younger than mine, not out of the nest yet. And you couldn't practice pediatric neurosurgery just anywhere the way you could obstetrics and gynecology.

If I believed that he loved me, all of this might be moot. But how could I believe he loved me? Oh, I didn't doubt he was sexually attracted to me. That was plain enough. It was the proximity, no doubt, and my own raging desire that prompted his interest. And his personal situation, being divorced and in low spirits about his work. Probably having someone lusting after his body had perked him up along with the Prozac.

But forever? I don't think so. Even the sexual attraction would fade, given time. There were too many beautiful, sexy women in the world. Why would Jack be satisfied with me and my oversized body? If he thought he was now, it was just an aberration which would pass in time. And where would I be left then, if I believed him? Flat on my ass, that's where.

By the time I reached this point in my reasoning, I was completely disrobed and thoroughly convinced. It was the merest chance that I happened to catch sight of myself in the mirror above the dresser as I reached into the drawer for my nightshirt. What I saw surprised me. I've seen thousands of women's bodies. They come in all sizes and shapes, all colors and conditions. The one reflected back to me was nothing so out of the ordinary.

My body looked healthy and rounded. My cheeks were full, my face on the square side, but with dimples to soften its planes.

I looked strong, with sturdy shoulders and staunch hips. Just looking at my breasts I could remember the pleasure they gave when Jack touched them, and how pleased he was at their size. My thighs seemed powerful, my legs robust.

Everything about my body looked alive and real in a way with which I wasn't completely familiar. For years I hadn't owned my whole body, and here it was, full of potential, the object of a loving man's desire. This was *my* body, my flesh, the outward symbol of an inward me, no more or less expressive of my essence than anybody else's body.

If I had to struggle every day to remind myself that being fat didn't denote some terrible character flaw, I would do it. This was just a body, the repository for my mind and soul and hopes and longings, pretty much genetically coded to be a certain size. How unforgiving of me to have consigned my poor flesh to the category of being unworthy.

Well, it was about time I changed, I decided as I pulled my nightshirt over my head. Because if I didn't, there was no way on earth I was going to accept the possibility that Jack loved me, and that we had a future together.

Decisions, decisions. Most of them seemed to hinge on whether I was willing to play the game by the rules my adversaries had chosen. I had always congratulated myself on being above the petty, backstabbing type of academic exercise that dominated politics in university settings. Which, of course, explained why I remained firmly entrenched in a position at my London hospital that hadn't changed in more than half a dozen years.

But when your personal happiness is at stake, holding the moral high ground may not seem a sufficiently strong position. Besides, as I'd decided the previous night regarding weight issues, the moral high ground wasn't always so high after all. It turned out to be personal prejudice as often as it did concern for the truth. And in the case of Doug Lattimore and Lavinia Hager, maybe a little beam of truth wouldn't do any harm. I just had to work up the courage to be under attack if I was going to attempt being the attacker.

Since Lavinia refused to find a spot on her calendar for me, I accepted Sarah Jamison's offer of assistance. Sarah was particularly concerned with the Effective Care in Pregnancy and Childbirth data that I'd been collecting, and she hated the idea that Doug would arrive and the whole project would evaporate. So it was on an academic as well as personal level that she was willing to put herself in a somewhat precarious position—by bringing me with her on an appointment with Lavinia.

I didn't tell Sarah ahead of time that I'd decided to play hard ball. Probably I should have, if I were still striving for the high ground, but having her an uninformed bystander would prove so much more effective that I couldn't resist the temptation. Besides, Sarah was no more immune to juicy gossip than anyone else in the department. She'd love hearing what I had to say.

Lavinia's expression became hostile as I followed Sarah into the office. "I don't recall being informed that Dr. Potter would be with you, Sarah."

Bless her, Sarah was not intimidated by her department chairwoman. "But we were planning to discuss the ECPC data, Lavinia. Amanda is the person who knows the most about it, and her report so far has some provocative findings."

She passed across two highlighted sheets of paper as she took her seat opposite Dr. Hager. "We're going to look a little lax if these figures aren't pursued and explained, and Amanda isn't sure Dr. Lattimore will be interested in doing that when he comes here."

Lavinia bent her frostiest gaze upon me. "The purpose of Dr. Lattimore's visit is to work on this project. Perhaps you've become too close to the subject to have an unbiased view of it, Dr. Potter."

"Oh, no," I assured her. "Doug doesn't have the least interest in ECPC. In fact, in the past he's spoken out against its findings."

"It was Dr. Lattimore who suggested the project, and who is on a committee of the RCOG which studied it."

"Yes, I believe he was the only one who voted against adopting it," I mused. "But he has more or less supported my work on it, since the adoption was inevitable."

Sarah urged her point again. "The University is not going to come off looking good if the ECPC project is dead in the water from here on out, Lavinia. We need someone like Amanda who will work with us and help us improve our compliance."

"Well, Doug might be willing to skew the results," I suggested. "After all, it's not like a clinical trial. I've known him to be influenced by people around him to make things look better than they were."

Both women stared at me. Lavinia's voice was harsh when she said, "Your suggestion that Dr. Lattimore would tamper with results is grossly out of line, Dr. Potter. I'm sure your accusations have no basis in fact."

I allowed my eyes to widen. "No basis in fact? Forgive me, but I've worked with Dr. Lattimore far longer and far more closely, at least academically, than you have, Dr. Hager. I could point to half a dozen studies that bear his imprint which skate a little wide of the truth. Nothing outrageous, of course. He could convince you himself that the results wouldn't impact on patient care in any negative way."

God, I'd wanted to say that out loud for years. Because it was *precisely* what Doug had said to me when I read in disbelief his conclusions about departmental problem spots. Any statistics which showed pregnant women felt they got better care from the midwives than the obstetricians on our staff disappeared without a trace. Any complaints against the males in the department also managed to get lost somehow, while those against the women popped swiftly to the surface. Complaints against doctors are a regular feature of medical life; how they're treated is the important element.

Sarah coughed to cover the snort of laughter that had escaped her. Lavinia scowled and said, "You're mistaken, Dr. Potter. Your jealousy of Dr. Lattimore is all too obvious. Be aware that I'll make him cognizant of this conversation."

"Please do," I urged her with obvious heartiness. "You might tell him, too, that when I spoke to my husband the other day Nigel informed me for the first time that Doug had been hinting to him for years that he and I were having an affair. I wonder why he would have done that? Nigel, being a proper English gentleman, had never raised the issue."

"That cannot possibly be true," Lavinia stated with an unbecoming flush.

"Well, it's not true that Doug and I have had an affair. But Nigel would have no reason to lie about Doug's hint. After all, I haven't kept all of Doug's affairs a secret from Nigel over the years. Maybe that's why Doug thought he could make Nigel believe it." I turned to Sarah with a shake of my head. "Men! Sometimes you wonder if they're born with borderline personalities."

"This is absurd," Lavinia insisted, though I could see she was thoroughly shaken. "Dr. Lattimore is a married man."

"True. I'm very fond of Mrs. Lattimore. In fact, the only reason I never reported Doug's affairs with patients to the professional ethics committee was because I was afraid it would ultimately hurt her." Again I turned to Sarah to comment, "Not that it would have made much impression, my complaint. The men on the committee would simply have shelved the whole matter, and threatened to make things difficult for me if I didn't shut up. So I never said anything, and look where it's gotten me. You might consider that a lesson."

Sarah's shoulders were shaking. "I will."

"I don't believe a word of this," Lavinia said as she rose. "Dr. Lattimore is a courtly, charming man with absolute integrity. I wouldn't be surprised if he decided to take action against you, Dr. Potter, for spreading such inflammatory rumors about him."

I had risen, too, and now stood my ground, facing her with the last remnants of my anger. "Perhaps I should have my husband call you, Lavinia, if you're interested in the truth of the matter. Do you think he'd lie to you, too? Not Nigel. He's listened to the whole saga over the last fifteen years."

"Just your side of it," she said.

"No, there have been corroborating witnesses—other members of the department who've chimed in from time to time. Nigel knows the truth." I sighed, sadness winning out over anger now. "I've been unable to put a stop to it. In order to keep my job I've turned a blind eye. After all, Doug was smart enough to choose only sophisticated women. He knew how to get the other men on his side, to exchange little favors for their support. And I've just accepted it as how the game is played."

"That's not how the game is played here," Lavinia said.

Her eyes searched mine, wanting to learn if I knew she was one of the sophisticated women. Did she want to hear the truth? Did I need to tell her? She had made my life miserable for weeks. Her prejudice against fat people made life miserable for a lot of people. But that was another matter. I met her gaze squarely, innocently, and she looked away in relief.

"I'd like to stay and finish the ECPC project," I said.

"I'll get back to you about that," she said.

Sarah and I exchanged a glance and quickly left the office.

CHAPTER TWENTY-THREE

"That wasn't so hard, was it?" Jack asked when I'd told him about the encounter. We were seated in the living area of his unit after dinner, both with work in front of us but as yet not ready to settle down to it.

"I've never wished to sink to that level of manipulation," I retorted with my haughtiest sniff. "Nothing I said wasn't true, but it was like tattling. There should be a better way of resolving things than hanging someone's dirty linen out."

"Doug Lattimore doesn't deserve your loyalty, and the reason it's dirty linen is because he *made* it dirty linen, not because you used it to get yourself a hearing. Besides, you didn't use what you knew about him and Lavinia, which must have been tempting. It was very smart of you."

"Oh, good, I'm learning how to play office politics," I grumbled. "It doesn't mean she's going to let me stay."

"But if she lets you stay, she's not going to have the same bitterness toward you that she would have if you'd embarrassed her about her affair."

"I suppose not." I released a long, gusty sigh. "You know, Jack, if I'd devised the medical hierarchy, things wouldn't work the way they do."

"But since you didn't, you're going to have to work the system in your favor. Pretending you're above all that isn't going to do you any good."

"Who's pretending? I *am* above it."

He rumpled my hair. "I know you are, sweetheart. But doesn't it feel good to fight for what you want, for what you know you deserve?"

"Not as good as it would have felt if I'd just been given what I was supposed to have. But, thank heaven, that's over."

"Nope. Not yet."

I looked at him, disbelieving. "What more can I do? I don't have a legal leg to stand on."

Jack nodded his head in agreement. "But you have a guilt-ridden husband who's not anxious for you to reappear in London any time soon and who could easily be put to advantage."

"I will not use Nigel in that fashion," I protested.

"Why not? He's managed to use you for years. You've got to get over this idea that you owe everyone a loyalty they haven't earned, Mandy."

"Nigel is my husband. I do owe him a certain amount of loyalty." When Jack raised a skeptical eyebrow, I retreated, saying, "I didn't say I owed him total loyalty. What could he do to be useful?"

"Have a little talk with Doug, in person, preferably. If Lavinia doesn't withdraw the offer to Doug, Doug might decide he isn't well enough to come, after all. I'm betting Nigel could convince him of that. If your husband has managed all these years to have things precisely the way he wanted them, I haven't the smallest doubt he's very skilled at this kind of game."

The concept wasn't entirely new to me. There had been many times when I'd felt myself manipulated by Nigel, but so subtly, so smoothly, that it had been hard for me to put my finger on what was truly happening.

My own attempts to have my way had been awkward and obvious in comparison. Even when I achieved my goal, I had found myself feeling like the loser. Because of my glaring insistence, I always managed to seem so selfish. On the other hand, Nigel could get what he wanted with a startling adeptness, and I would feel frustrated by my inability to recognize and express exactly how he'd managed it.

Jack beckoned me closer to him. If I thought this was in preparation for a little snuggling, I was mistaken. Though he put his arm around my shoulders and hugged me against him, that was as far as his touching went.

"When Karen and I were married, I was still in medical school. I came from an unsophisticated, almost reclusive family. I knew nothing about society or elegant manners. Karen, on the other hand, was raised in a very social, wealthy, old Madison family. Even at our wedding I felt like a displaced person."

"Poor Jack," I said sympathetically.

"Right from the start, Karen had that advantage over me. She could hint that I was doing something wrong, or that things were done a certain way, and I would accept her assessment, because what did I know? In some elusive way it gave her a free hand with our social life, with our dealings with our families, with our house and even our own children."

"But you were becoming a neurosurgeon, top of the heap. Didn't that make any difference?"

His fingers stroked the flesh of my upper arm, but I could tell this was merely an unconscious gesture while he considered how best to put what he had to say. "Some. But during training it also meant my interests narrowed down to just what I was doing and learning. You know how exhausting a residency is, and how long, for a neurosurgeon. I still looked to her for guidance on social issues, thinking she was the authority, *because she acted as though she were.*"

"But I thought you didn't really care about those things?"

As though I were a particularly bright pupil, he hugged me and said, "Exactly! I didn't, but Karen did, and by that time the kids did, and my lack of interest in social niceties constantly made me question whether I was going to do something to upset their apple cart. Which I didn't want to do. They'd been patient with me during all those years when I couldn't spend as much time with them as I'd wanted to. It would have been rotten to repay them by screwing up their lives."

"I can see that. In fact, I tried to point that out to you the other night, Jack. Your kids are going to be embarrassed if you bring a fat woman into your life."

Jack grimaced. "That's not a social faux pas, Mandy; that's a personal snobbery. You're missing the parallel here with your own life."

"My weight."

"Right. Nigel always had an advantage because of your dis-comfort around your weight, Mandy."

"But I accept my weight."

"Pretty much in the same way I accept my lack of social polish," he agreed. "It's fine for you, but you expect other people to take exception to it. And you think they have a *right* to take exception."

I thought about that for a while, wanting to dispute it, but knowing it was the truth. "All right, I do. It's realistic, though, because people *take* the right. I can't fight the whole world, Jack."

"You don't have to fight the whole world, just the people who use your weight to manipulate you."

"Nigel says very little about my weight."

"But you think you know how he feels about it, don't you?"

I could picture Nigel, sitting opposite me at the dinner table. "Sure I do. He thinks I could control it if I wanted to, that it's a matter of will power."

"Which made you vulnerable to his using your weight against you." Jack tilted his head so that he could see me better. "How long do you think you'd have accepted Nigel's lack of sexual interest if you'd weighed what you thought you should?"

"Not for a month," I admitted, feeling slightly uncomfortable.

He was observing me closely, a determined set to his mouth. "Exactly. And how long are you going to let your vulnerability about your weight keep you from recognizing that I could care about you? That I don't need you making excuses for me, like that I'm still too depressed to make a commitment or that my kids won't want me living with a plump woman? When are you going to handle all that anger and sorrow and fear, Mandy?"

His questions were like lightning bolts. They struck me with alarming force, illuminating corners of my mind where I'd felt safe to hide. Hadn't I just determined to be honest with myself about my body size? Facing the realization that I was screwing up again because of my weight, giving Jack a supposed advantage over me, was frightening and upsetting.

But mostly I felt angry and my anger spilled over onto Jack. I pushed away from him, as though he'd been responsible, and stood up to stalk across his small living room. I wanted to throw something; I wanted to make a lot of noise. If I'd been at home, on Netherhall Gardens, I'd have smacked copper pots together, or hammered some unnecessary nails into the arbor outside the back door.

"I have to get out of here," I said, my voice unsteady.

"I'll take you anywhere you want to go," Jack said.

"I want to be alone."

Jack tossed me his car keys. "There's a tennis racket in the trunk, and two cans of balls. Sometimes just smashing them against a wall helps. Try the stadium."

"I'll do whatever I want," I growled at him.

"Of course you will," he said soothingly, and winked. "Come back to me, Mandy. I need you."

"Well, I don't need *anyone*," I said stubbornly. "But I'll bring your car keys back."

It took me more than an hour to work the spleen out of myself. He was quite right about the effect of smashing the tennis balls as hard as I could against a surface that veered them back at me just as urgently. In the end I lost half the balls, but I figured I could replace them more easily than find them in the fading evening light.

I tried to give Jack his keys back in the hallway, but he was having none of it. "In, woman," he insisted, tugging me by my hand. "We have a little more to discuss."

When he had closed the door behind me, and taken me in his arms, I said, "Such as what?"

"Well, this," he said, and kissed me for the longest time, until the heat had started rising in my body. Then he released me with a sigh. "Did the tennis balls help?"

"Yeah, they did, and I'll try to be more honest with myself." I curled up on his sofa and crossed my arms in front of my chest. "But I'm not sure I like your knowing that much about me."

He crouched in front of me, his head at a quizzical tilt. "You've always seemed to know what my vulnerabilities were, from the day we met. You knew I was depressed then, which even I hadn't figured out."

"There's a lot of manic-depression in my family. I can recognize both." I traced the line of his jaw, a little rough now with a day's growth of beard. "Sometimes I think I got a tidbit of the mania without the depression."

"But you seemed to realize how distressed I was, too, about my work. How could you have known that?"

Time for another confession. I forced myself to meet his gaze. "I read your poem. I found it in the bike helmet with the maps. I know I shouldn't have read it, but, hell, Jack, it was like a cry from your heart."

He looked stunned. "But you never said anything."

"It was a very personal poem, a glimpse into your soul. I wasn't sure you'd want to discuss it. I'm sorry if I violated your privacy."

"I think we're both going to be especially careful about each other's personal issues," he said, taking a seat beside me on the sofa and drawing my hands into his. "We've both got some significant ones, but we'll help each other. And you fought to stay here with me, Mandy, which tells me you feel something for me."

"Of course I do," I said gruffly.

"And not just in some brief romantic fantasy?" he suggested.

"No, not just in some brief romantic fantasy."

"And what would you say those feeling were?"

I sniffed regally. "We are not in the habit of being questioned about our feelings."

"Then perhaps it's time 'we' got in the habit, your highness," he said. "Because I intend for it to be a regular element of our lives together. When we wake up in the morning, I'm likely to say, 'I love you, Mandy.' And I'll be hoping you'll have something to share with me, too."

"Oh, you Americans are so easy with your endearments. You love this and you love that. You love your lattes, and you love your BMWs. What does it means to say you love me, or I love you?" I flushed at saying it, and Jack's eyes danced. "It just means you're fond of this year's model or this week's flavor, doesn't it?"

He grinned at me. "For some it may. In this case, I'd say it means you *are* this week's flavor and this year's model, and next year's, and the next year's. Mandy, it means I feel an extraordinary affection for you, and a smashing sexual attraction to you. It means you've captured my head and my heart and a great number of other parts of me. It means I feel committed to you, to the two of us together. In short, it means I love you."

We British are known for keeping a stiff upper lip, but mine seemed to be quivering just then. His deep blue eyes were intent on me, and insistent that I reveal the truth to him. It was time for me to stop pretending this was all some game I could choose to play, and admit that I, too, had made a decision that was irrevocable.

"I love you, Jack. I'm just about overwhelmed with loving you. And I'll do everything I can to help us stay together, to make this work." My eyes dropped to our joined hands. "But you have to understand that there is nothing I can or want to do about my weight. This is me. This is how I stay."

"Your weight isn't an issue for me. It never has been."

I sighed, knowing it was true. "How can you not care that I'm fat?" I asked plaintively.

"The best English muffins are," he said, bending to cover my lips with his.

EPILOGUE

When Lavinia Hager announced that I was to complete the six month program in Madison, she made no reference to our previous discussion. Doug Lattimore, apparently, had decided that he was not, after all, up to making such a strenuous commitment at the time. "He's sure," Lavinia said, looking me straight in the eye, "that you'll handle the project in the best possible manner. And he looks forward to your return in November with the results of your study."

My guess was that it was a combination of Nigel approaching him—after all, what did Nigel have to lose?—and Lavinia's cooled interest in his arrival that had done the trick. In any case, when I told Jack the news, he hugged me and presented me with a saucily wrapped package which contained an adorable cream-colored cotton pointelle tank top and shorts set.

"This," he said, "is to remind you that I think you're the sexiest woman I've ever met. I hope you'll wear it for me when we're alone, but also as underwear when it might help to be reminded of that."

The soft cotton knit felt provocative in a way that silk and satin had never felt on me. Jack thought so, too, I believe, as this charming set never lasted long on my poor hungry flesh. I wore it at the Oconomowoc retreat and at Mayfield House to lounge in, and on numerous occasions underneath my skirts and jumpers. I wore it the first time Jack took me to have dinner with his children, and when I went to the airport to pick up Cass for her brief visit at the end of August.

I wore it when I returned to London in November. Nigel picked me up at the airport and regarded me with suspicion. "You've changed," he said.

"Not so very much." I accepted his chaste kiss and studied this handsome stranger whom I'd been married to for twenty-odd years. "You look more relaxed, Nigel. It suits you."

"Thanks. You look . . . glowing."

I laughed. "I'm not pregnant. Have you arranged to stay with Tony or somewhere else?"

He shrugged. "With Tony. His mum's getting more used to the idea, but she doesn't really like it. We've talked about getting a place of our own."

"Let's just see how things go, okay?"

Nigel nodded and picked up my carry-on. "Are you worried about Doug?"

"Not particularly. I'll probably only stay two or three months, and it won't be worth his while to make life too difficult for me. Jack is supposed to come after Christmas. If everything works out all right, I'll go back to America with him."

"You're sure?"

I smiled. "Oh, yes, I'm sure."

"And if that all happened, you'd let me buy you out of the house?"

Netherhall Gardens had been my touchstone over the years. My home, my place in London. When I felt Cass was alienated from me, and Nigel was distant from me, and Doug was giving me a hard time at work, Netherhall Gardens had been my haven.

"Yes, I'll let you buy me out of the house."

He glanced down at me, his face relieved. "Thanks, Mandy. You've always been the most remarkable person. I don't suppose I've told you that, have I?"

"Not as often as I'd have liked," I admitted, tucking my arm through his and heading toward the baggage claim area.

I wore the pointelle cotton knit underwear when Jack arrived on a snowy Boxing Day. He cocked his head to look at me and said, "Good. I was hoping you would. Do we have the house to ourselves?"

"Yep. Cass has gone off for the weekend with friends."

"Smart kid you have, Mandy," he said, grinning. He had liked Cass when she visited in Madison, and had helped me adjust to Cass's sudden decision to try art school instead of going back to University.

As we made our way through London, I pointed out landmarks that were important to me. Driving up the Finchley Road, turning into Netherhall Gardens, was like coming home with him for the first time. Every other place we'd stayed had been his, or foreign to both of us, really. This was mine, for now.

Winter was not its best season, but the lights I'd left on inside the old brick house welcomed us in out of the cold, dark night. Jack followed me into the foyer, his hand twined with mine. His gaze softened as he took in the cozy sitting room with its plump sofa cushions and garden of greenery.

"I've pictured you here," he said. "I had the one snapshot enlarged. I keep it in the living room, unless Cliff comes to visit.

They're doing fine, by the way. Angel told me to tell you she's pregnant, and very happy about it. If it's a girl, they're considering the name Amanda."

"Far too old-fashioned for an American girl," I said, though I was pleased.

"And my folks send their love."

The day I'd met his parents I had worn the pointelle set, too. My impression was that his parents weren't very sociable, and that they'd never much approved of his wife Karen. Jack and I had waited in the house in Oconomowoc until we heard a car pull into the drive. Then Jack gave me a bracing smile, said, "They're just folks, Mandy," and led me out into the sunshine.

Two people had climbed out of the car, a spindly older man with a fringe of white hair, and a sprightly, sharp-eyed woman as round as I was myself. I looked up at Jack and asked, "Why didn't you tell me?"

"Because you had to believe me first, sweetheart." He had proceeded to crush his mother in a bear hug, and shake hands vigorously with his father, before saying, "Mom, Dad, this is Mandy. We're planning to get married next year."

We'd talked about it, but the announcement seemed to make everything so decided. His mother's sharp eyes took me in at a glance. Then she nodded and smiled. "Welcome to the family," she said.

And now here was Jack standing in front of me, proving that none of this had been a dream, or a romantic fantasy. Jack, with his wiry brown hair and warm blue eyes, and his sturdy, athletic body. Jack, who wrote poetry about his sad patients, but who was no longer sad himself. Jack, who wanted to spend the rest of his life with me.

He dug in his coat pocket and drew out two small packages. "These are from the kids," he said.

"They have such lovely manners," I teased.

"Their mother's influence," he said, grinning.

Sandra had chosen a pair of dangling silver earrings and Luke a small framed photograph of Madison in winter. "They *do* like you," Jack said. "This was their idea."

"I'm glad." But my worries about his children were long past. We had our own lives to worry about. As I put away our coats in the closet I asked, "What did you think of my proposal?"

"Frankly, it blew my mind," he admitted as he followed me into the sitting room. "At first I wondered if it was entirely too English to go over in Madison. But before I had time to despair, Angel called, telling me it was exactly what was needed in the changing health insurance climate in America."

I knew I could depend on Angel's practical instincts. "Did she? That's great."

Jack drew me down beside him on the sofa. "A clinic staffed with nurse-midwives, supervised by a skilled and experienced OB/GYN, with the specific intent of seeing that every birth had as little intervention as possible—the perfect setup, according to Angel. She said she'd be your first patient, and she's convinced there are plenty of pregnant women in the Madison area who are unhappy with how high tech labor has become and want it given back to women."

"Yes, that's the impression I had when I was there."

Jack smiled at me, drawing me tight against him. "It'll happen, Mandy, if it's what you want—coming back to America with me."

"It's what I want." I glanced up at his beloved face and traced the line of his jaw with my forefinger. "But what I want even more, right now, is for us to get cozy on this sofa."

"I've been picturing that," he said.

Remembering that we'd finally ended up in bed together because of Jack's vivid imaging, I gave him my cheekiest grin.

"Then I think you should help me out of these cumbersome clothes, because the only way I'm going to be comfortable is in my underwear."

"Just like in your snapshot." He started to unbutton the red silk blouse I'd bought specially for his visit. "You know how dedicated I am to turning fantasy into reality, Mandy."

"Yes, Jack, and I'm very grateful," I said as the blouse slid to the floor.

About the Author

Elizabeth Neff Walker is the author of twenty-seven novels. Writing as Laura Matthews, she set most of her early stories in Regency England. Her more recent books, including *An Abundant Woman*, take place in the fascinating world of modern medicine.

With her children now grown, there is more time to spend at the computer indulging in her special love of writing about the relationships between women and men. She has also found outlets for her special research interests (the Regency period and medical sociology) by being active in the Jane Austen Society of North America and by volunteering at the University of California San Francisco Medical Center.

Ms. Walker has lived in England and enjoys traveling in the U.S. and abroad. Wherever she goes she indulges her passion for both old books and unique bookstores in her search for research materials and other literary treasures. She lives in San Francisco with her architect husband and two "interesting" dogs--a cairn terrier and a Lhasa apso.

On the Belgrave House website (www.belgravehouse.com) Ms. Walker has provided an overview of her writing career, including her past experiences with writer's block and the current rewards of writing reality-based escape fiction.

The Authors Studio

The Authors Studio is a community of small presses, each created by an established writer of commercial fiction. Being actively involved in the publication of our work allows us to produce distinctive books for discriminating readers. We want to offer our diverse readership fiction which will satisfy both the heart *and* the mind, as well as nonfiction (often about the craft of writing) with the stamp of experience and authority.

Writing is a challenge and a joy. The members of The Authors Studio realize that, in order to satisfy our readers and ourselves, we need to write the "books of our hearts." We believe we have an audience which appreciates the kind of high-quality, well-crafted work which it is our goal to publish.

If you delight in the written word, visit our website at http://www.TheAuthorsStudio.org to learn more about our authors and the titles offered by TAS members. The Authors Studio invites you to experience the special worlds we've created for you. Welcome!

Order Form

Belgrave House
190 Belgrave Avenue
San Francisco, CA 94117-4228

Please send me _____ copies of *An Abundant Woman* @ $12 each plus $3 for first book, $1 each additional, shipping and handling. (California residents add $.87 sales tax per book.)

Name_____

Address_____

City_____State_____Zip _____-_____

Phone_____

Payment:
☐ Check enclosed
Credit card:
☐ VISA
   Number:_____Exp. Date_____
☐ MasterCard
   Number:_____Exp. Date_____

Signature:_____

Books may be ordered toll-free by calling 1-800-929-7889

Order Form

Belgrave House
190 Belgrave Avenue
San Francisco, CA 94117-4228

Please send me _____ copies of *An Abundant Woman* @ $12 each plus $3 for first book, $1 each additional, shipping and handling. (California residents add $.87 sales tax per book.)

Name_____

Address_____

City_____State____Zip _____-_____

Phone_____

Payment:
☐ Check enclosed
Credit card:
☐ VISA
   Number:_____Exp. Date_____
☐ MasterCard
   Number:_____Exp. Date_____

Signature:_____

Books may be ordered toll-free by calling 1-800-929-7889